Hidden

ALSO BY DONNA JO NAPOLI

Beast

Breath

Bound

Hush

Storm

Hidden

DONNA JO NAPOLI

A PAULA WISEMAN BOOK

Simon & Schuster Books for Young Readers

NEW YORK   LONDON   TORONTO   SYDNEY   NEW DELHI

To the latest woman in my life, little Olivia.
Love, Nonna

SIMON & SCHUSTER BOOKS FOR YOUNG READERS
An imprint of Simon & Schuster Children's Publishing Division
1230 Avenue of the Americas, New York, New York 10020

SIMON & SCHUSTER BOOKS FOR YOUNG READERS is a trademark of Simon & Schuster, Inc.
For information about special discounts for bulk purchases, please contact Simon & Schuster
Special Sales at 1-866-506-1949 or business@simonandschuster.com.
The Simon & Schuster Speakers Bureau can bring authors to your live event. For more
information or to book an event, contact the Simon & Schuster Speakers Bureau at
1-866-248-3049 or visit our website at www.simonspeakers.com.
Book design by Krista Vossen
Map by Elena Furrow
The text for this book is set in Adobe Jenson Pro.
Manufactured in the United States of America
2 4 6 8 10 9 7 5 3 1
Library of Congress Cataloging-in-Publication Data
Napoli, Donna Jo, 1948–
Hidden / Donna Jo Napoli. — First edition.
pages cm
Companion book to: Hush.
Summary: When a marauding slave ship captures her sister, Melkorka, eight-year-old Brigid
is lost at sea but survives, disguised as a boy, and sets out to rescue Melkorka,
and as the years pass she becomes a woman, reputed to be fierce enough to conquer a man,
but desirous only of reuniting with her family.
Includes bibliographical references.
ISBN 978-1-4424-8300-2 (hardback) — ISBN 978-1-4424-8303-3 (eBook)
[1. Voyages and travels—Fiction. 2. Princesses—Fiction. 3. Conduct of life—Fiction.
4. Coming of age—Fiction. 5. Sex role—Fiction. 6. Sisters—Fiction. 7. Middle Ages—Fiction.
8. Europe—History—10th century—Fiction.] I. Title.
PZ7.N15Hid 2014
[Fic]—dc23
2014011732

FIRST EDITION

ACKNOWLEDGMENTS

Thank you to Ivy Drexel, Helen Everbach, Sarah Geselowitz, Abigail Holtzman, Christina Labows, Grace Leonard, Lena Lofgren, Kimberlyn McClendon, Julia Penn, Anna Rasmussen, Erik Rasmussen, and Valerie Shea for comments on an earlier draft. Thank you to Barry and Robert Furrow for discussing so many points with me. Thank you to Trinity College Dublin for a Long Room Hub Fellowship in spring–summer 2012 to work on this novel. Thank you to Damian McManus of Trinity College Dublin for help on the Old Gaelic, particularly the proverb at the end of chapter one. And a huge thank-you to my editorial team, Sylvie Frank and Paula Wiseman, both so quietly effective and so sweetly encouraging.

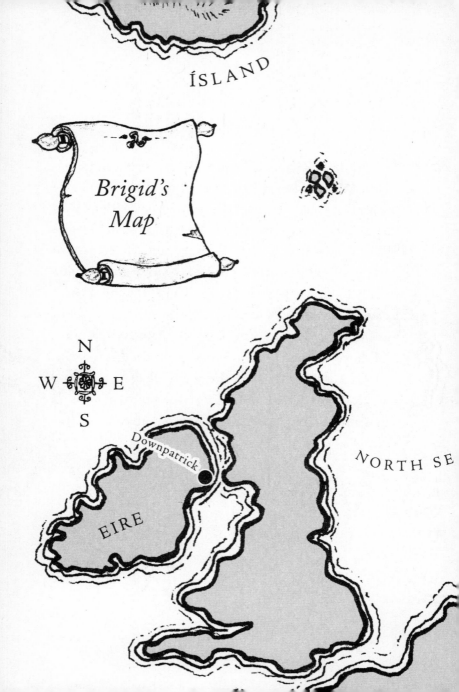

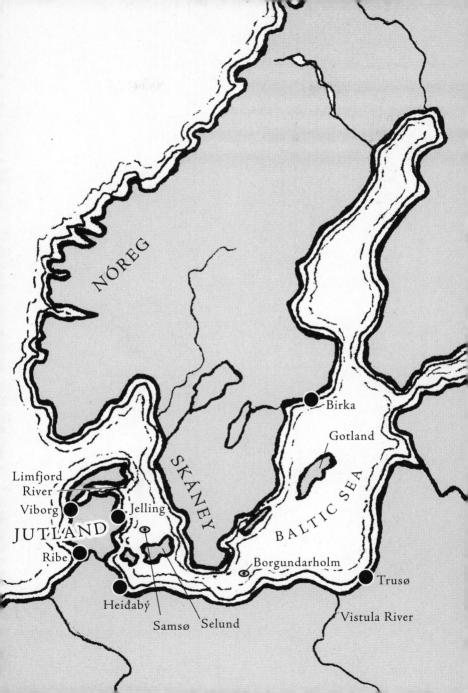

NOTE ON LANGUAGE

This story takes place in the first half of the tenth century AD. It opens in Limfjord, Jutland, in Denmark. A scattering of Old Norse words flavor the text and are gathered in a glossary at the end. Old Norse used some letters English does not use. The sound at the beginning of *thigh*, for example, is represented by þ, so the word *þing* ("assembly") was pronounced much like the English word *thing*. The sound at the beginning of *thy*, on the other hand, is represented by ð, and in this story you see it in the name of the god Óðinn. I am inconsistent about using these other letters, though; I prefer to spell *Thor* and all names that start with *Thor* with an initial *th* to make sure they are easily recognized.

Many vowels of Old Norse were written with diacritics over a letter familiar to us, such as ø, á, å. Some of these vowels don't occur in English. Further, even some letters we easily recognize are not always pronounced as we might expect (so written *f* can sound like [f] or [v]). I encourage you, then, to relax about the pronunciations and simply enjoy the sight of the words, allowing them to play in your mind as you wish. Alternatively, you could Google "recordings Old Norse" and visit a few sites—whose authority I cannot vouch for, however. And if you are a (budding) linguist, you could consult one of several fine books, such as *The Nordic Languages: An International History of the North Germanic Languages, Volume 2*.

Further, in Old Norse there was a case system, so nouns had endings that told their role in a sentence. For example, the root of the word for Norway was *Nóreg*, but if it was the subject of the sentence, it would be said *Nóregr*. In this book, however, I use the root form throughout, because I feared the reader would find it strange that most proper nouns ended in *r*.

Finally, Brigid calls her language Gaelic, even though Irish people today call it Irish. I do this with apology (since I wrote much of this novel in Ireland), because I believe it is more likely to be true to her time.

PART ONE

SURVIVAL

(EIGHT YEARS OLD)

SPRING

CHAPTER ONE

The shock of the cold makes me go instantly rigid. I lift my arms and break the water's surface and claw at my cheeks till I manage to pull the gag down, and I'm gasping. White glitters the water, the air.

Splashes come from somewhere. My arms flail. Shivers seize me. I clamp my jaw shut to hold down the chattering.

Monsters loom in the starlight. Snow accumulating on trees. I swim for it. It isn't far. It can't be far.

Crack! My hand protrudes through the ice it just broke. A thin layer lines the riverbank. A stabbing sensation shoots across my hand, and somehow I know my palm is sliced open. I make fists and beat my way through the chunky stuff, grabbing at stiff stalks, so many of them, all poky and horrible, my feet are digging into bottom now, and there's frozen mud at last. I pull myself up onto land.

"Mel?" I croak.

A groan comes from so close I can feel her breath. I reach out and grab. An explosion of strange words from a crazy language. It's one of the boys from the boat! I can't tell which one in the dark. I don't know what he's saying.

I look back at the river. The boat is far away now. I scream, "Mel!"

The dark bulk that is the boy gets up and runs toward the trees. But I won't follow; he can't know any more about where we are than I know. He was stolen too. All of us on that boat, we were stolen from our homes.

Home. Downpatrick, Eire. My Eire land. Where my mother and father and brother live. Where Melkorka and I should be. Across all that water. I'm so far from home now. It's been days. Days and days.

I crawl along the bank, touching everything I can reach. "Melkorka? Mel, Mel, Mel." My fingers can hardly feel anymore. I shake so hard, I think I may fall to pieces. Where is she? Where is my big sister? She always boasted that she and our brother Nuada could communicate with eyes alone, but she and I were learning to do that too. We were learning how on the boat. We did it even when our gags were off for eating; we kept silent. That was Mel's idea—to pretend we were mutes. I don't know why she did it, but I did whatever she did. I didn't need Mel's words to know I should copy her; I obeyed her eyes. And I'm sure an eye message passed between us the instant before I jumped. "Mel!" I'm screaming. She's a better swimmer than me. She has to be here! "Mel!"

I press on a stick and it slaps me in the face. I fall onto my back and hug myself.

I think back. There were only the boy's splashes. No one else. Two women, nine children, all captives on that boat, and only that one boy and I jumped. Mel didn't jump. Dear Lord, Mel, my Mel. Mother told us to stay together. "*Immalle*," she said. Together, together.

Mother put us on the nag, dressed like peasant boys. In disguise like that, no one would bother us. We were to stay at Brenda and Michael's ringfort until it was safe to return home to Downpatrick. But we rode along the shore, and that awful ship saw us and snatched us, as easily as gathering eggs. Still, we were together. Like mother said. *Immalle*. Until now. "Mel!" I shout.

But Mel didn't jump when I did. I already figured that out. She can't hear me, so it's stupid to shout. And maybe dangerous. Who knows what wicked creatures might hear? I broke so many of those stalks climbing out of the water. What if they were bulrushes? I could have crushed fairy houses. Fairies might be coming for me, screaming, shrieking. Like the damned. My ears are too cold to hear them, but my head knows.

That's why the boy ran off now. Not because he knows where to go—but because this is a bad place to stay. I have to get someplace safe. I have to get warm, dry.

I manage to stand and take a few steps. One shoe was lost in the silt under the river rushes. The other flops loose. I go to tie it, but it's already tied. Water sloshes inside it; that's what stretched it. I try to squeeze out the water so I can tie it tighter, but the water has made the leather strings almost fuse together. And my fingers are so cold they can't curl the right way to work the strings anyway. I tug hard and rip the shoe off and throw it in the river and stumble as fast as I can.

Nothing's visible now. The dark is solid. I head directly away from the river, smashing through the trees.

I was right—the line of trees is only three or four deep. Almost instantly I come out onto a meadow in hazy, snow-dampened moonlight. The thinnest dusting of fresh snow covers the ground; it's not thick and hard like I expected. Spring has started here, too, just a little later than in Eire, but winter frightened it today. Maybe a week ago that river ice would have been too thick to break through and I'd have been swept underwater forever. My whole body spasms.

The wind blasts me, and I drop to my knees to keep from being knocked over. Still, I saw what I needed to see—mounds beyond this meadow—houses, they've got to be houses. The people there will help me. Anyone will help a princess, especially a little one—I'm only eight, and

I'm small for my age. They'll want to bring me back to Eire and collect a reward.

I try to stand but the wind stops me, so I scrabble in a half walk, half crawl through the grasses. The ground is bumpy. Why? I let my knees gather the information: long furrows, long mounds. This is no meadow—it's a farmer's field. Sharp stubble a hand-width apart. Parsnips, I bet—and I'm hungry. They fed us almost nothing on that boat—a single boiled parsnip for dinner. So I should try to dig, but with what? It's so cold, the ground is too hard.

Everything is too hard.

My chest is ice. Just breathing hurts so bad I could scream. I want to be home, asleep on my bedmat in Mother and Father's room, with Mel asleep on one side of me and Nuada asleep on the other, our five warm breaths mingling, binding us together like the good family we are. I should have a tummy full of milk and leek soup and lots of meat, and be dressed in a smooth linen nightdress instead of this rough peasant tunic. My hair should be brushed to a gloss by a servant. My feet should be warmed by the hearth. Tears well in my eyes.

Stop that! Stop being a baby. That's what Mel would say. With her eyes if not with her words. I have to listen to her voice inside my head; I have to act smart. My wet clothes are freezing into hard clumps that will rub me raw. I need to get to those houses fast!

But nothing is fast. Every little bit of distance takes so long to cover, hobbling like this. A wandering spirit will find me before I ever get there. If not the vengeful fairies, maybe the vampire Dearg-due herself. Do I hear them? Or is that the wind?

Finally two mounds take on clear form out of the gloom ahead. But they aren't recognizable. My nose is no better than my ears in the cold air; still, one is a low building, oddly stubby—I don't think an animal of any decent size could go into it. I don't see how people could either. It might be for geese. Or maybe storage. But I don't think so. Something about it spooks me.

The other building is ordinary height—and not as big, not as threatening. Plus, it's closer. From what I can make out, there are no windows. That's all right, though—no windows means no wind. I pass through the opening in the wood fence, pitiful in comparison to the sturdy stone walls that separate fields back in Downpatrick, and I crawl around the outside of the more ordinary building.

No noise, no noise, no clues at all.

I stop still. What if the people inside are not good like folk from Eire, but all wicked, as wicked as the men on the boat?

But it's so cold. My teeth ache. Shivers rack me. It can't matter who they are. I can't think of anything else to do, anyway. I can hardly think at all. Mel should be here—she should be telling me what to do. She should be doing it all!

I press on the door. Nothing. I push hard. I ram with all my might, smashing my right shoulder and hip. The door scrapes open enough for me to squeeze through. Totally dark inside. But the air is hot breath, and my nose comes alive again. I stifle a cry of relief—hay eaters! I mustn't frighten them—these wonderful hay eaters. I can do this—I'm good with animals. I shove the door closed and feel through the dark to the closest one.

A cow. Best of all creatures at this very moment.

But beware: The animal closest to the doorway is the one easiest to see if someone comes.

I lift my head and breathe deep. The scent of pigs worms through the other sweeter smells—it sullies the air. They seem to be huddled together near the middle of the room, though their waste stink comes from the farthest corner. All the animals keep their distance from that reeking muck, of course.

I tuck my hands in my armpits and blunder along to the other rear corner, using elbows and shoulders to make a path past horses, sheep, goats.

I concentrate. I mustn't fall. I mustn't release my hands.

A taste of my blood could excite hungry pigs into a frenzy.

How hungry are these pigs?

At last, another cow. Thank the Lord, there are two. The most docile creature on a cold night is a cow.

I run my hands along her until feeling returns to my fingers. They ache now something awful. The cow's thin but not skinny. I rub and rub her. She rocks from hoof to hoof, coming awake at last. "Good. Good girl."

I move to stand at her head, and I shove my hand under her muzzle—the split palm. The smell of my own blood makes me woozy. The cow licks it. That's what I was asking for. This cow's a good girl. I press my forehead against hers in gratitude.

Then I crouch under her and feel. It's been long enough from her evening milking—her bag has rounded again. I yank on a teat, shooting the milk toward the center of the room. That should stop the fairies.

Pigs snort, and I sense them shuffling around one another, confused.

I should yank again and drink. But the pain in my palm is fierce now that the numbing cold has passed. I cradle my hand against my chest. My shoulder and hip hurt too, from slamming into the door to get inside this barn.

I sweep straw against the wall with the side of my foot, because the bottoms of my feet sting bad. I burrow inside the straw and roll side to side till my heart stops racing.

Everything is wrong. Only weeks ago my life was perfect. Then Mel insisted we go to Dublin for her birthday; she was turning fifteen and wanted to shop for fancy jewelry. And for no reason, no reason at all, a Viking boy cut off Nuada's hand. My poor brother. Father wouldn't trust a physician in that heathen town, so we rushed home and our royal physician saved his life. That would have been the end of it all. But the Viking chieftain who was in charge of that wicked boy sent a messenger with jewels and gifts, and the news that he would come in his ship to take Mel away as his wife. He was so rich he thought our family would forgive the loss of Nuada's hand if Mel became a rich queen. What an idiot! Vikings know nothing—as though Mel would marry a heathen, and after his boy had done such a horrendous deed! But Father was going to trick that Viking chieftain and slay him and all his men. So, before the battle, Mother sent us off on the horse. She gave Mel a pouch with her old teething ring in it; it was gold, so we could trade it for shelter. That would keep us safe. That, and the fact that we were dressed as boys.

But we weren't safe. Not at all. We got stolen—not by a Viking ship, no, but by another kind of boat entirely. A boat with two sails, instead of one. And fat men with scars, whose hands smelled of clay and whose breath smelled of goat and who shouted that ugly language, men who stole children and women who were unlucky enough to be near the shore when their boat passed. Like Mel and me. We captives huddled on the deck, hands bound, mouths gagged. They freed our hands only to eat.

Except tonight. After dinner they hadn't yet tied us up again. And for once we weren't out on the open sea; we were going through a river with land close on both sides, which was why they put our gags on, I'm sure. But free hands were enough. It was our chance—I took it; Mel didn't.

All of it is wrong. No fair, no fair, no fair. I'm supposed to be in Downpatrick with my mother and father and sister and brother. I'm supposed to own pigs instead of sleep with them. I'm not supposed to be alone. *Ar scáþ a céile marait in doíni*—"people live in each other's shadows." That's how we survive. That's what the priests always say. But right now I'm in no one's shadow, no one's shelter.

Neither is Mel.

A little cry escapes me. Tears burn the cracks in my lips. I lick them away.

Mel's on that boat with those men.

And where am I?

CHAPTER TWO

I wake with something nasty in my mouth. Straw? And it's rank! I go to spit, when I remember where I am, what happened.

Mel. Oh, Mel. Oh, sister.

I press my lips together hard to hold in a sob.

Weak dawn light seeps through the building. Someone has opened the door wide. How did I not wake at the very first sound? My throat constricts; I can't breathe. I'm hot. Hunger squeezes my stomach.

The one in the doorway shouts. But he yanks at the rope around the first cow's neck. It's her he's shouting at, not me. He hasn't spotted me.

My throat eases and breath comes harsh. I shrink back till I'm pressing with all my might against something rough and pitted. And good Lord, how much it hurts to move. I can't even say the source of the pain, there are so many.

The boy shouts again in some garbled language, and how on earth will I make people who speak like that understand who I am and that they should take me back to Eire? The boy tugs so hard his whole body is at a slant. He's urging the cow outside. The idiot. That's no way to get an animal to do what you want. Or it is, but a stupid way. At least he's putting all his effort into budging that one cow. He knows that if he gets the one at the front, the others will follow.

At last the cow moves sluggishly. The other animals turn too, jostling one another, blocking my view of the doorway. All I see is a crowd of different-sized hairy legs. But I hear the boy shouting at them, and even not knowing the words, I can tell he's mean. I'll have to find another home to ask for help—with nicer people. Once I'm feeling better. I reach out to grab more straw to hide myself, and alas, the scab on my hand breaks open. It feels like I've just grabbed a fire poker. Who's the idiot now?

I curl tight and small and stop my breath voluntarily this time. Please, Lord, don't let that boy notice me.

Shuffle, shuffle. Bleat. Baaa, baaa, baaa.

Then quiet.

Really?

Or is someone waiting to pounce?

I keep still.

But it's getting colder, and my body wants to move. I stretch my neck to peek out from my little burrow. The door still stands ajar, making a pool of light on the floor that rises up with little motes of dust and straw swimming through. An open door makes sense. It gives the barn a chance to air out. And it will warm up again fast from the animals' body heat once they come back. But who knows how long that will be? The animals might graze on new spring shoots all day. The barn door might stay open till evening. And there's a wind again today. I hear it outside. It crisps my skin like hide held too close to the fire—like the vellum they make in the monastery at Dunkeld that Mel and I visited with Mother. The sweat that rolled off my forehead when the animals were here has dried and left me chilled.

I lick my hand—which won't cure it the way a cow's lick does, but at least soothes it—and look around. Nothing but straw over hard earth and open boxes built into the side walls—for feed in deepest winter, I'm sure. The walls are tree trunks split vertically and placed standing in the ground, each tight against the next with something shoved into the crevices to keep out the wind. I put my face to the damp wall behind me and sniff: dung. Not mixed with hazel wattles or heather or even grass—just plain dung. It can't be as good insulation as a proper mixture. These people don't know how to treat their animals.

I swallow and my ears pop and then buzz loudly, and I feel all dizzy for a moment.

Mel should have jumped. She should be here now, taking care of me. *Immalle.* Together. As Mother said. Sisters don't abandon each other.

But maybe Mel couldn't help it. Maybe someone grabbed her and stopped her. Maybe she's right now searching for a way to get back here, to find me. She'll do it. Mel can do things.

I snuffle back tears and get to my feet and immediately sink to my knees again. My feet are no use. I feel them with my good hand. They're ripped up on the bottom from going barefoot across the frozen ground last night. I imagine Mel scolding me. When Mother put us on the nag dressed as peasant boys, Mel insisted we keep our shoes. Princesses can't go barefoot.

But last night I had no choice. I had only one shoe, and I couldn't hop on that one foot with all the water inside turning to ice and stabbing my toes. I had to rip it off. Anyone would have done the same. Even Mel.

I crawl on my knees and my one good hand, till I'm against the wall beside the open door, and I lean sideways to see out.

A woman passes so close I hear the flap of her long undershift with each step. She could have reached out an arm and touched me, easily.

I fall back on my heels and scrabble away to the nearest corner, pressing into the shadows. I don't know what to do. And I have little strength. I wait.

I'm hot again.

I lift my tunic clear and relieve myself and then move to the side, away from the wet.

I need a plan. I want Mel. I'm always the one who comes up with plans, but she's the one who knows which plan will work. My eyes feel like huge, hot balls. They keep closing. I have to think. But I can't keep my eyes open. My head falls to the side and hits the wall. I don't bother to lift it.

Scrape.

I jerk awake.

The door has been closed. A person moves inside the barn and plunks something down on the ground with a heavy *thud*. Light comes dimly through cracks around the door, and I make out a form. The person lifts off a wide cloak and drops it. A man. He's wearing a huge floppy tunic over those funny baggy things the Norsemen in Dublin wore—trousers. Lord no, have I found myself among Norsemen? I swallow, and my ears ring now.

He lurches forward, and though his back is to me, I can tell he's sick. He groans in pain. He yanks wildly at the drawstring on his trousers, and now he's ripping them off.

He squats and he's stifling yells, I'm sure of it. His head writhes on his neck and the pain goes on and on. Misery like that can only come from a struggle with the devil. I hug myself hard and wish I could shrink to invisible.

At last he lets out a cry, just small and wavery, a pitiful cry, and seems to go all heavy and slack. He takes something from between his legs and throws it into the center of the room, the pig area. It lands with a *slop*. It was a large something. The smell makes my nose wrinkle. Stale eggs.

He reaches into that something on the floor beside him, and I hear splashing. It's a bucket and he's squatted over it now, washing his privates. He stands and stuffs something between his legs and pulls on his trousers and dumps the bucket and struggles into his giant cloak. He turns. But this time he spins toward me, not away.

Our eyes meet.

His mouth drops open, and his face crumples.

I stare back.

He says something. Quiet. Like he's trying to convince me. Like he's making a pact. His face is young and hairless. It shivers with fear at me seeing what he did. He won't tell on me, no he won't, because what he did was secret.

My heart beats so hard I hardly hear him, but I wouldn't understand anyway. I nod.

He opens the door wide and leaves.

I can't stay in this corner, that much is clear. And something's gone wrong with me; I can't crawl anymore. I wriggle and thrash my way along the wall, heading for my corner. When I pass level with the center, I stop a moment and listen hard.

A snuffling noise.

No! I shouldn't have stopped. I shouldn't have listened. I can't do anything. How could I do anything, all messed up the way I am? Besides, if I went over there, with the door wide open, anyone looking this way would see me cross the floor. I can't do it.

But I can't not, either.

I move slow slow toward the snuffle. It's covered in slime. But it moves. It moves. I'm clearing that slime away now, as fast as I can. Energy has come from nowhere. I'm cleaning off the head frantically—the head has to be first. I may be only eight, but I know that much.

The baby lets out the smallest noise, like a chick that doesn't realized it's hatched yet.

I slip the body from the caul and feel. It's a boy. A sweet boy. I can't use my tunic to clean him, because it's so filthy and the coarse nettle would be too harsh on his tender skin anyway. But the only parts that really need cleaning right now are his eyes and nose and mouth and ears. The rest can wait. So I lick him. That's what animals do. I gag at first. But I mustn't do that again. I pretend to be a cow. And he's my calf. I can do this. I have to.

Then I push on my back the rest of the way to my straw burrow, holding this babe on my chest. We need to burrow away. I'm dripping sweat. It rolls into my ears.

When Father's men came home from slogging through wetlands last summer, the horses got hot like I am now. They bled from their nose. They died.

But my brother Nuada got through his fever when the Viking youth chopped off his hand. That was when? Only weeks ago. It seems like forever ago. Nuada had Liaig, the royal physician, looking after him, though. This babe and I have only each other.

I pull the straw around us and bite my bottom lip hard. I don't really have the energy to cry, but biting my lip seems a good precaution anyway. I am not a cow, and this babe is not my calf. So he's sure to die, but I'd rather be damned for all eternity than let crying be the last thing he hears.

CHAPTER THREE

Oof! Something smashed into my back.

Oof! Now it's pulling on my tunic. I'm curled with my arms around the babe and my knees up behind him. My back is to the room, but I know it's a pig behind me. The animals have returned, and I slept through it. I slept the entire day.

Oof!

If I don't react fast and hard, the lot of them will attack. I go rigid; I've seen pig attacks. Though these pigs are short, I know they can get vicious. There's got to be at least three, and there could be four, even five. But there's nothing in this barn—no stone, no club, nothing I can use to fend them off.

He's tugging harder. My tunic tears.

I clutch the babe tight, turn over as fast as I can, and slam my head into the pig's snout. He screams and runs off. The others snort and squeal as he pushes through them.

I lower my face to the babe's head. I think he's still warm—I'm so hot myself I can't be sure, but I think he is.

His forehead is soft under my lips. I feel his back and legs. He moves just the slightest.

Good. I grit my teeth. Fight, fight. We both have to fight!

I reach around and feel for the cow, up her hind leg, to that udder. It swings empty, a withered sack. Of course. They milked her just before putting the animals back in the barn for the night.

My stomach is a pointed flint that jabs at my gut. And the babe needs food even more.

And, most of all, pigs are smart. It won't take them long to realize we're defenseless.

I can't think what to do, though. These are Vikings. Oh, I know not all Norsemen are Vikings—only the bad ones. But these ones are bad. It's dreadful enough to kill a baby. It's worse by far to kill an unbaptized baby. And it's the worst thing ever to kill a baby by throwing it to the pigs. Because that's what he—she—meant to do.

I have no understanding of a girl who would throw a child to the pigs. I have no understanding of Vikings.

And why does she dress like a boy? Something's wrong in that girl's life. She's afraid. I swallow. I know the kind of fear that makes a girl dress like a boy. Mother made Mel and me dress like boys when she shooed us away from Downpatrick before the battle.

But it doesn't matter how bad the girl's fear is. Nothing can excuse what she did.

The baby moves again. I hug him close, and he somehow manages to lift an arm and close his fingers around the thumb of my mangled hand. That's all it takes: I love him. If only he lives, he can be mine.

"We won't die here with the pigs," I murmur into the matted wisps of hair on his roundest of heads. "I promise you that, little one, little egg, because that's what you are, hardly more than an egg. I name you Og, then. And in my heart I baptize you." I'm not a priest, so it doesn't count. But he's a baby; he can't know better.

I take a deep breath. No one beside that disguised girl knows about Og, I bet, so maybe no one else wants him dead.

And, in the end, those people out there are the only chance we have. They have food and warmth; we have nothing.

I get to my feet, trying to hold in the scream from pain. But maybe it would be better if someone heard and came running.

Unless it was the girl.

No. I bite my tongue and stumble through the animals.

A pig noses at my side. I hold Og tight with my good

arm. Then I lean over and jab my elbow hard into the pig's face. The pig shrieks. I must have gotten his eye.

And I like pigs. The old sow back home won't let anyone else near her baby piggies. She charges all the others, but with me she lies there on her side as I tie ribbons around their ears.

It's a gift I have, this way of understanding animals. Mother says that.

And now I've injured this pig when all he did was what any pig would do.

It's unfair I had to fight the pig. It's unfair I'm here at all. I hurt all over and this baby, my Og, is hardly alive, and he didn't do anything to deserve such a rotten start in life. We've both been cheated. I'm screaming now. I can't help it. I'm screaming as loud as I can.

I plow through the rest of the pigs and stop short at the door. The hatefully heavy door that hangs all wrong so it drags. These people can't even hang a door right.

I can't put Og down or the pigs will snatch him. So how am I to pull open this most horrible of doors?

I lean my cheek against the door and practically slide off, I'm so drenched in sweat. A wave of nausea washes over me.

I pull off my tunic with my bad hand, and it starts bleeding again. The blood rolls along my arm. The smell must be driving the pigs crazy, because one's already back nuzzling me hard. I'm scared to be naked like this. I have to hurry. I struggle and twist and pull and every move hurts so bad, but I manage to make that tunic into a sling that hangs around my neck, and I tuck Og in it—he's so tiny and limp, it's easy. Poor little starving thing. I throw all my weight into lugging the door open.

The pigs rush past me, stupid with the excitement of stirred-up hunger, baffled by being let out at night. I stumble after them and look around.

There's nothing but that other building, the squat one. I don't understand, because these people are normal size, tall even, but they have to be in there. Where else could they be?

I go to the door, every step a torture. Yesterday's light snowfall has frozen into a stiff layer that crunches under my broken feet. The cold air nips at my skin, and I know Og doesn't have enough heat of his own to last out here much longer. Tears make warm rivulets on my cheeks. It's a reaction to the air. It's not crying. I can do this.

Finally I'm there. I bang on the door with both fists.

It opens inward, and the blade of an ax shines, backlit by a fire that hisses loudly. The ax stops just short of my eyes. Beside it a startled, yellow-bearded face makes a shout and stares at me. I stare back. The man's nothing more than a chest and head. His eyes reach level with my waist. I don't understand. And if he doesn't put down that ax, I might just faint dead away. I'm shaking all over.

He moves downward, and I can see he was on a strange kind of ladder. I go to take a step down and fall, tumbling head first, holding onto Og for dear life.

Arms catch us, though they hurt maybe more than a flat fall would have. Screams fill my head, but I keep my mouth shut tight. We are hauled, Og and me, to a wooden platform built into the side of the room. They stretch us out, a naked babe on a naked girl. A woman—the one I saw pass the open door of the barn this morning—pries my arms apart.

"Og," I call in protest as she takes him. My voice that seemed so loud in the barn is barely more than a whisper now.

"*Øg!*" says the woman, changing the sound a little. She holds Og at arm's length, her eyebrows furrowed, her face alarmed. But slowly her expression changes. "*Øg?*" She looks at me in doubt.

I blink.

A blanket is already around me. I didn't see who covered me.

"*Alf.*"

I turn my head to the voice.

It's a child, no older than me. She comes to stand beside me and reaches out a hand toward my hair.

A man slaps it away. He chatters at her. I make out the sounds *alf* and *øg* in the quick stream of odd words. The air is warm and peat-smoke heavy, with the odors of a meal hanging in it. Fish. Barley. The room swirls with my hunger.

The woman calls out something, and then the boy who is really a girl shows up with a bucket that sloshes water, and his eyes won't meet mine. I see the lines of fatigue on his face, and I know it must take all his will to keep up the act, to not let anyone know he gave birth just this morning. He's pitiful weak. But not as pitiful as Og and me.

He turns to me purposefully, still not looking in my face, and I tense up. He snatches away that blanket that I've already grown attached to. There are so many people in this home that is half den in the ground—I hear their voices, and I know not a one of them will save me from the boy/girl.

He grabs an ankle and swabs my foot roughly. I jerk my knees up, but the girl child at my side throws herself across my legs, clearly to help the boy/girl, only she knocks my bad hand, and it hurts like the devil is shredding me. I curl around my pain, calling, "Mel, oh, Mel." I need my sister so badly. "Mel," I sob again. *Please, Mel, make them stop*, I pray inside my head.

The woman holding Og, who is now wrapped in a cloth, says something to someone beyond my view. A moment later a pelt is thrown across my chest. And another. And two more. All white. They are fox skins, I'm sure.

"*Melrakki*," says the woman holding Og. She puts a hand on my chest on top of the furs. "*Mel . . . melrakki*." She leans over me. "*Sefask*," she says softly. She stands tall and calls out something.

A younger woman with a toddler on her hip appears quickly. She taps the little girl who is still lying on me, and the girl eases off and stands. The woman hands her the toddler. Now she undoes the brooches that hold the wool sheet wrapped around her body over her long shift. She opens the front and faces the woman in charge, taking Og from her and cradling him to her breast.

Og turns his head and bangs his face into the nipple, but finally opens his mouth and latches on. She puts out her free hand and strokes his arm, and he grabs her thumb.

Just like that, Og goes from being mine to hers. My heart breaks.

The air smells of honey.

Fire! What are they doing to my wounded hand? It's on fire! Everything goes black.

AUTUMN

CHAPTER FOUR

I've been living with these people for many months—all through spring, all through summer, working with the women, busy absorbing their chatter so I can master this language. But right now, on this fine autumn day, I'm in a boat with a man—Thorkild, the one who held the ax just a hand-width from my nose the night I showed up naked with a babe in a sling.

The wind blows in my face, which is not a good thing—it makes rowing harder, and we're already going against the current. But I expected it would be like this; the wind always blows from the west along the water here. I don't know why. It's so consistent that the trees actually lean to the east. We passed a stand of them a long while back, reaching out low, over the water. But there are no trees in sight now. Just land stretching out as far as I can see on both sides. In the past half year I've gotten used to this strange place—this awkward and stark Jutland—but right now the flatness makes me miss Eire almost more than I can bear. I want to see cliffs, or at least big boulders along the water's edge. I want to see rolling glens with grasses stretching over them like the softest green cloth. I want to see my sister and brother, my mother and father, all running toward me, saying how hard they've been searching for me, how much they've missed me, how they're going to shower me with treats now.

"Alf, can you see it?"

I blink away those wishes and sit tall, grateful for an excuse to pause and pull the oar up so it rests across my thighs. "What? What am I looking for?"

"If you see it, you'll know."

A challenge. I perk up and scan the area closely. The marsh grass ripples around us. A large clump of yellow-green seaweed dangles from the neck of my oar. The waters are thick with it. I look over the side. This grass has to be rooted into the silt. If this *feræringr*—fishing boat—weren't so shallow, we'd get stuck on the bottom here. We might anyway. Being on water makes me anxious. This is my first time in a boat since that awful boat I fled from. I hate boats. "The water is shallow. We'll get stuck."

Thorkild gives me a light tap on the back of the head and laughs. "You're just trying to divert me because you can't see anything and you hate to admit it. I know you."

"If we get stuck, we'll be late. Thora will be mad."

Thorkild makes a groan of exasperation. "I liked you

better all those months when you were silent. Ever since you started talking, all you do is annoy folks."

"It's shallow here. Take a look."

"Swing that oar in, no no, this way, Alf. Good."

The boat rocks.

I twist my neck to see what's going on, and there's Thorkild standing right behind me. I'm about to warn him it's not safe standing like that, but he lifts me up under the arms and tosses me overboard.

Splash!

I'm underwater, and panic seizes me. All at once it's night on the river, freezing, and I'm alone, lost, without Mel. I scream, and the brackish water rushes into my mouth. It brings me back to the present, and I break the surface of the water and gasp at the air. This isn't a river— it was never a river. It's an enormous fjord with water that's not quite sweet, only I didn't notice the salt that first night because the gag over my mouth kept the water out. And it's morning now. The water is cold, bracing, but nothing like that night. And the fishing boat is much, much smaller than that hateful boat that night. This is now. Everything has changed. This is now, now, now.

I swim to the edge of the boat and throw a hand up over the gunwale and hang there, panting, trying to calm myself.

Thorkild smiles down at me. "What? You too much of an elf to pull yourself up?"

I wipe my eyes and nose and mouth with my free hand. "Why did you do that?"

"It was easier than having a debate with you over the depth of the water."

It is deep here—he's right. But that's no excuse. "I almost drowned."

"You swam like a fish."

"What if I didn't know how to swim?"

"I'd have reached over and plucked you out."

What if he hadn't been able to pluck me out? What if the current had carried me off? Or some Fomoiri water monsters had held me down low out of his reach? And here I forced myself to overcome my loathing of boats in order to go with him, because last week he took me to cut peat and it was fun. It was like an adventure. Staying home has no adventures. It's nothing but boring spinning and weaving and sewing and cooking and brewing, the same thing all the time. Girls have no fun here. But despite his talk, Thorkild's just as dumb as the rest of them.

"Help me," I say in a weak voice.

He stands—good—and leans over, stretching out a hand for my free hand.

I plant my feet against the side of the boat, catch his

hand in both mine, and throw myself backward, pushing off as hard as I can with my feet.

The big man falls into the water beside me. He comes up, spluttering and red-nosed. I make a fake laugh, but he doesn't join in. He climbs into the boat by rocking it hard and then heaving himself over the side. He stands and shakes off like a dog, then he sits on the rear bench and rakes his fingers through that long beard, without looking at me.

"Don't be mad, Thorkild. You threw me in first."

Thorkild twists his beard into two tips that strike me as demonic. Water drips from his bushy eyebrows. "I don't know what Thora sees in you, you little ruffian. She thinks you're special because Åse named you Alf. You're stubborn as an elf, I'll give you that, but you're no more a real elf than I am a real giant. And that boy Øg of yours is no more a terror than any other baby."

"You're right."

He widens his eyes in surprise. "You admit it, then?"

I want to get out of the water too much to fight. "You're always right."

If Thorkild realizes I can't possibly mean that, he doesn't show it. "You're a true human child. That's what you're saying?"

"It's what you're saying. And you're always right."

He rests his forearms on his knees and leans toward me. "So what's your real name?"

"I'm cold, Thorkild. You felt the water. You know how it is."

"I won't lift you in till you tell me."

"We're drifting backward. And after all that rowing."

"Who cares? We're already there really, even though it's clear you didn't detect a thing."

"Right again. I saw nothing."

"Don't think you'll trick me by agreeing with me. Hmmm. You might be deceitful as an elf too. But I still know you're not a real one." He points at my nose. "What's your true name? Tell me."

"Brigid."

"What?" He drops his hand and laughs. "Did they name you after a dog?"

"Well, what about you and your sister Thora and your little brother Thorsten? Thor, thor, thor. Whoever named you had a stump of a tongue—thor, thor, thor."

His face shows instant alarm. "Don't go getting so mad at your ugly name that you say bad things about the god Thor, child."

Oh. Oh how stupid I am. I know about Thor. He's their favorite god. They tell stories about Thor nearly every night, all full of thunder and lightning and a crushing hammer called Mjølnir. Only I never connected their names to his. I'm so dumb—and after being named myself after Saint Brigid, the healer. I should have realized. "I'm sorry."

He looks at me as though assessing my face. "No more tricks?"

"No more tricks." I try to look pathetic. It isn't hard; I'm chilled deep.

Thorkild pulls me into the boat. "Listen, I won't tell anyone about your ugly dog's name. Parents shouldn't do that to a child. Maybe that's what made you naughty."

Brigid is a beautiful name, the name of someone exalted, as a princess should be. And it sounds like "fiery arrow." That's what I love about it. I told Mother that once, and she laughed and said I was her arrow of inspiration.

Mother. I swallow. I used to sit on her lap and she would rest her cheek on the top of my head, all heavy and warm. She smelled of the oil she put on her wrists: vetiver. It was lovely. The last time I saw her, her hair made a yellow cloud around her pale, worried face. I want to bury my head in that hair. I want my mother. I want my sister. I want my home and my old life. When are they coming for me?

Longing makes me suddenly tired. "Thank you," I murmur.

"You're welcome."

I slick the water from my arms and wring out the bottom of my wool shift.

Thorkild picks up his oar and rows us into the middle of the sea grasses. He ties our boat to a thick pole I hadn't seen before. It sticks up from the water only a foot's length and the grasses are taller than that, so it's hidden unless you're practically on top of it. I look around. Nothing seems special about this spot—no easy landmark. "How did you spy it?"

"Ah, so you're ready to agree that I know some things you don't, are you?"

"You know lots of things I don't. That's why I came with you. So you can teach me."

Thorkild looks around. "Tell me what's here."

Flat land. Grasses. Bulrushes. "The same stuff as everywhere."

"What about the different stuff?"

"What different stuff?"

"You want to learn from me? Really? Think about what I said, child. Don't be lazy."

Different stuff. I look around anew. A tall gray-and-white bird with a long neck and a narrow, pointed beak picks its way on orange legs and feet along the shore. I don't know the name for this bird, not in any language.

But I don't see how it could help anyone find this particular spot. Seabirds come and go, after all.

Four birds I do know pass overhead, wide black wings, gray tummies. They fly so low I can even see the little hook at the end of their beaks. Frigate birds—though what Thorkild calls them, I can't guess. They're no use either.

A low clunking noise is followed by a quack. Immediately offshore a male and female shoveler swim along. I shout, and they take to the air; hurrah, for now I can see that blue on the male's forewing feathers that shows only in flight. I love shovelers. They're all over Eire all year round. I love shouting at the males.

I shift on my bench seat. That's when I see them: a family of swans. The parents are pure white, of course, but the young—four of them, all adult-size now that autumn is coming—are ashy gray. Swans nest in the same place every year, not like shovelers. They're as regular as the cuckoo that used to call outside our bedroom window from midspring to early summer. Mother always trimmed our hair when the cuckoo returned each year. The swans are looking at me, and it seems they're more annoyed at my shout than worried.

I turn to Thorkild in astonishment. "Can you really tell one swan from another?"

"Can't you?"

"No!"

He laughs. "Neither can I. But I can judge time. I row till the right amount of time has passed, then I look for swans." He reaches under the water and pulls up a rope. The mussel shells on it glisten blue-purple as he pulls the loaded strand into the boat.

My job is to lean over the other side of the boat and scoop up armloads of kelp. Then, as Thorkild pulls up a rope of mussels, I push the mess into the center of the boat, to clear the way for the next ropeful, and I cover them with kelp to keep them wet on the journey home.

We don't talk as we work, but it feels good to be doing it so smoothly. I manage to get each load of mussels covered properly before the next load comes. I like working together. It would be nice, if only it didn't involve a boat.

When the fifteenth rope comes up—I was counting them—Thorkild announces that's the last. I can't guess how many mussels we have. Tons! It'll be a feast.

Then he attaches fifteen new ropes to the pole, and we push off.

The boat is heavy now, but we're going with the wind and the current, so it's still easier than it was coming here.

"Hey." I point up ahead. "A baby seal." He's lolling on the shore. There are lots of seals in the fjord, but this is the first one I've seen today. The water is clear here, so I should be able to spot his mother swimming around, but I don't. "He's all alone."

"His mother's off fishing somewhere."

Or maybe she's off someplace mysterious. She might be a selkie, who sheds her seal skin and becomes a maiden some of the time. "Can we pass close to him?"

Thorkild steers us closer.

I call out, "Hey, little seal." And I sing a melody from my homeland, but without the words—just with *la la la*. None of them—not Thorkild nor anyone else—know I'm not a Norse girl, because I kept mute till I could speak properly. That's what Mel did on the ship that stole us . . . so that's what I did here. And I'm glad I did it. I'm not about to let them know I'm Irish. They don't like foreigners. They say horrible things about a people they call the Franks.

The little seal humps to the water and slips in. He comes to our boat, crying. We keep rowing, and his cries turn to howls.

"He's hungry, Thorkild. I bet something happened to his mother."

The pup goes under our boat now. He comes up on the other side. I pull my oar in and kneel, looking over the side. "His eyes are sad, Thorkild. He's asking us for help."

"On second thought, pull him in." Thorkild leans forward and smiles. "He'll be delicious."

"Delicious! No!" I grab my oar and shove the pup away from the side of the boat.

"What's the matter with you!" Thorkild kneels and lunges toward the pup.

I bring my oar down hard between his shoulders.

Thorkild grabs the oar from me and shakes it in the air.

We stare at each other.

"I have a mind to leave you here," he growls.

My insides go quivery. I can't be left here. The boat is moving with the current, and the little seal has given up and gone back to his place on the shore. That's where he belongs anyway. I know that really. If his mother's alive, that's where she expects to find him. I shouldn't have lured him to us.

And I never should have hit Thorkild.

I'm doing everything wrong today.

I look at the rust-colored scar on my palm. I think of the scars on the bottom of my feet. This time if I die, it's my own fault.

Thorkild blows through his lips in disgust. "I was wrong. Alf is your rightful name. Better yet, Alfhild. That's who you really are. You've proven it. You're nothing but trouble."

I know that word: *hild* means "battle." He's dubbed me

"the elf warrior." I listen closely to the stories every night. So I know there are elves of light and elves of darkness. Only the darkness ones are warriors. "Even the elves of darkness are needed." I try to keep my voice steady, but it wants to turn into a cry.

"How? What did they ever do of value?"

"Think of Fenrir, that vicious wolf. He grew so big the god Óðinn—Thor's father—was afraid of him. He thought Fenrir would eat him. So the elves helped. They made the strongest chain and bound him up."

Thorkild runs his tongue up inside his top lip. I watch the bulge of it move slowly. I can't hold on to my strong face much longer. I will beg him if I have to. I will throw myself on his mercy.

He hands me the oar. "Row."

I row hard.

For the moment, I'm safe. But it could change. At any time, it could all change. And I'm not strong enough to live on my own. Especially with Øg to take care of. I'd never leave him behind.

I need help. *Come for me, Mel. Come for me, Mother, Father. Come! I am so very weary of this prayer. Make it come true. Save me.*

CHAPTER FIVE

The autumn days are short now, so we retreat to the pit house earlier than in summer. I don't much like the pit house. It's not unfit for humans, like I thought that first night when I saw it looming in the dark. No, the eight of them, plus me and Øg now, all live fine inside here. But there are no windows, so when the door is closed, the only source of light and air is the hole over the fireplace in the center of the single big room. And there's the fire, if it's lit. And now and then a lamp. But none of that is enough. Each night I fall asleep staring into the dying embers surrounded by total blackness. From our bedroom window back in Downpatrick, I could look out over the whole farmyard inside the fort walls and see people milling about, and I could look up at the never-ending sky. Here there are no people to watch mill about: This is an isolated farmstead. And if you want to see the stars at night, you have to go outside. I feel caged.

But tonight is better than most. By the time Thorkild and I came home with the mussels, his wife, Gunhild, and

42

sister, Thora, had already piled the axes and tools and buckets into a corner and pushed the loom and the vats of pickled fish for this winter against the rear wall to make space. All because a stranger had arrived while we were out on the boat. It turns out that's who the mussel feast tonight was for. We roasted so many, we'll have mussels tomorrow, too. And still more wait in the current, the ends of their ropes tied to a tree that leans out over the water. They'll stay fresh that way.

The stranger calls himself Beorn, and he says his father was a bear, some kind of huge, ferocious animal. Beorn is even taller than Thorkild, so I half believe him, though I can't understand how his mother wasn't killed by the bear that was his father. She was human, after all.

Where Beorn comes from, the bears have white fur. Like the fur of the white fox—the *melrakki* that Thora thought I was asking for that first night when I cried out Mel's name. Beorn was the original source of those fox skins. He's a traveler, by boat if he can catch a ride, or by land if he can't. He carries things from one farm or settlement to the next, allowing trade all the way from the north country Nóreg, where his home is, to Heiðabý, a big city down south and the biggest port in all the lands around here. That's where he's heading when he leaves us. He says it's a wonderful place, with traders from all over the world who have the most beautiful wares he's ever seen. He'll board a ship there and go back home before winter sets in. Then he'll start his journeys next spring again, arriving at this farm in autumn, like always.

Trading isn't all he does, though; Beorn is a storyteller. All Norse people are storytellers, it seems. But Beorn's special. Here the best kind of storyteller is called a *skald*. A *skald* goes from town to town, telling stories to the chieftains—just like *seanchais* do in Eire. Beorn is a *skald*. Thora announced that proudly after dinner, for the benefit of Randolf and me. We're the only ones who weren't here in past years when Beorn has come through. And maybe for the orphan Åse's benefit, too, since she's young enough that her memory might not hold that well. Åse turns out to be only six—though I thought she was my age when I first saw her. They're all so tall here.

I'm glad that these people love storytelling; at least they have that much in common with the people of Eire. My own brother Nuada can tell tales that make you fall on the floor laughing or huddle together terrified. Now that his hand is cut off and he's no longer perfect, he can never become king. So I wonder if he'll become a great story-teller instead—a *seanchai*. If I could only see him again, I'd tell him he'd be the best *seanchai* ever.

I press my fists against my cheeks and sit back on my heels and try not to think about Nuada. It only makes me sad. And angry. They should have come for me by now. But I won't think about that. Tonight is a celebration, because Beorn's visit is a treat.

I look at him now and wonder what it's like to travel so much. I bet Beorn doesn't have a home. Not really. Housing a *skald* would be like taming a wild bird; it makes no sense. When he gets on that boat and heads north for winter, I bet he doesn't nestle in a house with ordinary people. I bet he does something extraordinary. Maybe he wanders with the bears till spring comes. Maybe he turns into a bear himself.

I imagine him all white with blood smeared across his face fur from eating a human. My stomach turns.

"Who wants to drink blood?" says Beorn.

I flinch. It's as though he's heard my thoughts.

Beorn takes a flask from a pouch that hangs off his belt. He holds it up so the firelight flickers on it. The silver is as shiny as the host bowl for communion in our church back in Eire.

Øg makes an appreciative gurgle and reaches both hands toward the flask. Everyone laughs. I wince. I want to snatch Øg from Randolf's lap. He should be sitting with me. I'm the one who saved his life, after all. It was Randolf who meant to throw him to the pigs. Øg practically lived in my arms for months, except when Gunhild nursed him or he napped. But today, because I was off getting the mussels with Thorkild, Randolf took over his care. Randolf is a thief.

"This feast was good enough for a god," says Beorn, "so . . ."

"That's because you're a god," interrupts Gunhild. Little Gudrun on her lap nods happily at her mother's words.

"True. You look like Ægir himself," says Thorsten.

I know about Ægir. He's a sea giant or a god or something important like that. But in our nightly stories, he's the one who gives the parties, not the one the parties are thrown for.

"I'm no Ægir." Beorn smiles ruefully. "I have no goddess wife, no nine maiden daughters, alas. My family consists of my dog. And I'm grateful for the luck that brought him to me." He jerks his chin toward the dog Vigi, curled near a post. "But I have this flask of blood, and it's a way to repay you for such a fabulous feast." He waves that silver flask around. "If you drink blood, you become strong. As strong as . . ." Beorn raises his eyebrows and looks around.

"A troll," says Åse. "As strong as a troll."

Beorn smiles in a superior way. "Exactly. Strong as trolls, with their tusks and claws and lizard tails." He moves his hands as he talks, making his pointer fingers curve out and down from his mouth, so I figure out tusks are long teeth. And I already knew trolls were special giants, but now I know what they look like. "But this . . ." Beorn taps the side of the flask. "This is not ordinary blood. This blood does much more than what ordinary blood does. Can you guess what kind of blood it is?"

"Bear." It's Thorkild. I bet he's right.

"Wrong." Beorn looks around. "Any other guesses?"

"Wolf."

"Reindeer."

"Walrus."

More guesses are coming out of everyone's mouth and I don't know half the animals they're naming—they can't be animals from around here, because I've learned the name of every animal I've seen so far. But it doesn't matter, because Beorn keeps shaking his head no.

"Dragon," shouts Randolf.

Beorn jumps around and stabs his finger at her. "Right!"

Randolf smiles at Beorn in delight.

Beorn smiles too. "Clearly you're a person who understands we may meet a dragon at any turn, in any cave, under any wave. You're a person of discernment."

Randolf blushes.

I look around quickly. But the others don't seem to notice. How is it that no one realizes Randolf doesn't behave like men do? And what about how small Randolf is? Size alone should make them suspicious. Even Thorsten, who's barely fourteen, towers over Randolf. And Randolf doesn't have a hint of a beard. And Randolf wears that huge cloak—even on the warmest days. They should figure out Randolf's hiding something under that cloak. They shouldn't just let Randolf sit there with Øg, my Øg, on that lap. I glare at Randolf.

Randolf looks at me, then quickly down. My eyes told her she's acting girly.

I look away. Randolf is right. If they figure out she is a woman, they might figure out Øg is her baby. Then not only is Randolf's secret out—with whatever consequences that carries—but no one will think Øg is the terror born of the elf, which is what he and I are supposed to be, which is why we weren't thrown out at the very start. No one feeds an extra mouth for nothing; they feed us because they fear what would happen if they didn't.

But I'm growing bigger. Somehow I didn't grow all spring or summer. This autumn, though, I've started to. My head comes up to the brown blotch on my favorite cow's horn now. It isn't a lot—she's a short cow—but it's something. Pretty soon they'll have to notice. And Øg, well, that egg of a baby has turned into the sweetest little giggler anyone ever knew. It's ridiculous that his name means "terror" in Norse.

We're in danger—Randolf and Øg and me.

Gunhild touches me on the shoulder. "Alfhild," she says softly. "Didn't you hear me?" She uses my new name. Thorkild came home today and told everyone I was to be called Alfhild from now on.

Gunhild's holding the silver flask out toward me. Clearly it's been going around the room. And everyone whose hands it has already passed through is now talking about how different they feel—stronger, wiser. The dragon's blood has an instantaneous effect.

Dragons here are different from dragons back in Eire. Norse dragons are huge serpents, and instead of protecting the world, they cause horrendous problems. But their blood is good. I remember a story about a man named Sigurd who kills a dragon named Fafnir and saves his blood in a trench. Then he bathes in it—and that makes him invulnerable, except for one of his shoulders, where a leaf stuck, so the dragon's blood didn't touch it—a big mistake later, of course. Anyway, Sigurd drinks the blood, and that makes him able to understand the language of birds. And he roasts and eats the dragon heart, and that makes him able to see the future.

Maybe dragon blood doesn't do the same thing to everyone. But no matter what, it makes you better than you were. I look at Beorn. Where did this man find a dragon? How did he dare to confront it? But no one else asks, so I hold my tongue. It doesn't matter anyway. All that matters is the power of the blood. I take the flask and bring it to my lips, but Gunhild stays my hand. "Just dip in a finger and lick it, like everyone else."

I do. Then I pass the flask along. The blood is thick. It coats my fingertip. I lick half of it, then I walk over to Randolf and Øg and put my finger in Øg's mouth. Obediently he sucks it clean. I knew he would; Øg sucks anything clean.

Am I different now? Did the dragon blood work? I hug myself and rub my arms.

The flask finally returns to Beorn, and he closes it and puts it away. "Now you're all dragon-strong, so listen close to my dragon tale." And he's practically singing now, telling the story of a young and brave king named Frotho. "Frotho needed money to pay for his country's battles—for it costs a lot to build ships and arm the brave men who sail them."

As Beorn describes each weapon and every step of building a ship, his audience nods in agreement, nudging one another knowingly. I wonder if any of them has ever been on a real ship. This farm seems to be their world.

"One day King Frotho overheard a farmer singing about an island where no one lived but dragons. And one of those dragons kept a magnificent treasure in his lair, deep in a mountainside."

Beorn describes that treasure, and all of us are oohing and aahing, even me. Thora fingers her brooches as though imagining them much more elaborate. Gunhild clinks her bracelets together. Even Åse touches her arm ring.

"King Frotho immediately decided to go to the island and claim that treasure. The farmer tried to dissuade Frotho from going to the Island of the Dragons." Beorn points at us. "Wouldn't you?"

And we all agree, the farmer is sensible, yes yes, King Frotho should listen to him.

"Indeed. And I bet you're envisioning an ordinary dragon. But the dragon that guarded that treasure was no ordinary dragon. His flickering tongue ended in three points, his teeth were sharper than razors, his tail could coil around you, around and around and around, and squeeze out your last breath." Beorn pauses. "And if all that failed . . ." His voice is quiet now, and we strain to hear. ". . . he could spew poison from his mouth. That poison blinded you . . . then drove you insane . . . then killed you . . . all so slowly that you screamed for someone to stab you in the heart."

I hear the swallows of the people around me as my own ears pop.

"But Frotho was determined, and he sailed to the island. Ah, you're groaning." Beorn points at each of us.

"But you knew he would do that, you knew he had to take the challenge. He sailed all alone, of course . . ." Of course? It's not "of course" at all. It's crazy to go alone into that den of dragons. ". . . for he wouldn't endanger his men." And we all gasp at Frotho's honor. "Frotho entered the dragon's cave quiet as your most secret thought. He drew his sword and brought it down hard on the dragon's back. But no sword could pierce that thick hide." We wait, open-mouthed, aghast as the possibilities. "The dragon's wrath was now awakened, and he stretched to his full height and glowered down at Frotho." Beorn looks around at us. "And that's when Frotho spied the creamy spot on his underbelly, the weak point of any dragon, and he plunged in the sword." Everyone leans back in relief as Beorn tells about Frotho hauling away the dragon's treasure and going home wealthier than ever.

They're drinking beer now, the very beer I helped Thora make from the early barley harvest, before we planted the rye. Everyone's swilling it down except Øg and Åse and little Gudrun and me. The four of us curl up on our berth built into the wall, wrapped in one another's arms and covered with hides. The steady, hot breath of my companions warms my neck and back. But I can't sleep.

The treasure belonged to the dragon. Didn't it? So Frotho was just a wicked Viking, not a hero at all. Unless the dragon had stolen the treasure from someone else. In the story of Sigurd, the man who killed the dragon Fafnir and bathed in his blood and drank it, Sigurd also was after the dragon's treasure—which Fafnir has stolen in the first place, so that wasn't so bad. But no one tonight asked about how the dragon got his treasure. That wasn't part of the story. It was as though just being a dragon was enough to justify robbing and killing it.

I shiver. Could they find a way to justify doing something awful to me and Øg? No one has threatened us. But no one really likes us either. And winter is coming. Thora already pickled herring and eels in salt water, and everyone's been drying salmon and plums for the long months ahead. And, alas for us but lucky for her, Gunhild is with child again. Resources will be scarce soon. Øg and I are extra.

They're hospitable to Beorn; he brought things to trade, after all.

Øg and I are empty-handed. No. I wriggle around and manage to pull Øg into a tight hug. We can't be thrown out now. We'd die on our own.

We have to work our way into their favor no matter what, until my family finds me.

CHAPTER SIX

They're killing animals today, because we won't have enough food around in winter to feed them all. Their meat will be dried, and we'll chew on it in winter's harshest months. It's not winter yet by any means. But everyone says the rains are coming—which is strange to me, because it seems to rain here most of the time, just as in Eire. But apparently it's soon going to rain and not stop, just rain, rain, rain for two or three months. And it's best to dry the meat in the sun—so we have to do it while there are still sunny days ahead.

Besides, Beorn is here—we have to take advantage of that. Thorkild and Thorsten need him to help with the slaughtering, because Thora's husband, Karl, fell from an apple tree and twisted his back, so he's trying to mend. The animals—two goats and a cow—have to be skinned and gutted and cut into quarters before the women can slice thin pieces to hang from the racks Thorsten built. It takes lifting and lugging.

They're also killing a pig today, but not to dry. Pigs

have a lot of fat, and fat goes rancid if you dry the meat. So last week we collected apples from the two trees behind the barn and squashed some to ferment into vinegar. The pork will be pickled in that vinegar.

It doesn't really bother me that the goats and that pig will die. The animals have been left outside since spring, day and night, like they do in Eire, except there it's year round. That means there have been no jobs in tending most of them, and that means I haven't really come to know them well, not like I knew all our animals back home. Besides, I'm no baby. I'm nearly nine. I understand how life works. I understand that some have to die in order for all the others to live.

Killing that cow, though, that's different. The cows are milked twice a day, and once my hand healed, I proved to be the best at milking. It's not that I have especially strong hands—I don't. Nor that I have some special technique with my hands—I don't. It's that I talk with the cows. I whisper in their ears. I rub them in the direction their hair whorls, and I put my eye right up to theirs and blink. I scratch them under the chin and call them by name. They didn't have names before and they sort of still don't, since no one knows their names except me, because I'm the one who named them. They're happy around me, and they give their milk freely to me. I can fill a bucket higher and faster than anyone.

The cow that's going to die is Ciaran. My sweet little friend Ciaran. She's old now, and there are two milkers younger than her and a new girl calf who seems strong and promises to contribute a lot eventually. Ciaran gives hardly any milk these days. After I first heard them talking about how useless she was, I started pouring milk from the other cows' buckets into hers. But Thorsten caught me doing it and told. Besides, even if Ciaran was producing more, she's the oldest, and they all prefer goat and sheep milk to cow milk anyway. So I couldn't save her. She's doomed.

When they asked me to gather the animals for killing and put them in the barn to wait their turn, I refused. I won't have any part in it. Thorkild looked angry at first, but then he flapped me away with his hand, saying I was more trouble than I was worth.

I went cold at those words—he says them too often— but I looked around and it seemed no one else had heard them. I don't want his attitude toward me to spread. They have to keep me until my family finds me. I rub the scar on my palm; they have to keep me and Øg both. In the meantime, I must make myself tolerable.

Still, I won't help kill the cow Ciaran. I won't watch the slaughter. So I've volunteered to help Randolf gather the honey today, despite the fact that I don't like her one bit. No one volunteers to gather honey because it's a nasty job; it's easy to get stung. When we get back, I'll hand the brimming honey pot to Thora, and she'll remember I'm a value to the farm and maybe even Thorkild will notice.

I don't want Øg to watch the killing either, so I'm bundling him along with us.

The three of us are swathed head to foot in woolen strips, to keep out the bees. Øg rides on my shoulders—which is getting harder for me, because he's growing fast. But when Randolf offered to carry him, I snatched him quick and swung him up. I have to hold on to his chubby legs with both hands so he doesn't fall off backward.

Randolf carries a pot of smoking pine needles in one hand and an empty pot in the other. A knife tucks into her belt on one side, and from the other side hangs the pouch I prepared with a toy for Øg.

The bees live in hollowed-out logs way at the other end of the meadow. We march around the cabbage patch and through the grazing animals. I wonder if these ones know how lucky they are today. Will they miss their companions? Out in the meadows it must be easy for them to lose track of one another. Maybe they won't even realize there are fewer of them.

When we're still a sensible distance away from the hives, I set Øg on the ground. Randolf puts down the pots and digs around in the pouch. She takes out a smooth crescent of something white and brown that looks like horn but it's solid, not hollow, and hands it to Øg, who immediately gums it.

I didn't put that crescent thing in the pouch. "Give him the doll," I say.

"He likes this toy."

"He has two hands—he can hold the doll in the other hand."

"Don't be stubborn, Alfhild. He'll be perfectly fine like he is."

"I take care of him more than you do."

Randolf looks away and purses her lips. But she takes the bone doll out and holds it toward Øg, who quickly tries to shove it in his mouth alongside the crescent.

"See?" I say. "He likes it."

"He likes the other better."

"What have you got against little Gudrun's doll?"

"Nothing. It's just . . ." Randolf puts her hands on her hips. "The antler's mine. It was my toy as a baby. I brought it with me."

That crescent is part of an antler? Deer in Eire don't have antlers anywhere near that thick. I've seen deer here—they're not enormous. One variety is tiny. But the deer that grew that antler must have been enormous. "Where did you come from, Randolf?"

"It doesn't matter. It was a long time ago." She rolls the wool swathing back from her hands, so she's bare from above the wrist to her fingertips. "Let's get to work."

"But your hands will get stung."

"With the cloth on, I'd be too clumsy. I'd upset the bees and get stung a lot worse. Move slowly." She lifts a swath of cloth from around my neck to across my mouth. "Don't let them sense your breath or they'll sting you bad." She covers her own mouth.

For a moment I think of turning back. But this family loves honey nearly as much as Irish people do. And Irish people adore it. My brother Nuada tells a tale about King Lir long ago. His wicked wife turned her stepchildren into swans, and the girl, Fionnuala, cried all the time, remembering the wonderful mead made from golden honey and crushed hazelnuts. Everyone loves honey. So if I do this today, they'll all be grateful. I raise the cloth so it covers my nose as well.

We go to the logs on stealthy feet. Randolf swings the pot with the smoking pine needles around the holes. Then she hands it to me and nods. So I swing it just like she did. I swing and swing, walking from hole to hole. The bees gradually seem to realize something's up. They go on alert. They crawl around the brown, dripping honeycombs, eating like mad. They gorge themselves. I wonder if there will be any left for us at all. And the whole while, I have to keep swinging the smoldering pot. My arm aches.

Finally Randolf stays my arm and pushes me gently aside. She reaches one hand inside a hole to steady a honeycomb, and with the knife in her other hand, she cuts off a slice and places it in the empty pot at her feet. The bees hardly react. There are five hives in all, and Randolf cuts a piece off the honeycomb in each one. I watch because I want to understand. It seems she's avoiding the parts of the honeycomb that contain larvae. This way the hive will have a next generation. And taking only part of the honeycomb means the bees will still have plenty to eat through the winter. How smart this is. I wonder if this is her own method—if she figured it out herself.

A bee crawls on Randolf's hand. She stops moving. But I can tell from the sudden stiffness in her shoulders that the bee stung her anyway. She doesn't jerk away, though. She just waits. Then she carefully slices off a part of the honeycomb she's holding.

Randolf finishes and backs away slowly. I go with her.

Some bees follow the honey pot, but few. And they move lethargically, as though they're heavy, satiated with their own honey. It's still the middle of morning, and we've finished our work. Randolf is efficient, and I'm duly impressed. And the fact that she hasn't complained at all about that sting forces respect.

A shriek comes! It's Øg. The screams sound as if he's dying!

I run to him. The poor babe has somehow managed to get from the spot I planted him into a dense growth of stinging nettles.

Randolf runs to him too. And that sends what bees remain in pursuit into a frenzy. They go for her bare hands.

Randolf's shouting and slapping at her hands, and Øg's sobbing and pressing his already reddened hands into his mouth, and I'm the only one not burning with stings. I pick up Øg and yell, "The water," and we're running for the fjord as fast as we can go.

We splash down among the tall grasses at the edge, and I rub Øg all over with soothing mud, while Randolf dives underwater and swims and swims. Then I lie in the shallows with Øg.

When we're finally all three together again, Randolf laughs. Øg looks at her in surprise and then he laughs, though big tears still cling to his cheeks. What can I do but laugh?

We climb out of the shivery water, and I strip Øg and hang his clothes to dry from a tree branch. I do the same for myself. Then I turn to Randolf. "You might as well. I already know you're a woman."

So Randolf strips and hangs her clothes to dry. It's funny to see how thin she is without all those clothes. I bet she's only fifteen—Mel's age.

We lie in the sun, protected from the wind by low bushes. Øg crawls back and forth over me, as though I'm his warming rock. At last he tires and falls asleep, half on my belly, half in the grass. Randolf is asleep too. I blow thick kisses into the soft part of Øg's arm, up near the shoulder, then close my eyes. Time is passing. I feel half-grown already.

"A dream come true."

The voice startles me.

"Don't be afraid. I thought a swim would refresh me." Beorn stands there, wearing only a cloth wrapped around his waist. His chest and arms glisten with water. His hair drips on his shoulders. The dog Vigi noses his way around us. "Slaughtering always makes me feel like I need to do something . . . different . . . afterward, you know? Something to remind me I'm still alive."

We just look at him.

Beorn shrugs and walks over. "Maybe I'm not making much sense. I feel like I'm dreaming." He sits at Randolf's feet.

Her knees are pulled tight to her chest. Her arms encircle them. A visible tremor goes through her.

"I watched you last night. I was drawn to you in a way that confused me. I tossed and turned all night long, wanting . . . I couldn't fathom what. Now I know why."

Randolf's eyes are wide with fear.

"Don't tell," I say.

Beorn looks at Randolf, not me. "Why the secret?"

Randolf shakes her head.

"If you expect me to keep a confidence, then you have to give the confidence."

Randolf sucks her top lip inside her bottom teeth. I know she's trying to keep from crying.

"Being a girl isn't a crime." Beorn wipes the water off his nose with the back of his hand. "So are you hiding from someone? Is that why you're playing a boy? Is that it?"

Randolf gives a single nod.

"Tell me. I want to know the whole thing. Breathe deep, then talk."

"I was taken, as a girl."

Beorn lowers his head toward her. "Taken?"

I'm straining forward too. My heart speeds. I was taken.

"I was pulling in crab traps by the water. And a ship came by and they took me. Just took me. Across the sea. And sold me to a family."

"A slave ship." Beorn's lip curls. "You were a Norse girl?"

"Yes."

"From Nóreg, like me?"

"No. I'm not sure where I came from, but I know it wasn't that far north."

"It doesn't matter. You are good Norse stock." He seems comforted by that thought.

I will never tell him where I came from.

All at once Beorn frowns. "And a Norse family bought you?"

"Yes."

"Most Norse families don't have the money to buy a slave."

"The fully grown girls were the expensive ones—especially if they were pretty. I was little. I cost little. And the family needed extra hands."

"Did . . ." Beorn clears his throat. "Did the family mistreat you?"

Randolf shuts her eyes. She buries her face in her knees.

"Tell me."

"They were good to me. Until I grew up, and the father . . ." Randolf talks into her knees. "When I realized I was with child, I knew the mother would turn me out. It would break her heart. And ruin the family." She's whispering now. "So I ran away."

"Disguised?"

"As a man, I could work in exchange for a home, and no one would expect . . . more."

"So you came here, to these people."

"It wasn't far. The settlement the family lived in was just on the other side of the Limfjord. I walked for three days—that's all—and I found this farm."

"But then . . ." Beorn looks around and his eyes settle on Øg, who is doing that funny stretch-and-curl thing as he wakes up. "Then you had the child. So . . . didn't they find out?"

Randolf shakes her head. The saddest look I've ever seen on anyone clouds her face. She opens her mouth.

"I pretended he was mine," I say quickly. Beorn doesn't need to know more than that. Randolf has a right to at least that most awful of secrets.

Beorn looks from me to Randolf and back again. "I'm bewildered. You're a child. Who on earth would believe you had a baby?"

"They think I'm an elf. Don't tell."

"What? Where did you come from?"

I shrug.

Beorn slaps his forehead. "So they don't know anything about you, either?" He looks at the sky. "How can that be?" He stands and picks up Øg, who rides in his arms, leaning away circumspectly. Beorn walks the shore, talking to the babe—my babe.

Randolf puts on her clothes, though they're still mostly wet. I do too. My head swirls with thoughts I can't catch long enough to make sense of them.

Beorn comes back. "I won't tell. On either of you. But I have a proposition. For one or all of you. Secrecy is a bad life. There's a better alternative."

CHAPTER SEVEN

I tie a knot in the end of the thread that attaches the sole
to the top, and my new pair of shoes is finished. I put them
on and draw the leather strings tight around the ankles.
In Downpatrick my shoes were made of a single piece
of hide, so they had wrinkles that got hard and rubbed
when they were wet. The good part, though, was that you
could always work them with a stone to reshape them as
your foot grew. Norse shoes, instead, have two parts sewn
together, which means you have to make new ones as your
feet grow. But it also means they're smooth all over. And
goat hide is lighter than cowhide, and tougher, too. My
last pair is still in decent shape—and I've worn them since
I got here. The only reason I made myself a new pair is
that I want to start this journey with the best protection
my feet can have. We're walking, after all. And the scars
on the bottom of my feet are a constant reminder of the
importance of shoes.

I have a sack with apples—nothing else. I came to this
farm with nothing—I have no right to leave it with more.

But, oh, what a stupid thought. I'm leaving with Øg—and he's so much more. I get to carry him. I insisted. And Beorn agreed, even though Randolf wanted to carry him too.

I kissed little Gudrun good-bye, and Åse as well. I'll miss them. They're Øg's and my sleeping buddies. I expect they'll miss us, too. And I kissed Gunhild good-bye. She cried, which made me blink back tears. She's always been kind to us. The rest of them just gave me a nod or a wave. And Thorkild didn't even do that.

I'm happy to be leaving this home where I didn't fit and starting out on a journey. It's a strange happy, like walking on a high log over a raging current in a fjord and being giddy with the joy of not falling. I've never walked on such a log, but I'm imagining what it would feel like. I sense my breath floating in front of me, as though my spirit leads me. I don't know what will become of me in the next place we go to, but I have to believe I'll find a home. After all, I found a home here at this farmstead when I was so wounded and could offer nothing. Now I'm strong; it will be easier this time. So when Beorn offered to take Randolf and Øg and me away, to a town farther south, I didn't hesitate.

Randolf, likewise, is happy. Her feelings are a lot like mine. She owns nothing, just the new shoes I made her as well, and the outfit that she stole from the father of the family who owned her—the father of Øg. She's still wearing it, cloak and all, still hidden. She doesn't want this family to know a girl lived with them almost a year. She doesn't want word of her to ever find its way back to that family she left. Legally, they own her.

But how can it be legal, really, if she was stolen in the first place? Still, I keep silent. Randolf needs protection—whether she should need it or not. I suspect the reason she accepted Beorn's offer is to put more distance between herself and Øg's father.

Beorn is standing beside Karl, hanging his head forward like dogs do. Randolf is half behind Beorn. Beorn and Karl stayed up late last night arguing—and it looks like the argument isn't over yet, though we're standing in the yard by the house, ready to leave. I hear the word *fuð-flogi*. *Fuð* is the word for a girl's private parts. *Flogi* is a man who flees something. What would it mean to be a man who flees a girl's privates? I swing Øg onto my shoulders and come up behind Karl to listen.

"It's a man's duty to take a wife and have children, no matter what his pleasures are." Karl's voice shakes with anger. "You can do both—but you can't ignore your duty."

"I know my duty." Beorn thumps his chest with his fist. "I plan on fulfilling it."

"Then why steal Randolf? He's better off here."

"I'm going of my own will." Randolf lifts her chin. She's holding a small clay jug in each hand—she made them, so she's allowed to take them—full of cow's milk for Øg. Somehow knowing how small she is without all those clothes on makes her look pitiful to me now.

"We took you in. We treat you well. Like family."

"And I worked hard for you. I earned my keep. I'm grateful, but now I'm leaving."

"But you're supposed to marry me." It's Åse. She's inserted herself into the middle of the group. She grabs a corner of Randolf's cloak and hangs from it, insistently.

I laugh at the idea of six-year-old Åse thinking about marriage, but no one else does.

"Who told you that?" says Randolf.

"Thora." Åse looks at Karl. "That's right, isn't it? Randolf's supposed to marry me." Åse's mother died in childbirth, and her father died of an ax wound that turned his leg black. Gunhild told me. So she's under Karl and Thora's care, even though they're not blood relatives. Living together on this isolated farmstead made them family. Karl and Thora are the oldest couple; they're the ones to arrange a marriage for her.

Karl puts his hand on Åse's head. "It would be a good match someday," he says to Randolf. "New blood. You'd have strong children."

"And Alfhild shouldn't go either," says Åse, looking at me with accusation on her face. "She's my sister now. And she's supposed to marry Thorsten."

I drop my jaw in astonishment. Thorsten's eyes meet mine. His face changes from surprised to hurt. He's never been nice to me, and now he's hurt I won't marry him? I make an ugly face. He raises a fist. I move closer to Beorn.

"You can pick up all your belongings and go north, across the fjord, to the settlement at Aggersborg," says Beorn to Karl. "There are advantages to living with several families, all together. There you'll easily make good matches for the children."

"Don't talk like you know things." Karl folds his arms across his chest. "I bet you wander all year. I bet you don't even have a home in the north. You never name the town— never. You don't fit anywhere. You know nothing."

I'm stunned. Beorn was treated like a king when he arrived. Or more—like an angel. I wonder if he feels like Lucifer now, fallen so far from grace.

"Rubbish." The word bursts from Thorkild. He's been leaning over a shovel, looking at the ground through all this, but now he looks straight at me. "I knew you were rubbish. You'd be dead without us. And this is how you repay us. Leave this place. Now."

"Farewell, Karl." Beorn puts on his leather pack.

Karl turns to Randolf. "It's going to rain."

"It often rains," says Randolf.

"Not like this. It's going to pour. I can tell weather. This won't be like usual. You have no idea what it means to travel by foot in a rain like the one that's coming. Every day will turn a little colder till it's sleet night and day. You'll be so drenched, your bones will hurt."

Randolf and Beorn walk away. I follow.

"Don't think you can come crawling back to us when you're sick and weak," calls Karl. "You've never been strong anyway. Thorsten can do more work and harder work than you, and he's younger. You think you earned your keep? Bah!"

But we're walking. Vigi races around us, ecstatic at having so many companions to keep track of—and the sky is clear and our bellies are full. The world is wonderful.

We walk, keeping the fjord to our right. The general direction is southwest. We walk. And walk. Time passes slowly. We plod. I count steps. By midday, I think I'll die. With every step, the pouch of apples bumps against my thigh. And Øg is heavy. He wanted down so many times and I couldn't let him, and he pulled my hair and screamed and then fell asleep, his head on mine. Somehow asleep he's even heavier. "Can we stop a bit?"

Beorn smiles. "Tired?"

"I've got apples. Don't we want to eat them?"

Beorn tilts his head. "Can't you eat and walk at the same time, Alfhild?"

"It's better to eat sitting down."

"You're tired," says Randolf. "Admit it. You're tired from carrying Øg."

"I didn't say that. I'd never say that."

Beorn laughs. He leads the way through the little stand of trees at the fjord's edge and sheds his leather pack. Randolf puts down the jugs, then lifts Øg off my shoulders and sits with him sprawled across her lap. I feel instantly lighter—as though I weigh nothing—as though I could walk for days, weeks, without getting tired. I drop to the ground and stretch my legs out in front of me, enjoying the carefree flyaway feeling.

"Thorkild told me you were stubborn, Alfhild, but he didn't tell me you were the most stubborn girl alive." Beorn hands me a horn he's filled with water from the fjord.

I drink it down. "What are you talking about?"

"I've been waiting for you to pass Øg to someone else."

I bite into an apple. The sharp sweetness soothes me. "I could allow you. If you really want."

"Ah. These are not going to be easy days ahead, are they?"

"She can behave when she wants to," says Randolf,

shooting me a quick warning look. "Don't regret taking us. Please."

"I don't." Beorn hands an apple to Randolf and takes one for himself. "It's autumn." He jerks his chin toward Øg, who's starting to squirm. "The boy's waking."

And Øg comes awake with a screech. He sits up on Randolf's lap and screams.

"He's starving!" I reach for a jug.

"Not that one." Randolf quickly passes me the other jug.

I'm confused. I thought both held milk. I open the one she gave me and dip in a finger and stick it in Øg's mouth. He pushes my hand away. He's never eaten anything but milk from Gunhild's breasts. I dip in my finger again and push it into his mouth again. He bites me. I yelp. He's got two bottom teeth now. What am I to do? He's got to eat. I dip again and make a quick jab at his mouth. He grabs my face and scratches in fury.

"You're living up to your name," I cry. "What will become of you? You'll starve."

Randolf puts her hands on Øg's cheeks and turns his face to her firmly. She's chewing apple, chewing and chewing, and now she puts her lips to Øg's and I'm scared for a moment that he'll bite, but he doesn't, he just waits, and she spits. I smell the apple mash. It's like a mother bird with her young. Øg's eyes go wide. He splutters and pulls away. But then he opens his mouth and lunges for Randolf's mouth again. She feeds him the whole apple that way.

And now Randolf takes a swig from the jug. She feeds Øg milk from her mouth.

It's as natural as water sinking into the ground.

"It's autumn," says Beorn. These words make no more sense now than they did when he said them before.

But Randolf nods. "I think today is Freyjudag."

Freyja is a goddess who knows magic and healing, and a day of the week is named after her. I'm about to ask why on earth anyone should care what day it is when Beorn says, "Yes. I noted that." He rubs his nose with the back of his hand. That's what he did when his nose was wet yesterday, but now it's dry, so I don't know why he does it. "But we won't be to Viborg—the next settlement—for at least two days at the rate we're going. And we can't start anything without *mjød*."

Mjød . . . mead? Why is he talking nonsense?

"Look in the other jar," says Randolf.

Beorn opens the jar and smells. He smiles.

"We gathered the honey," says Randolf, "so I figured I had a right to a small slice of the honeycomb. I added water. I added yeast. If we take just a tongue-dip each day, it should last a moon. It won't run out."

75

"The whole moon—and the *mjød* will simply grow better with each passing day." Beorn puts the stopper in the jug. "What do we call you now? Will you go back to your birth name or forward, with a new name?"

Randolf presses her lips together. "I want a new name. Do you want to give me one?"

"Never. That's a father's job. I'm not a father to you, nor anything like one. But I'll rename the boy."

Randolf's cheeks flush. Her eyes shine, and little crinkles of pleasure form at the corners. "What will you call him?"

"Búri. Like the god Búri, who preceded everything. This boy preceded our union. And at the same time Búri is a good name for a son of Beorn."

"And I'll be Ástríd." She looks at me. "It's a good name to go with Alfhild."

I know what's going on. Finally I know. "I'll make you rings from pine needles."

Beorn nods. "That will do till we get to Viborg. Thank you."

We walk the rest of the day, stopping only to gather hazelnuts and hawthorn fruit. Beorn carries Búri on his shoulders, perched on top of his leather pack. My hands are free to snatch at wild celery and pigweed, both of which are delicious to munch on as we travel. Ástríd swings the jugs and sings. I never heard her sing before. She has a lark's voice.

That night of Freyjudag in early autumn, with a moon's worth of honey mead in a jug and pine needle rings, Beorn and Ástríd join hands and say their wedding vows.

Afterward, I lie with Búri on my chest. But my insides are too jumbled to sleep. For some reason, I didn't realize it till this moment, but now it's all I can think about: Ástríd and Beorn and Búri—they make a family. They already talk about having a farm down south.

Where does that leave me?

I cradle Búri's head in my hands. Such a nice round head. When I named him Og—said the Irish way— I was right: He's like an egg. But Beorn said Búri was a good name "for a son of Beorn." And I know he meant that it sounds right, because Búri and Beorn start with the same sound. Gunhild told me that if Thorkild's and her new baby is a boy, he'll be named Thorsten, just like Thorkild's younger brother Thorsten. And if it's a girl, she will be named Groa—to go with the names Gunhild and Gudrun. She said that was an old custom in the village that they moved there from, and she liked it: All sons' names started with the same sound as their father's name, and all daughters' names started with the same sound as their mother's name. But, she added, you could always name a child after Thor, as the father of Thora and Thorkild and Thorsten did.

So those names sound like a family, at least to some ears: Ástríd, Beorn, Búri.

Then there's me, on the outside.

But, oh, Ástríd chose her own name—she said it went with me, with Alfhild. Oh! She meant that she and I should have names that start with the same sound. No one would take her for my mother, she's far too young. But we could be sisters. Just like Thorsten came to live with his big brother Thorkild and his big sister Thora, when their parents died. Just like Åse said I had become her sister—our names made us sound like sisters.

Ástríd's making me part of her new family. She's going to pretend I'm her sister.

But I'm Mel's sister. Now and forever. Mel. Mel. My eyes burn with longing.

Still, I can pretend to be Ástríd's sister. I can do what I have to. And it's only till I'm big.

I stare up at the stars. It is beautiful to see the stars again. It feels like a miracle. And it strengthens my new resolve—the decision I made today as we were walking.

Ástríd was stolen by a slave ship. That's what happened to Mel and me, as sure as there are stars above. I know that now.

Ástríd was sold to a family.

I run my fingers around the edge of Búri's ear. Mel has undoubtedly been sold by now. Who was she sold to? How is she treated?

Mel is fifteen and a half. Fully grown. Beautiful.

I could drown in tears. But I won't. I won't cry. *When Mother and Father and Nuada find me, we'll come find you, too, Mel.* I swallow. *And if they never come, it doesn't matter, because I'll grow big and I won't need anyone. Wait for me, Mel,* I pray. *I've changed my plans, dear sister, true sister. As soon as I'm big, I'll come find you. We'll go home to Eire together. Stay strong. Wait. I'll come.*

CHAPTER EIGHT

We arrived at Viborg in the sun to a proper *skald*'s welcome. I don't know how many houses were there—but certainly forty or fifty, arranged in groups rather than scattered over the land. They have a huge hall for everyone to gather in, and it's fully above ground. When people learned that Ástríd and Beorn had been married only two days before, the feast turned into a true celebration, and we left enriched by two goats, a pig, and a cow with various sacks of woolens, tools, pots, and bowls hanging across her back. All because Beorn said he was ready to settle down here in Jutland.

Gifts are wonderful. And animals are the best kind of gifts. But that cow certainly slowed us down. It took six days to travel from Viborg to Jelling, despite the fact that there was a dirt road the whole way, so we didn't have to skirt around bushes and rocks, like we did getting to Viborg. Then, to make things worse, rain came steadily the last two of those days. Baby Búri caught a cold, and since he slept on me, I woke in the morn with his drippings across my neck, like slug paths.

So I was delighted when we arrived in Jelling and slept in a real home again, with blankets and hearty meals, knowing it was raining outside but unable to hear it for all the noise inside. Beorn did his *skald* routine, which by this time I was disappointed in. Irish storytellers embellish their stories with each telling, but Beorn repeated his word for word.

Not to be outdone by the people of Viborg, the folks of Jelling loaded us up even more. We now have a horse with a saddle and straps that hang off it and end in iron bars called stirrups to rest your feet on. No one's riding the horse, though, because her back is packed with other things: a plow and a shovel and a second ax—Beorn had an ax already; no Norse man goes without one—and a slew of other things people insisted we'd need.

My birthday passed while we were there. I'm sure of it, because the days are getting shorter than the nights now, and that's when my birthday comes—just a fortnight after that. No one knew, of course. But it felt like some of the presents were for me, too. I am nine now.

We are back on the road again, with Jelling four days past, and rain our constant companion. The sound of rain on the surface of a pond is *plunk*. Heavy and deep. The sound of rain on a leather pack is *thud*. On a hazel leaf it's *smack*. On grass it's nearly silent. On a puddle it's *splash*.

On the cheeks of my upturned face it's *plink*. Rain is all the good things of the land of my birth. Rain is why the earth of Eire has so many shades of green. Rain gives birth to rainbows. I love rain.

But I am very sick of being wet.

And today there's a wind, so the rain drives at a slant. It's behind us, at least, which means the rain hits our necks and ears, rather than our faces. But the north wind forces the rain down the back of our tunics and it chills—oh, how that rain chills. I look over at Ástríd's ears, red as flowers. She should have a shawl over her head, but she wants her short hair out, because the rain curls it and she says it makes her pretty. After nearly a year of playing boy, she's reveling in womanhood again. People in Viborg and Jelling marveled at her short hair. Married women grow their hair long and wear it in braids or a bun. I suppose that's what Ástríd will do. But for now, her hair is free and curly. I don't understand her not putting on a shawl, though. No one should suffer just for beauty.

The road we took from Viborg runs down the center of this land, gradually veering east. Beorn explained that this land is a large peninsula jutting northward, hence the name Jutland. From what Ástríd has remembered of her childhood and her passage on the slave ship, Beorn pieced together that she probably lived in Skáney, across the sea to the east. Since Ástríd knows as little as I do about where we are, Beorn gives us lessons as we go.

The northwest of Jutland is a mess of islands, but fortunately, we started out south of there. The rest of the peninsula is vast areas of meadow and bog, crisscrossed by rivers, but most of them originate to one side or the other of this country road, which is why the road is located where it is. The traveler who sticks to the road can avoid marshes and wetlands. The one stream we had to cross was nothing but a narrow slop of mud at this time of year. Beorn said in a month, with all this rain, it will be impassable without a raft, but all we had to do was cut bunches of brushwood and throw them down ahead of us as we tramped over.

Yesterday we left the big road, though, and headed west, walking beside a river. I've been watching the changing land, and I'm not happy.

"Beorn," I call. It isn't easy being heard in the rain.

Beorn waves me over to him. He's leading the horse, and Ástríd is at his side, leading the cow with baby Búri secured on her back. I'm swatting the unruly pig with a hazel switch to keep her moving forward, and the goats are running free with Vigi yapping and nipping at them whenever they stray.

I drive the pig toward Beorn and wait for a slowing of

the rain so I can be heard. "Why are we going this way?"

"I told you. I know people in the town ahead. We can have a farm."

"But this land, have you looked at it? It's sandy heath-land. The land was more fertile up near Jelling and Viborg."

Beorn tilts his head. "You're smart. But think about it. Viborg is too close to things Ástríd needs to get away from, and Jelling is too far from the water for me."

"Isn't there a coastal town with better land than this?"

"Heiðabý has good land. It's on the east side of the peninsula and more south."

Heiðabý. I remember Beorn singing that town's praises. "Let's go there."

"No."

I think of kicking him, but I don't know him well enough to predict his reaction. "How come you get to make the decision all by yourself?"

Beorn leans toward me. "Heiðabý," he says in a low voice, so I can hear but Ástríd can't, "has the biggest slave market of the Norse world. Ástríd could never bear it."

His words crash around inside my chest.

Soon enough we cross a wide ditch and enter the town of Ribe through a gate in a tall rampart. The houses all face the central street or the river. The people give a *skald*'s welcome, and Beorn performs night after night in the big hall, with the chieftain presiding. Over the following weeks, I come to find his repetitions consoling; they can be counted on. I love especially the story of the world Ásgard, where Óðinn rules. It's more fertile than anywhere else, with green glens and rivers and hills. It sounds like my Eire land.

That's what Beorn wants for us, a life that feels like Ásgard, and when he says it, Ástríd nods. She believes we can do it. Beorn can make anyone believe anything.

We live with a family while we build our own home. That's proper Norse hospitality. Ástríd wanted to build in town at first, but Beorn said no. If you live within the area marked off by the ditch, you have to follow all rules and perform all duties of the town. But if you live outside the ditch, you're free of many of those rules. So we claim a plot inland and clear it of trees and dig up roots and move stones into a pile. We dig a well and make water troughs for the animals, which are many now, since the people of Ribe added generously to our motley crew. The weeks and months pass in hard work. When the rains of autumn and winter finally cease, we burn off brushwood and plow and plant.

We are farmers. Ástríd busies herself, moving from one task to the next; contentment eases her quick eyes. If Beorn misses wandering, he doesn't show it. He has a knack for building things. He's going to be good at making things grow, too, I can tell. Búri learns to walk and say a few words, and his sweet nature deepens every day. They adapt to this new life. They belong here.

One night in spring, I realize I've been gone from my home, from my life, for a whole year. I belong in that life. But there's nothing I can do about it yet. I can't go off alone. I know what can happen to women and children who get caught someplace all alone.

The biggest slave market in the Norse world is in Heiðabý. And Heiðabý is east across the peninsula, then south. I never forget that. I never will.

Mel's birthday is well past. It was her birthday that started all this—her birthday, with our family trip to Dublin and everything that went wrong after that. I am nine now, and safe. Mel is sixteen, and I cannot know if she's safe. Or even . . . no, I won't think further.

I sneak outside to the stone pile and arrange some in a circle, with an opening for a door. Then I pile another layer on top. I keep adding stones, building a circular wall that I can lie inside of if I curl on my side. It's hard working in the dark, but the moon is bright and my hands feel every crevice. I jiggle and jiggle until one rock falls snug between two others. When a rock doesn't fit, I choose another.

I build through the night. When the wall's high enough that a person could crawl through the opening and the sides would be above her back, I try to make the rocks at the opening extend just a bit more on each new layer, so that they'll come together and form a roof. But the rocks fall off when I try. I work and work. I smack rocks against each other hard so they split and fit better. But they never fit perfect.

"Alfhild." Ástríd has come up behind me in the dawn. She walks around the wall. "I never saw a stone fence before." She touches it tentatively, as if afraid it will fall. She doesn't ask whether or where I've seen such a wall. Neither she nor Beorn ever presses me for information on where I came from. They seem to know I won't tell. "You're good at this." Her eyes go to my hands, and her mouth drops open.

I hold my hands up. The fingertips are bloody. Only now do I realize how sore they are. I suck on them, all of them at once.

"Come inside."

"It's not finished. It needs a top. It has to close, like a beehive."

"You can finish later."

"I have to do it now. But the stones keep falling when I try to make a roof."

Ástríd takes a deep breath. "A few split logs would make a fine roof."

I shake my head.

"Do you have to be stubborn all the time?" She puts her hands on my shoulders. "All right. We'll help. We'll build it together. Come inside now and soak your hands. Then we'll all go hunt for the right stones."

We make me a stone hut, the kind that hermits inhabit in Eire. The kind that Mel and I went inside before the slave ship stole us. It was the last place in our home country that we were free. And together. *Immalle*.

I take up sleeping in my stone hut. I eat with the family. I work with them. I love them. But this is my spot, where I whisper my home language to myself, where I sing the melodies of my Irish heart. Tucked away by Latin prayers, this is where I belong.

At least for now.

PART TWO

GROWING STRONG

(TWELVE YEARS OLD)

AUTUMN

CHAPTER NINE

We have been living on this farm outside Ribe for three years now, and I've never seen a sky like this. Clouds billow in from the west in quick profusion. More and more of them. It makes my skin prickle. Eire had wild storms. My Eire land. But nothing like that happens here.

I run my hand down my throat and swallow. It's not just the clouds; there's something strange about the air itself.

"Come, Búri. We have to hurry to gather the last of the cabbages and get inside."

The boy's a good help. I cut the leafy clusters off the stems with the big knife, and he hugs them to his chest and carries them to the wide swath of cloth I spread out at the end of the row. I cut fast, and he trots back and forth on legs that have just lately grown lean and long. He's proud to help me, just like I was always proud to help Mel. My heart beats a double drum of loss and gain.

These are good people, but they're not mine. Time passes far too slowly. I need to grow up and leave; I need to find Mel.

I look at the sky again. It changes even faster than we work. It suddenly goes dark. It's November, so the sky darkens fast anyway, but this is the middle of the day. And it's different from a night sky: The bottoms of the clouds are black.

I stab the knife into the dirt up to the handle for safekeeping—because I don't want it swinging around loose, not with how fast we'll have to move. I tie up the ends of the cloth and throw the sack of cabbages over a shoulder, then grab Búri by the hand and we run. He laughs—Búri is a great laugher—but when I don't join in, he hushes and runs harder.

We just make it into the house when the first drops fall. Our house has three rooms: a big central room, where we sleep and eat, with a smaller one to each side. All three rooms have doors to the outside. We enter through the door into the central room, and no one's there. The hearth fire in the middle of the room licks at the dark air and makes everything eerie. Evil spirits seem to rise from our sleeping berths along the walls and creep up to the oak rafters. I quick dump the cabbages in the room that we use for preparing food, then I check the other room—the one where we keep the animals at night in winter. It's empty.

Búri stands at the open central door. The rain has turned hard already; it thuds on the thatched roof. The wind howls. "Where's Mother?" Búri pulls on his fingers and turns in a circle on the packed dirt floor. Each stamp makes a small cloud of ash rise around him, for we scatter hearth ash on the floor to help keep it dry. He's over three and a half now—old enough to worry. I notice that he doesn't ask where Alof, his little sister, is. I'd smile at the sweetness of jealousy, except I'm as worried as Búri is.

But, thank everything good, I don't have to answer, for the animal room door bangs open and noise enlivens our entire home. Búri laughs and races into that room. Horses and cows, pigs and goats, sheep—and best of all, Ástríd with Alof in a sling at her chest, shooing the animals inside with nervous words of comfort. I'm the one who knows how to bring the animals in right. It's just accident that our roles were reversed today, and I wound up bringing in Búri while Ástríd wound up fetching the animals. But I shouldn't criticize her in my thoughts; she got them in, after all, even the ornery pigs. She did well.

Búri runs to Ástríd and throws his arms around her legs. I move from animal to animal, a scratch behind the ear, a pat on the rump, a rub between the eyes, until they're all quiet. They huddle close, as though they, too, realize this is not a normal rainfall. By the time I return to the hearth, Ástríd's got stew going in the iron cauldron over the fire. She and Búri sing loud, and little Alof crows along. It's as good a response to fear as any, for I know that Ástríd's mind is where mine is: Beorn went out on the boat this morning.

Beorn has turned out to be a rather poor farmer. Try as he does, he can't quite deal with farm rhythms—the way one season is all planting and the next is all tending and the next is all harvesting and the next is all preserving. It bores him. He likes variety in his day—that's what he had when he was a wandering *skald*. So now he leaves the farming to Ástríd and me, and he spends his day in a boat. He fishes some. And he trades along the west coast of Jutland, going by boat because it's faster. He sings and tells stories everywhere he goes. Lucky for him, small farmsteads keep popping up; it's easy to find people who want a *skald*'s services. And he always comes home with something useful or beautiful.

Today he went fishing.

I try not to picture him in his boat. I still hate boats. No Irish girl should hate boats. No Norse girl should hate boats. But I loathe them. They make me think of Mel, lost somewhere across some sea, in who knows what country. I feel stricken.

But Beorn is not lost. He's just fishing. Close by.

We smell the ocean from our farm, but we can't see it. The town is a good ways up the river from the sea. I'm sure the sea is wild, though. It has to be with a wind like this.

The house shudders. Now I can see why the farm up north had a pit house; they're sturdy. The homes down here are aboveground. But the roof is held up by posts, not just walls. So it shouldn't come apart. And Beorn is a good builder. We're safe.

Where is he? *Please, whatever god or gods there may be, please, don't let Beorn be lost at sea. We need him. We love him.*

Muffled crashes puncture the air. I imagine flying debris. Uprooted trees.

We sit with the firelight flickering on our faces, and I hug myself tight. Ástríd speaks very softly, so we have to strain to hear. I recognize the trick—that's how Beorn gets everyone to listen close. She tells the story of when the god Thor visited the giant Hymir and ate so much the giant got mad at him. So when they went fishing and Thor asked for bait, the giant told him to take care of himself. Furious, Thor ripped off the head of one of Hymir's oxen. So Hymir got scared and they rowed fast, but they were rowing so hard, Hymir feared they'd disturb the horrible serpent that lived there. And they did! That was Thor's plan—to make the serpent take the bait so he could smash his skull. But when the giant saw the serpent floundering there, he quick cut the line. The monster serpent sank back to the murky depths, defiant as ever.

Ástríd gives a triumphant laugh, and I know she's trying to soothe us. I know she's telling stories because if Beorn were here, that's what he'd be doing. But I don't see the comfort in this story.

As though she reads my face, Ástríd goes quiet. She nurses Alof while I measure out stew for Búri and me. The handle of the ladle is a carved bird head—Egill, a boy in town, made it for me. We eat greedily. Ástríd sings with her bird lilt. Finally Búri plants a kiss on his mother's cheek, on my cheek, and, honorable boy, on his sleeping sister's cheek. He curls up in his berth. I recognize the method: Sleep is a good escape.

The noise outside feels far away, because Beorn packed the spaces between the wall timbers so tightly. But we know the storm is right there, right outside. It screams.

I bring Ástríd a bowl of stew. She shakes her head. "You're nursing," I say. Her lip quivers. I work to keep mine steady. "Don't think the worst. It'll only wear you out."

Ástríd takes the bowl and eats. "Thank you, Alfhild."

"You made the stew. Don't thank me."

"I mean thank you for all of it. Thank you for saving Búri at his birth. Thank you for not telling Beorn what I did. Thank you for living with us and helping us."

"What else could I do?"

"Any number of things. Don't think I don't know that.

You're the most unusual child I've ever known. I'm glad you chose to stay with us. You filled a hole." She drops her head. Her braids flop on her chest. "The sea has stolen so much from me. I had a sister once."

I didn't know that. When she says no more, I move closer so that our sides touch. "So did I." I pray the sea steals nothing more from either of us.

I undo her braids and comb her hair. Then she combs mine. And we rest once more side to side. We fall asleep that way.

Then the door crashes open and the hearth fire is blown out, and Beorn stumbles in and drops Vigi on the floor. His wet clothes slap around him. He fights the wind to shut the door. He and Ástríd hug while I get the fire going again and Vigi whimper-barks.

Beorn tells how he was fishing when he saw the clouds and knew it would get bad. He rowed toward shore, but the pitch of the ocean was too strong, and the boat flipped. The sea was totally crazy. It took all his strength to swim to the beach. He wanted to rest there, but it was clear the sea was rising, so he dragged himself to the closest home. By then the rain came down in torrents, and the man of the house begged for help getting his animals to safety. Beorn thought about us, but he knew we would have already done it—he knew we were strong. So he helped that family, and when he saw other families struggling, his energy came back and he helped another, with the winds furiously ripping at him. And all at once he panicked at the thought of us alone. He practically crawled his way home against the buffets, clutching Vigi in his arms so the wind wouldn't steal the hound away.

I give Vigi a bowl of stew. The dog eats it in three gulps. Beorn is almost as fast. He finishes the stew and drinks beer from his big wood cup and burps loudly. The room sighs with the smell of bog myrtle—the spice Ástríd adds with hops into the barley beer.

"I'm glad the boat is gone," says Ástríd. "Do you want my advice?"

Beorn smiles. "Even the god Óðinn asks Frigg's advice."

"Yes," I say, boldly interrupting, "but he doesn't listen to her."

Beorn hesitates briefly, then laughs. We all do.

We are together, safe. That's all any of us needs now. Tonight I am glad not to be sleeping in my hermit's hut. Tonight I am very glad to have this family. I make a final prayer, the one I make every night—that my Irish family, far and scattered, should be well and safe—and I fall deep asleep.

In the morning the beach is a mess of broken branches and seaweed. Most of the townsfolk are back in Ribe, cleaning up there. The only ones out here on the shore besides Beorn and Vigi and me are the scavengers. We walk slowly, even Vigi, for the dog has aged quickly. He moves like an old man now, his legs stiff.

Fortunately, the scavengers have discovered the remains of an old ship washed up on the rocks at the far south end, so they've converged there in hopes of finding treasures in the wreckage. They're stupid, it seems to me, since if the hapless sailors who sank with that boat had their wealth and jewels with them—an admitted likelihood—those coins and precious metals and stones would have been in their personal wooden chests. The chests would have sunk straight down; the ship, most likely, as well. Over time the ship was buffeted by the currents and busted apart—as the wreckage proves—but the chests simply sank deeper, as heavy things will. If there are treasures to find, it will take deep diving to do it, and I doubt anyone could dive that deep. Besides, who would know where to dive?

I look at Beorn, and he looks back with eyes that tell me he also finds the scavengers foolish, but he enjoys that about them. I like living with Beorn. I like the way he uses his eyes. I like that he's not as critical as I am. And I'm grateful that he is not lamenting the loss of his fishing boat. He's lucky to be alive; that fact stays his tongue.

The sea is still high, with perfect waves that crest, linger an instant, then crash silver white. I love the sound, even though I know what destruction they brought. But there's a quiet sound now too. A little pop. *Pop, pop, pop.* I look at Beorn quizzically.

He's already smiling and kneeling. With both hands he digs through the sand. I help. And we're scooping up scallops by the tens. They've been washed out of their grassy beds somewhere in the shallows north of here. I set one on the surface of the wet sand, and it opens and shuts its shell in a quick flap, making a soft *pop* as it disappears under sand.

Beorn works at filling our bucket.

But I'm walking past sponges and shells and seaweed to a large, golden hunk, about the size of Alof's head. I hold it up to the sun. It glows, almost translucent. I know amber. Everyone here prizes it for making beads, amulets, and delicate carvings of animals. It's soft, easily scratched. And sometimes it has parts of creatures inside—a bee wing, a spider leg—which makes it more valuable.

Inside this piece are three ants, whole and perfect. I turn it over. Not a scratch.

I am the daughter of a king. I knew gold, silver, all precious stones, when I was still small enough to sit on people's laps. And Ribe is a trading town. So I've seen the finely worked jewelry that traders bring. This is by far the most precious object I've ever seen.

I look back at Beorn, piling scallops up past the bucket brim. I open my cloak and ease my treasure into the pouch that hangs from my shoulder strap, attached by a brooch.

Then I gather the smaller pieces of amber scattered across the sand. There are many. A forest of submerged pine trees must have been washed loose by the violence of that storm. Some pieces are dark reddish brown, some straw yellow. Resin is a marvel that way. I set aside the darkest one for Alof, the lightest one for Búri. I'll let Ástríd choose the pieces she wants. The rest are for Beorn. For I know he'll build himself another boat. He has to travel, he has to tell stories. He can trade these amber pieces away.

All but one.

When Mother put Mel and me on the horse's back and told us to ride away from Downpatrick and not come back till after the Vikings had been killed, she gave Mel a pouch. Inside it was Mel's gold teething ring from when she was a baby. Mother said anyone would recognize it was worth lots of money, so anyone would know we were the children of royalty, and they'd take us in. Mel never showed it to anyone, though. Or not while I was still with her. She was saving it.

It's good to have something valuable. You never know when you'll need it.

I pat my pouch.

CHAPTER TEN

"What will you do with a boat that size?" Ástríd's voice is an accusation.

Beorn ushers her off to the side where Knud, the boat's owner, can't overhear them. "The same thing I did with my smaller boat."

"You can't manage that big boat alone. It could hold six people!"

"Not six. It's built to be managed by three."

"You're but one."

"I'll hire help."

"And pay them with what?"

"I won't need more than one. I'm not crossing the ocean. I'll simply skim along the coast. With one strong boy—who will be grateful for the opportunity to travel and learn a skill and earn his keep on the boat as we trade. I even have a boy in mind."

Ástríd walks in a tight, angry circle with Alof on her hip. "Maybe this boy, whoever he is, would be willing to work in exchange for experience on a trading trip—but never for just daily fishing off the coast right here in Ribe. And we can't afford to share your meager fishing catch with anyone. So tell me, are you going to give up fishing altogether? Will you make your living entirely by trading? Will you leave me for weeks on end while you go on those infernal trading trips?" Her voice gets higher pitched with every question.

"Of course not! I'll fish. Even more than I did before, because now I'll be able to go after bigger fish. I'll sell to everyone in town, not just our neighbors." He looks around in desperation and his eyes light on me and Búri, who are watching tensely. "And I don't need to hire a boy for daily fishing, because I have Alfhild."

I flinch.

"Alfhild?" Ástríd looks at me, her eyes wounded. "Did you agree to this?"

I shake my head. "It's the first I've heard of it."

"But you'll do it, won't you, Alfhild?" Beorn's voice is raspy. "I'll teach you."

I look at the boat. It's far smaller than the slave ship that stole me and Mel from Eire, but it's still big—bigger than the little boat Thornkild had. How on earth could two people control such a boat? Beorn has a lot of experience . . . but so do I, more than I wish, and my experience with boats makes my stomach churn.

"Farming is a good life," says Ástríd, more softly now.

"I know," says Beorn. "But it's not for me." He touches my shoulder. "Alfhild?"

I turn to him. Beorn's face is rigid with need. He can't possibly stay on the farm all the time—he wouldn't survive. Where would I be without this man? I swallow down the sick that has risen in my throat. "All right."

Ástríd turns her back on me, while Beorn barters with Knud. From now on, one third of his catch will be Knud's for as long as the man or his wife shall live. It's not a bad arrangement, since the couple is old and not long for this life anyway. But I know that Ástríd is holding in a little scream of worry. I can hear it in the pulse in her neck. And it's nothing compared to the wail I'm holding in. But she doesn't know that.

The very next day Beorn takes me out to the river. There's hardly any farmwork this time of year, after all, and I've never shown aptitude for weaving or other home skills. So why delay? Nothing Ástríd says can dissuade him. I don't even try.

I follow his broad back, praying that cold weather will come early this year. *Let it come now, in fact. Today. Allow me the winter to get used to this idea, please. Oh, please. I can face it in spring, not now. Let a storm come again. Please, something, anything.*

But the water stays calm, the skies stay clear, the wind is what Beorn calls auspicious. And so we sail, down the river, out to the sea. There are oars for use in dead air, of course, and chests to sit on if we need to row. But this boat was built for sailing.

We start with lessons about wind. Wind can come from ahead, the side, behind—well, of course I knew that. So you have to wait for wind to come from the right direction in order to sail where you want to go. Either that, or use oars. Or, in a small boat, if you are strong and swift, you can learn tricks with moving the sail, but that risks capsizing the boat. All this means it is important to stay within sight of land, because wind can quickly change direction and confuse you. If the land gets suddenly cold, as when night approaches, wind will blow from the land. But when the land warms up, it draws the air to it, making a sea breeze. And if you didn't notice the shift, you're lost. It's all very tricky.

We have a sunboard, which measures the sun's height and lets us know whether we're going south or north—but that's only to use if we lose sight of land and, naturally, it can't help in fog. We have a sunstone, too. It's transparent and sparkles in the sun, and on foggy or cloudy days it shows the sun's direction, but only if there's at least a sliver of blue sky. It's best not to count on the sunboard or the sunstone. Sailors know safety nets shred.

So, basically, we are never to lose sight of land. That's the first rule. Once on the open sea, it's easy to get lost and not have any sense of where the closest land is. If all else fails, follow the birds. At this time of year, especially the pink-footed geese. Or seals. They have to rest on dry banks. But really, never let that happen. Never lose sight of land.

This rule is fine with me. I'd rather be on land anyway.

It isn't just seeing the land that matters, though— because if you lose track and don't notice for a while, when you look back at the land, you might be looking at something that isn't the land you set out from. It can happen, even to seasoned sailors. You can think because the land is to your right, you're heading north, when really, it's land across the sea, and you're turned around heading south. If the sun is out, that helps, but the sun is often hidden by clouds. So we have to memorize the landmarks. Islets. Little peninsulas. It's important to distinguish between small inlets and bigger bays and which have undersea reefs; between soft ochre beaches and white silky beaches, and know which one is south of the other even though there are tens of them. It's important to recognize the shape of hills, even low ones, and to know the areas where the red deer are most populous. At certain times of the day you can count on seeing them, and that can send you in the right direction—or not. Sand dunes characterize one stretch, gravel beaches characterize another. And if we see tall cliffs, white with black stripes, we know we've gone too far, all the way back to the Limfjord. This, too, must be memorized, although if we stick to plans, I'll never see it—so my mind's eye has to paint it clearly enough to stand firm as reality. All of it—fact and mystery—must be committed to memory. Beorn is adamant that I do this.

I have a good memory. And my arms and legs are strong from farming. Between memory and strength, I take to boating as though born to it, which in a sense I suppose any child of Eire is, since it's easier to get from one town to another by water than by land. This country is the same. All the settlements of any size are on the coasts, and even isolated farms are always near rivers, so boats can arrive much faster than walking or going by horseback.

Reciting the rules in my head helps me to quell the initial abhorrence. And gaining skills with the sails actually makes me feel proud of myself. Who knows, maybe being able to handle a boat will help me rescue Mel. Now that I think of it that way, I can look forward to each thing I learn.

Soon I enjoy looking around as we glide through the water. We're just moving into winter, though the air is yet mild, and sunrise and sunset are filled with clutters of skylarks, their forked tails well defined against the red to yellow to white backdrop of sun glow. I laugh. In just a couple of weeks, I've come to savor the spray of salt water on my cheeks. Something about this is so very right. I'm coming, Mel. I'm coming to get you as soon as I can.

I am sitting now in the calm of a bay created by a barrier island just a little out from a curved rocky shore thick with oak and beech. We were on our way home when we stopped here. A large beaver came out of the forest and swam across the salty water right in our path and disappeared on this island—which means there's a dam in there. Armed with his ax, Beorn went over the side of the boat in pursuit of what he claims is the darkest, moistest, tenderest meat on earth. So I am entirely alone—a rare experience.

I scan the bay simply out of habit, when I see the ship. It enters the bay on the north side of this island. And it has two sails. Norse ships have only one. The slave ship that stole Mel and me had two. It's going slowly, as though trawling.

Sweat beads across my brow and stings my eyes. Maybe they haven't seen me. Our sail is down, of course. I pull up the anchor. I can't paddle the boat around the south point of the island to the far side before they see me. So I hoist the sail. What else can I do?

They have seen me now, definitely. No one could fail to see a boat with its sail up at this distance. I gasp for breath; I feel smothered. I go south. But they are coming south. So I head out, away, into the sea. The wind is at my back. The boat flies over the waves, faster and faster as though it will take flight. The world blurs and I'm shaking, but it doesn't matter because nothing about me can affect the motion of this ship; it moves on its own now, as though at one with the changing shape of the water. We go, go, go, the ship and me.

When I finally dare to look behind, there is nothing but sea. Blue-green everywhere.

I loosen the sail so it luffs, then lower it. Within just a moment, the ship bobs on the sea like a dead body. My hands are numb. I look at them, at the indentation from the rope I held on to so tightly, but I can't feel them in the least. I sit in the middle of the bottom of the boat and hold my face in my hands.

But what am I doing? I jump to my feet. I've lost sight of land! There are no markers in the sea, nothing to give me a sense of direction. I no longer know which way the boat faces, which way is home.

The sun blazes distantly. And it's setting! It's like the single eye of Óðinn. The god traded his other eye for a drink from the well of wisdom. He knows almost everything, and he's counseling me now. I hoist the sail, but the wind is small. So I reef it, folding up the bottom part and lashing it to make the right size for this weak wind. I turn so the sun is to my back, and I sail due east. It takes a long time to see land—or maybe it only seems so long because it's getting dark fast and I'm squinting. The wind blows against me now, at first just a little, but it's gaining strength. I turn south, even though I don't yet know which direction the island is, because I have to turn one way or the other.

There's a beach I recognize because the strand is so deep—even in high tide, the sand goes back enormously far before grasses start—so now I know the beaver island is to the north. I spin the boat and head north. It isn't far. Beorn stands at the island's tip and waves, the fool—as though I'm not heading straight for him. I stop and anchor while he swims out and tosses into the boat first three dead beavers, then his ax.

He climbs in, hand over hand on the rope, and wraps himself in a blanket. He swam to that island in the first place, so he's been wet all afternoon—and the temperature has dropped precipitously. He shivers. His teeth chatter. He doesn't speak a word.

I spin the boat again and sail us home. All these weeks my mind has been filled with the challenge of learning to sail. And, yes, the joy of being in control, and the hope that this will help me find Mel. I hardly thought of anything else. It was as though I was someone much stronger, someone who could do anything, right now, today. Someone who didn't have a past that taught her better.

But that ship reminded me.

I could have been snatched. Again.

And Mel is still somewhere else. Maybe somewhere awful.

It's my job to find her. I must!

I'm yet only twelve; I can't do it now. But I will. I will find Mel. She is my sister, and I love her. I will bring us back to Eire. Once I'm older, stronger, able. Once the sight of a ship with two sails doesn't turn me into a quivering mass. I must find a way to prepare myself properly, so that I can succeed in rescuing her.

As we finally turn up the Ribe River, Beorn moves close and says, "Don't tell Ástríd."

Does that mean he saw the boat? Does he guess why I fled? It's too dark to see the message in his eyes, if there is one there. "I won't."

"You scared me, Alfhild." He rests his hand heavy on my shoulder. "You were out of sight—so I know you couldn't see the land. You broke the rules."

I turn my head away. I had no choice. If he saw the boat, he knows that. What's the point of an argument?

"You're a fine sailor, though it will take years to make you sea wise. Remember that. Don't get complacent. Ever. I don't want to lose you."

I stifle a cry of pain. I love Beorn. Ástríd . . . Búri . . . Alof. And Mel, too. And Mother, Father, Nuada. I love them all. My head could burst with all this love.

CHAPTER ELEVEN

We walk past the smithy to the great hall where the feast is going on.

"Look up, Búri." Ástríd stops, holding the boy by one hand and pointing to the sky with the other. "The god Frey is riding over the earth tonight on his magnificent boar. If you look hard, you might see him, like a streak of gold."

"Boar? The god is riding on a boar? Our boar won't let me ride him."

"Frey's boar isn't ordinary. His shines so bright, he lights up even the darkest cave. And he has a name: Gull-inbursti."

"Our boar has a name: Collach."

"What a strange name to give him."

"It's not strange. It's what Alfhild calls him."

Ástríd looks at me.

I shrug. *Collach* means "boar" where I come from. I've given Gaelic names to all the animals—it's one way of holding on to the words that would slither away from the edges of my mind. I keep my face blank.

Ástríd twists her lips. "Well, it makes sense then. After all, Frey is king of many things, including Álfheim, the world of the light elves. And Alfhild's name is elfin. So Alfhild has things in common with him." She looks at me as if to check whether I object to this account, but I simply shrug again. "Anyway, have you noticed that the days have gotten shorter?"

Búri shakes his head.

"Well, they have. Now Frey is bringing back the light. Today was the shortest day of the year, but tomorrow will be longer. Each day from now on will be a little longer."

"Forever?"

"No. Just till summer. Then it changes again and the days get shorter."

"Don't think about it too hard," says Beorn. He's holding Alof, and he kisses her on the forehead. Then he stoops and kisses Búri, too. "It's the way the world works, and thinking won't make sense of it, and it surely won't change it. The important thing is to move quickly to the great hall, and if anything strange greets you, just keep walking."

"Anything strange? Like what?"

"Someone on an eight-legged horse."

"A horse with eight legs! Really?"

"His name is Sleipnir. And the god on his back is Óðinn. You don't want to stop if they show up, because behind them run the dead."

"What are the dead?"

Beorn straightens the boy's leather cap. "I'll tell the tale later. For now, let's go eat."

I'm ready. I don't want to hear about what the gods are doing tonight. It bothers me that I already knew everything he said about Frey and Óðinn. It's impossible to sit around the hearth at night with a *skald* and not know all the god stories. I know about the long line of Danish kings who were always waging war with someone too—the first of whom was Skjøld, a son of Óðinn. The stories about these gods and kings are fabulously entertaining, I admit. But I worry that they're entering me, sneakily, insidiously. Sometimes I can't remember stories from Eire, and I used to love those stories. I used to make my brother Nuada tell them over and over.

When I was lost on the boat, when Beorn was on the beaver island, it was the god Óðinn who I thought of, not Jesus. Sometimes I'm not even sure of the words to the Lord's Prayer. Mel and I used to say it together, and without her, it's hard to remember. The thought makes my tongue feel fat, like before I cry. It's almost a foreign feeling to me now; I haven't cried in a long time.

I focus on the feast ahead. We've been fasting all day so we'll have a hearty appetite now. Jól is the most important holiday. It starts tonight and goes till the new year.

We enter the hall, and the aroma of roast pork slaps us in the face and practically makes me fall over with hunger. People are drinking ale—no, not drinking, they're sloshing it down—and the room is so packed we have to weave our way through. A piper follows us, with a goatskin covering his shoulders in honor of Thor. His tune is all lively, so that my feet naturally want to dance. The two harpists at one side of the room join in. As one, people get to their feet, and in a snap the center of the room is cleared of food and game boards. It's like magic. They dance, partners hand in hand.

Something tickles my neck, and I turn to find Egill's face thrust in mine. I laugh. "What are you doing with that feather?"

"Since I haven't much of a beard yet, I thought it was a good substitute. Come." He grabs my hand, and we join the dancing.

The music goes on and on, and it's fun shuffling about. I love dancing, of course. At banquets when I was tiny, Mel and I would grab opposite corners of a kerchief and swirl each other around the hall to horns, pipes, whistles, harps. Then she got too old for such behavior, so I danced in circles by myself, waving the kerchief over my head. I'm dancing for her now, dancing out my pledge. *I'll find you, Mel.* I kick and turn. *I'll save you, Mel.* I flail my arms. *I'll come in a boat and whisk you away.*

But it's been a long day, and finally my stomach clenches. "Aren't you hungry?" I practically yell above the laughter and music.

"Always."

So we stop and eat, and Ástríd comes over to ask Egill to watch Búri, so she and Beorn can dance for a while. She feels fine about asking Egill for a favor, since Beorn has promised Egill to take him on as his helper once spring comes and he goes trading again. And, of course, she doesn't even ask me; she simply plants Alof in my arms and leaves. Little Alof promptly grabs at the meat on the tip of my knife, but I swing it away in time.

"Good thing you're quick," says Egill.

"I've had lots of practice." I hold the knife tip at a slant so Búri can take off the meat, and then I look at Alof, who's staring at me with eager curiosity. This child will be eating everything lots earlier than Búri did, I bet. I kiss her, so the grease of the meat from my lips coats hers. She understands instantly and licks her lips in surprised glee.

"Can I have one of those?"

I spear a piece of meat on the tip of my knife and hold it out to Egill.

"No. I meant the other."

A kiss? I'm appalled. I've known about what happens between men and women for as long as I can remember.

I'm the girl who passed as much time as I could among the livestock, after all. But I have no interest in such things. Not yet. I pull away.

Egill grabs me and pushes me down.

I jump up, ready to let loose a fury of invectives, when I realize that a huge bone just got hurled across the room. If Egill hadn't shoved us flat, Alof and I might have been hit.

The man who caught the bone calls out a challenge, and people clear the way as he casts it back. The other man catches it and falls back a few steps from the force of it. And the bone's flying through the air our way again. But we are safely crouched on the floor. I've seen this sport before and always thought it was stupid—drunk men making absurd challenges. But now I realize the bone-casting contest isn't just dumb; it's dangerous. Gnawed bones are heavy. I don't like how these men show off their strength all the time.

The bone goes back and forth faster, flung harder each time. The laughter of the onlookers becomes strained. Egill tugs on me and we crawl away, over near the gaming boards.

"What's going on?" I ask him. "What's at stake?"

"They both want to marry Helga, and Harald hasn't decided who will win yet."

Harald is Helga's father, and Helga is my friend, to the

extent that I have any friends outside the family. I keep pretty much to my work. We haven't really talked since last summer. I spy her now, standing against the far wall, her arms crossed at the chest, her face a mask of indifference. I wonder who she prefers. "It's rotten that she can't choose."

"Choose? What a crazy idea." Egill laughs and pushes me in the shoulder.

I push him back, a little harder.

"You have too many crazy ideas," says Egill. "Like working with Beorn on the boat. He'd be better off with me helping all the time, not just when he goes trading."

"I'm good on the boat."

"You might be. But that doesn't make it right."

Suddenly one of the men throws up his hands. "I won't fight you. I won't break Jól."

And the contest is over just like that. That's a good thing about Jól—it's a festival of peace. Even men who fight all the time can act nice during Jól. I watch the tension drain from Helga's shoulders as she turns back to her plate of food.

Egill reaches a hand toward me, and for a moment I fear he'll touch my hair, but when I lean away he touches Alof's cheek instead. "Will you skate with me tomorrow?"

The weather changed this past week, as though getting

ready for Jól. It's so cold now, the stream is frozen. "I don't have skates. You know that."

"I made you some."

"Really?" I've watched skaters with something bordering on envy. It's like dancing, but infinitely smoother. "Who died?"

"Kjartan's old stallion. And I was the first to ask for the foot bones."

It's a lot of work to make skates. I watched Beorn make a pair for Búri. You have to grind the bottom of the bone flat and make it smooth on top. And unless you want to use a spiked stick to propel yourself across the ice, you need to add holes in either end of the bones so they can be fastened by thongs to your shoes. Though I coveted those skates, I didn't ask Beorn to make me a pair for the very reason that I knew how much work it was.

I shouldn't accept such a gift, especially not after how Egill behaved tonight.

Still, I'd love to learn to skate. I'm sick of standing on the side and swallowing my envy as I watch Búri play ball games on the ice. "Thank you," I say at last. "But skates aren't payment for kisses, you understand."

He laughs. "I know that."

"Know it well. If you want thrills, you'll have to find them elsewhere."

"Oh, there'll be plenty of thrills this week, with the *papi* and all."

I don't know that word . . . *papi*. "The what?"

"Aha! Something the know-it-all Alfhild doesn't know. A *papi* is a foreigner."

"So what? Lots of foreigners pass through Ribe."

"A *papi* is different. He's not a trader. He's a religious man from some other religion. He's come to find converts."

My ears are starting to ring. "What religion?"

"He calls himself *Kristinn*."

Kristinn? Christian!

"And he's from Írland. It's to the west."

Írland—Eire land.

An Irish monk.

CHAPTER TWELVE

"What do you think it is?" Egill stands looking at the box on the floor inside the poled enclosure they've built for the monk. It's a poor excuse for shelter; the wind blows right through. The monk sits on the dirt with his back to us. He's slumped forward, and his tunic is so thin, the ridges of his backbone stand out distinctly.

The box is the length of my forearm and half that in width. It's made of thick yew. Sheets of pounded-thin copper are nailed to the outer surfaces and secured at the edges by nailed-on bars of more copper. The bottom is a normal rectangle. The lid is attached by hinges and is in the shape of a pitched roof, with four sides: two large ones and two smaller triangular ones to close off the ends. A ridge pole goes across the apex of the roof, and it holds together the four roof pieces. The ridge pole sticks out a little on both sides and curls into loops, where each end of a chain is fastened. On the sides and lid are circular and rectangular decorations, all of bronze.

"What do you think it is? Go on, make a guess."

I don't have to guess. I know exactly what it is: a reliquary. Monks carry them hanging from their necks by those chains. But I don't want him or anyone else to think it's important—because who knows what people will do if they think it's important? "It's a box, Egill. Just a box. All the travelers who come through Ribe carry boxes."

"Well, yeah, of course, but guess what's inside?"

I shake my head. "I don't want to know."

He grins. "Bones. Human bones!"

The bones of a saint. Probably bits of the saint's clothing, too.

"And a tooth."

"How do you know?" *Please tell me no one touched them.* They shouldn't touch what they don't believe in. They shouldn't touch without reverence.

"Arne showed us. He opened it up yesterday morning and held it out for us boys to see. Then he stripped the man and made him turn in a circle." Egill points toward Arne, under the bushes. I hadn't noticed him there before. "When he wakes, he'll show you."

The ruddy-faced man is wrapped up in blankets. After a feast, drunk people sleep where they fall. But Arne's big—I'm not sure even Beorn could win over him in wrestling—and big men stay sober longer. Arne stayed sober long enough to roll up in the blanket.

The monk has no blanket. And no cloak. The world spins a little, and I have to shut my eyes a moment. "Why is Arne there?"

"He's guarding the monk."

"From what?"

Egill laughs. "Not from anything. He's keeping him from running away."

I hug myself. This is not a shelter; it's a cage. I've never seen a man in a cage before.

"I have to go now. Meet me in the afternoon? I'll bring your skates, the ones I made. I can be like the god Ull, who hunts on skis and skates, and you can hold on to my arm. Say you'll come."

"All right." But I'm not thinking toward the afternoon. The moment holds me fast.

Egill lopes off, and I notice how long his legs are these days, how big his feet are. For an instant, I'm afraid of him.

I walk around to the other side of the cage and sit in front of the monk.

He looks at me, but stupidly, as though he's the one who spent last night drinking instead of Arne and all the others. Maybe that's what happens to a man when he's caged. I saw a caged wolf once when I was small, and it looked all listless like this monk does now. The monk's clothes are loose, but I can see how skinny he is. Not just his back, but his arms, his legs. He appears shrunken, like a wizened child. His eyes have sunk into their sockets. How long has he been wandering? And how did he get here?

He makes the sign of the cross. *"Pater noster,"* he whispers.

That means "our father" in Latin. I wish he was speaking my language—the language of my lost childhood. But Latin is good enough. Latin is what I heard in church, what I use in some of my prayers at night; it's what my memory grasps at. I move closer to his cage.

"Pater noster, qui es in caelis, sanctificetur nomen tuum."

Our father, who art in heaven, hallowed be thy name. This is what I mumble at night in the hermit's hut. Or try to. I need to hear what the monk says. I need to be reminded of the right way to say it. I lean forward to catch the holy sounds.

"Is he bothering you?" Arne stands behind me. I don't know what woke him. The monk was whispering, and I didn't say a thing. We're just unlucky. He jabs a finger toward the monk's face. "Shut up, Ansgar! My head is hurting from last night's drink, and the last thing I want to hear is your babbling."

"Is that his name?" I say softly. That's not an Irish name I've ever heard.

"Who knows? He speaks nonsense."

"So why do you call him that?"

"Ah, you haven't heard about Ansgar yet? How many years have you lived here? You know the black earth, on the south side of the river, across from the marketplace?"

It isn't black earth at all. It's just open land. But everyone calls it the black earth and they skirt around it, as though it's filthy. Or cursed. I nod.

"Ansgar was a missionary monk from somewhere south. He built a church there." He picks meat from his teeth. "Do you know what a church is? A Christian church?"

I nod.

"Always with their crazy languages and incomprehensible rituals. They talk about drinking their god's blood and eating his flesh. Did you know that?"

Holy Communion. That sacrament is not at all how he describes it. But I nod.

"After Ansgar, there was another monk. When he died, no more came. So we burned the church. That's what made the earth black. It's scorched. Hideous people, monks."

"Did you know Ansgar?"

"Me? Of course not. Ansgar came forty years ago."

"Then how do you know monks are hideous?"

"My grandfather knew Ansgar. And he hated those bells. They scared away the land sprites. There was no one to guard the flowers and the trees. And the next monk did the same. I knew that one. I was thirteen when he died. I helped burn the church." Arne brushes his hands together as if cleaning them off. "You won't find any more monks coming here."

I look at the monk. He's watching the two of us, and energy has come to his eyes.

"We just did," I say.

"Well, he won't be here for long."

"Are you going to send him on his way?"

Arne shakes his head and looks at me reprovingly. "It's a mistake to pass your problems to others. No, the only thing to do with a monk is make him a slave or kill him."

Arne already said the monk won't be here for long. Knowledge is heavy as an ax head. I stand, holding on to a cage pole because my knees wobble. "He'd be a good slave."

"That mess? He's skin and bones, child. You're stronger than he is."

"But he's a holy man."

"So what?"

"It's wrong to harm a holy man, no matter whether he has your beliefs or not."

"Who told you that? He's a scourge."

I won't win this battle. "What if someone wanted to take him as a slave?" I say.

"He's useless. I told you."

"But what if someone did?"

"No one does. So the *þing* has decided to hang him."

A ball of pain forms between my eyes. But it's not too late. It's not like with kings in Eire; Irish kings can make decisions and stand firm no matter what the others think. These people, the Dan, they come together in an open-air assembly—the *þing*—and talk it over. They vote. "What if someone spoke up now?"

Arne looks at me with bleary-eyed interest. "You know someone who'd be willing to take him as a slave?"

"I do."

"Who?"

"Me."

Arne laughs. "Go home, Alfhild."

I shake my head and back away, moving my steadying hand to another pole. "What if Beorn comes and asks for him? The *þing* would let Beorn have him as a slave, right?"

Arne puts a hand to his forehead. "You're making my head hurt worse, child."

"But they might, right?"

"You talk as though Beorn has an interest in a Christian monk."

The tone of his words scares me. "I'm not sure what Beorn will say." I use my most childlike voice. "I haven't asked him."

Arne shakes his head like a giant dog. "Good. For a moment you had me worried. Don't bother asking. Beorn is sensible. I'll see you at the hanging. Before nightfall."

I turn and run. The sky is far too dark for morning. Snow comes, light at first, then faster. It gathers on my eyelashes. *Pater noster.* The only noise is the jangling iron fastenings on the collar of a horse pulling a wagon along the lane. *Qui es in caelis.* I run as fast as I can, slipping and sliding in the new snow. *Sanctificetur nomen tuum.*

They are all home, seated around the hearth.

"Alfhild!" Ástríd smiles at me with relief. "You went out early. I checked your stone hut, but you weren't there."

"Ástríd, Beorn, help me."

Beorn's eyes widen. "How?"

"We have to save the monk."

"The monk?" Ástríd sets Alof on her knees and bounces her. "Why would we care about that monk?"

So she knows. Everyone must know. Of course. Maybe she even went to the *þing* when they met—women don't have a duty to go, but they're allowed. "Let's buy him."

"I hate slavery." The words burst from Ástríd like a cough.

"He doesn't have to be a real slave. He can be like a family member."

"A family member?" Beorn throws up his hands. "I can't afford to feed another mouth. Besides, he's weak. Useless."

That's what Arne called him. "No one's useless."

"He can't plow the fields."

"Neither can Búri or Alof."

"Children are good for—"

"He's good too! He's done no crime. It's wrong to hang him."

"He's a danger," says Beorn.

"How can that be? You just said he's weak."

"You don't understand, Alfhild." Beorn slaps his thigh. "He's a dangerous influence."

"He can't speak our language. How can he influence us?" I look at Ástríd. "Tell me."

Ástríd's eyes are large with concern.

Beorn rubs his nose with the back of his hand. "We can't feed him."

"Yes, we can." I go to my personal chest and take out my amber.

Beorn holds it to the fire, staring at the ants within. It's even larger than I remembered it to be. It looks like a heavenly vision. "Where did you get this?"

"I found it on the beach."

"Do you have others?"

"No. This was my treasure. In case I needed it. If you sell it, we'll have plenty of money. Especially if you sell it in Heiðabý. You said everyone pays top price there."

"Alfhild." Beorn looks quickly at Ástríd, then back at me. "I haven't been to Heiðabý since I married. I'll never go to Heiðabý again."

"Then you can get someone else to go there and sell it for you."

Beorn drops his head. "I won't keep a foreigner in this home."

"He can sleep in my stone hut. I hardly ever sleep there these days anyway."

"What work could he do?"

"I'd find chores for him, like I do for Búri."

"I don't want him near the little ones."

"He won't hurt them."

"How do you know?"

"I know."

Beorn shakes his head.

"Please." I fall to my knees in front of him. I have to save the monk. I might never be able to really save Mel; I might never even be able to find her. But this monk is here, and I can save him. I have to. "Please, Beorn." I'm wiping away tears. "When spring comes and people go off to Heiðabý to trade, they can bring him along with them and send him on his way. But we have to feed him until then. We have to shelter him and make him strong. We have to keep him through the winter. Please."

Ástríd comes to stand beside Beorn. She puts a hand on his shoulder. "I hate this idea—but I owe Alfhild heartily. It's only till spring. Please, husband, can we do this?"

"There's no owing within a family."

"Then do it out of love. We all love each other. We want each other to be happy."

Beorn puts his hand over Ástríd's and looks up at her. "I never go to the *þing*. I never vote. In this town, only the rich men go. What if they turn me down?"

"Then they turn you down."

Beorn leans toward me. "I don't understand why you want this."

"A good man cannot be hanged."

Búri comes to stand at my side. He puts his hand on my shoulder, mimicking his mother. "A good man cannot be hanged," he says.

CHAPTER THIRTEEN

"Alfhild." Beorn stands over me. He's opened the door to a cool dawn breeze, much warmer than usual. The winter months have slipped away. "Things are going to change."

I sit up and question him with my eyes, even as I wipe the sleep from them.

"Spring is here, and there's work to do. Papi's lived with us more than three months, and he's done no work. Well, that's ended, starting today. You're in charge of him. Understand?"

"Not really."

"I'm going to the river to work on my boat with Egill. Got to repair winter's damage. So it's up to you to make that monk work." Beorn stomps outside.

A sinking feeling weights me to the berth. I hate to admit it, but Arne and Beorn were right: Papi is useless. Egill's told me a thousand times that I'll regret taking in the monk. I hate hearing it. I stopped skating with him, his refrain got so grating.

When Beorn brought Papi home last December,

he stood outside our door, touching a red streak across his neck. I looked close and saw that it went all the way around; it was a burn mark—someone had already tightened a noose on him! I expected him to scream at the horror of the memory. But he just looked detached, tap, tap, tapping his fingers. I couldn't for the life of me understand why a person would do that to him. What's to be gained from scaring a man witless before hanging him? Unless someone considered it fun.

I took Papi gently by the hand and led him to my hut, feeling apologetic for the lack of a hearth fire, but at least I had put my blanket inside for him. And two goats I named Gabhar and Meigeall. One has a long beard that Alof likes to pull. Goats can be excellent company. Papi crawled inside. Then he pushed the goats out; he prefers to be alone.

He sits in the center, so there's no room for anyone else. I know because I tried to enter; he wouldn't move aside. He acts as though the hut was built expressly for him. It is a hermit hut, so I sort of understand. Some monks live in monasteries, others live in isolated huts.

But I don't understand how he can be satisfied sitting alone all day. Nothing can entice him to come out—no pleading or shouting. All he does is pray. Loudly. It would drive me to despair to act like that. I listened to his prayers at first, but that got monotonous. He speaks only Latin. To tell the truth, by midwinter I was sick of him.

The months have passed with the only acknowledgment of his existence being the bowls of food I bring him and the empty bowls he passes back. Gradually I have come to understand that he enjoys a life of no communication other than with his God. This makes me wonder if he's done something terrible. Maybe he went on this mission of converting Norsemen as a penance, and he now accepts life in the hut as more penance. I even wonder sometimes if he feels cheated because he wasn't hanged. So much of my early religion has melded together with the religion surrounding me today that I'm not sure of much anymore, but I remember penance. If you do something wrong, you must repent. You must say prayers. And suffer somehow. And I think somehow that if you suffer enough, if you die, you become a saint.

I blink at the thought. Maybe Papi is trying for sainthood.

The whole idea is ugly. Like Beorn and Ástríd, I now resent feeding Papi while he does nothing. And since Beorn hasn't yet sold the amber, feeding Papi is a daily hardship.

Papi is a good-for-nothing.

I eat my porridge, kiss the children and Ástríd, and go

outside in search of Beorn. He has attached the wheeled cart to the back of Capall, as I call our horse, and he holds up two large knives, swinging them by their wide cross handles. It's a message—this is the task. He puts them in the back of the cart, which I can see already has two giant baskets, and turns and heads off on foot toward the river.

So Papi is to do the worst job of all: cutting peat. It makes sense. There have to be some advantages to having one more mouth to feed.

I walk to Papi's hut—because that's what it is now, his—and stand outside with his bowl. I call, "Good morning."

He doesn't answer, though you'd have to be an idiot not to know what those Norse words mean after all winter long of hearing them every day. He never answers. The man is as stubborn as the stupidest beast I've ever known. Well then, I'll treat him like one.

I put the bowl down outside the opening of the hut, but far enough away that his arm can't reach it. Then I wave my hand over the bowl, so the smell wafts into Papi's hut.

Within minutes his head appears. I gasp. He's become a matted hairball. He stretches his nose toward the bowl, eyelids fluttering. It's been so long since he's been out in the light, I wonder if the sun hurts his eyes. He reaches toward the bowl with one hand.

I move it farther away.

He tilts his head at me, like a curious beast. But not even a smart one—a sheep perhaps. He doesn't appear to suspect anything. He crawls forward.

I move the bowl away more.

He stays on all fours, still as stone. Then he lunges at the bowl.

And I lunge for the doorway. I sit there, blocking his way.

Papi holds the bowl to his chest and sits on his heels. He eats with the spoon. When he finishes, he rests the spoon in the bowl and sets it on the ground and waits.

"You're working today," I say in Norse. "And that's that." My tone is forceful, and I'm hoping that carries enough of a message to make him behave. "Stand up." I stand as I say it.

Papi still sits on his heels.

I walk toward him.

He tries to crawl around me, but I jump back and block the hut entrance. "Stand!"

Papi sits back on his heels and drops his head. He prays out loud.

"Stop that with the *pater noster*," I say. And I pound him on top of the head with a fist. Just one pound.

He looks up at me, and his eyes are fully open now.

Maybe the dark of the hut hasn't bothered his vision, after all. "*Pater noster*," he says.

"You can't use prayers as an excuse to do nothing. You're coming with me." I grab his arm and pull. He's heavier than he looks. I yank. "Come on! We're going together. *Immalle*." The Gaelic word bursts from me without thought.

"*Immalle?*" Papi takes my hand in both of his. "What do you want of me, child of Eire?" he says in the language my father used, the language my mother used.

I am transfixed. I haven't spoken my old language for so long, I don't know how to begin. My throat has grown all thick. But I remember basic things. "*Tar*—come," I say.

Papi stands. We walk to the cart. He wobbles; there's no chance he can make it to the bog. So I urge him into the back of the cart, then push him up when he can't do it alone.

"Thank you, child."

I take the cart reins.

Papi sings as I lead Capall. His songs are unfamiliar to me, but at least they are in Gaelic, not Latin. Clean, clear Gaelic. The songs run through me like water.

Though the horse is surefooted, I still choose the driest path. Beorn has taught me never to court disaster with the wagon. We stop at the bog edge. It spreads out vast and beautiful, all orange and green. I help Papi out and show him how to slip on the straps of the basket. When it's secure on his back, I give him a knife. I put on the other basket.

Papi sucks in a huge breath and heaves a sigh. Then he sets out, slow and plodding, leaving foot impressions in the spongy peat that quickly fill with water. I step to the side of his path, for fear of sinking so much I get stuck. I call out for him to stop. He's so weak, I expect him to fall any moment, and then I'll have to lug him out of that muck. If I'm strong enough. I call out again. Even if he manages to cut peat from the middle of the bog, that's too far to carry it back to the cart. But Papi slogs on, mindlessly.

All right. Let him wander. The man spoke my child-hood language; I can forgive him anything now. Besides, I'll probably work faster alone. And now I bet Beorn knew I'd have to work alone. He didn't think I could even get Papi out of the hut. He hasn't been able to, after all. So he's teaching me a lesson—reminding me it was my idea to take the monk in.

I stop and cut into the turf, grabbing the two ends of the handle that go perpendicular to the blade with both hands and pushing that blade straight down. I slice out neat bricks. It was Thorkild who taught me how, back up north, near the Limfjord. I remember how impressed Beorn was with my skill the first time I did it with him.

That was gratifying. It's backbreaking work, but it's necessary. I make a stack of ten turf bricks. Then I stop and load half of them into the basket and carry them back to the cart and return for the next half and carry them to the cart, and then go to work cutting ten more. I let the rhythm of the motions fill me. There's a chill in the air. Good—without it I'd be far too hot.

When I'm just coming back into the bog after putting my fifth set of ten into the cart, Papi shouts. I don't recognize the words he says, but he repeats them with urgency, so I hurry to him. He's standing in water that fully covers his feet, and the surface of it changes from blue to purple as I approach. I touch it; it films my fingers, like oil.

Papi smiles with teeth that are gray and pitted. It is a horrible smile. But I try not to show that on my face. He stabs down into the soggy mess so inexpertly, I'm afraid he'll cut his feet. But then he sets the knife aside and peels back a layer of peat. He kneels on it and digs into the orange mud with both arms and comes up with handfuls of rocks.

I smack two together. They're solid! I smile wide. This is bog iron. It's the only metal that Jutland doesn't have to buy from foreigners, but it's still hard to find. "Go maith— good!" I'm so glad I remembered how to say that.

Together we feel around in the mush for hard lumps.

We fill the baskets, but then Papi is too weak to carry his, so it's up to me. That's all right, though. I'd be willing to carry bog iron all day. We gather another three baskets of iron. We have to stop because we're down to clay now; it would take a shovel to dig through. But what we have is plenty. Beorn will be able to sell it to the smith for smelting, and who knows how many ax heads he'll make from it? Axes are prized; some men insist on being buried with theirs, and hundreds are lost in battles. There's always a market for axes. This iron will more than pay for Papi's keep, even if he stayed another year.

Why, I can ask Beorn to give me back my amber! Then I'll have money when I leave to find Mel.

I lead Capall homeward, and Papi rides on her back because the cart is full. He talks the whole way. He tells how he grew up knowing he'd travel the world and devote his life to Christ. His sisters and brothers were rotten, disobedient, and lazier than sin. But he had a mission from the start. Then these Norsemen invaded his area and robbed the church and murdered innocents. That's when he knew that his travels had to start immediately and in the land of the most vicious people of all. So he came here. He'd thought he had failed, but now he had me and I would help him. I would be his voice, since he never learned Norse. Together we could convert these people.

I listen, but only for the words, the plain old words. *Máthir, athir, bráthir*—mother, father, brother. I don't care how holy he is. I don't care that he's crazy and thinks he can turn Norsemen into Christians. All I care is that he keeps speaking Gaelic. I laugh in joy.

Then, suddenly, I realize the opportunity. "Do you know of the town Downpatrick?"

"Everyone knows of Downpatrick."

"Have you heard of King Myrkjartan?"

"The unfortunate? Of course."

A chill seizes me. "Unfortunate?"

"His son was mutilated. His daughters were lost."

Ah, that. I know all that. "Does he search for them?"

"For a whole year he sent out soldiers to scour the countryside. But no trace."

"Did he look abroad?"

"Everywhere, they say. He's posted a reward for anyone who can bring him news of them. And he's promised a treasure to anyone who can return them."

Faithful Father. Faithful Mother. A wound inside me that I hardly knew existed heals in a quiet instant. The Lord has not denied me love, after all. "Can you tell me about them—the king, the queen, the prince?"

"They say the king is a great strategist; he's the leader of the most feared army in Eire. They say the queen was always beautiful, and tragedy has only enhanced that beauty."

I'm breathing hard. "And the son?"

"His name is Nuada."

I smile. "So his name has become known? He's famous?"

"Of course. His hand was cut off, like the arm of the mythical King Nuada. The coincidence fascinates everyone. But unlike the mythical king, this Nuada refused to have a silver limb made. He wears a sleeve that ends empty but for ribbons. They say one of his sisters loved ribbons. He wears them for her memory. He strokes them as he tells stories."

I knew it. I knew Nuada would become a *seanchaí*. "And I bet they say his stories are the best anywhere. I bet he tells about handsome Cúchulainn and his warriors." And I'm so happy to remember that hero. His name just bubbled up in my head after all these years.

"No one hears Nuada's stories. He tells them only to the queen and king. So maybe the bit about stroking the ribbons is fanciful. You know how the Irish like to embellish."

But it's not fanciful; I know it. I'm the one who tied ribbons around the piggies' ears. Nuada wears ribbons for me. Far to the west I still have a family who loves me, who longs for me. They did come looking for me—they did! "I'll make you strong, and then we can go back to Eire together."

"I'll never go back, child. I told you. This is my destiny." Papi talks about how all these months of sitting on the frozen ground praying, all these bleak months, are now ended. The Lord answered his prayers by bringing me to him.

It's nothing but nonsense. Maddening nonsense. I could slap him silly for saying it. He believes it, though. This monk is completely beyond reasoning with. He's never going back to my home. He's not my answer.

Still, I vow to myself that before Papi leaves Ribe, I'll get him to promise to find a way to send back a message to Father. That's it! That's the real answer. Then Father will come for me. And we'll find Mel together. I laugh in happiness.

When we get home, Beorn is already there. As Papi and I enter, he's telling Ástríd what a good worker Egill is and how the youth is coming for dinner. Beorn looks at us with amazement. I was right: He thought Papi was still sitting stubbornly in the hut and I had to do all the work alone. I'm prepared for this. I hold out both hands palm down, but cupped. Obligingly, Beorn looks at my hands. Good! I turn them over with a grin.

Beorn takes the iron rocks from me. "How did you find them?"

"Papi did. He stood in this oily stuff."

"A *járnbrák*—iron slick," says Beorn.

"A *járnbrák*," I say, happy to learn the new word. Norse is a good language, too. "He found it and dug out rocks and showed me. We got baskets and baskets full."

Beorn looks at Papi.

But Papi's leaning against the door frame, muttering in Gaelic, "*Cotlud.*" Sleep.

"He's weak, Beorn. Can he rest here?"

Egill arrives right then. His face is flushed. "I see the cart is full. I'll help unload it."

"We can stack the peat together," I say.

Egill doesn't answer. He doesn't nod. He doesn't look at me. He's been moody all winter. Probably he hates being close to Papi. He hates foreigners, like most people here.

"Leave the iron in the cart," says Beorn. "I'll bring it to the smithy tomorrow." He turns to the monk. "Papi, will you eat inside with us tonight?"

I feel all warm at the unexpected invitation.

Papi seems to recognize the name we call him. He looks at me, as if asking me to translate. Oh no! I spin on my heel and go out the door before he can start spouting Gaelic to me.

Egill follows me. We stack the peat under the awning that Ástríd has strung up along the side of the house for this purpose. We make tripods of peat bricks, so they'll dry faster and be ready to use in the fireplace sooner.

We're finishing and Egill still hasn't said a word to me. "Papi's not awful," I say at last. "And he's not useless. He discovered the *járnbrák*."

"Wrong. He is awful, Alfhild, or whatever your real name is."

I fall back a step, but I keep my mouth shut, eyes down. I won't ask what he means.

He steps toward me. "I heard you. I heard you speaking that foreign language."

I shake my head. "Papi spoke. Not me."

"You understood him. I know. I was following the cart, because I was going to surprise you, and then I saw. I saw you laugh."

"I laughed at the sounds of the words."

"You laughed at the meaning. Will you deny it? Will you lie?"

I stare at the ground.

"I know you're not Beorn and Ástríd's child. And I know you're not her sister—you couldn't look less alike. But no one says where you come from."

If I run into the house, Egill will follow, and who

knows what he'll say to them all. There is nothing to do but let him finish. I lift my chin. He's gotten much taller this winter.

"You're a slave, aren't you?"

"No!"

"You are. Look how short you are. I'll buy you. I'll buy you from Beorn. You'll be my slave. And then you'll have to kiss me. Whenever I want."

I force myself to put my hand on Egill's arm. He jerks to his full height. It is all I can do to keep from shuddering. "We can talk. We must talk. But not now. I have a secret, Egill, but it's not what you think. And neither Ástríd nor Beorn knows it."

"Tell me."

"Not now. The telling will be long. They're waiting."

"Tomorrow, then."

"I'm exhausted, Egill. I cut peat all day. I'll need to rest tomorrow."

"Tomorrow, or I will tell Beorn my suspicions tonight."

"Tomorrow, then."

CHAPTER FOURTEEN

I disentangle myself from sleeping Búri's arms, gather my clothes and pouch, and creep to the door. Vigi stirs. I exhale onto the dog's eyes. He gives a *humph* and lets his head fall back onto the floor. But now I realize I can't leave the others without a farewell too.

Alof has thrown off the covers in her sleep, and her clothing has bunched around her chest. I rub my nose along the soft skin of her back. Then I bend over Búri and flutter my eyelashes against his cheek. I blow kisses to Ástríd and Beorn, across the room.

I grab my cloak off the hook and open the heavy door just enough to slide out, so the whipping wind won't enter. There's no moon, the clouds are so dense. I move as quickly as I can without stumbling and go all the way to the river before I stop to dress. I'm thoroughly chilled. It was stupid not to dress before going outside, but I feared disturbing their sleep; if they woke, they'd try to follow. They'd want to protect me.

I want to protect them, too. So I'm leaving. This way

they don't have to face people's condemnation for harboring a foreigner who isn't their slave. And I don't have to put them through the agony of figuring out how they feel about having an Irish girl in their home.

When Egill returns in the morning and sees I'm gone, he may keep his mouth shut. After all, there's nothing to gain from exposing me now. But if he should talk, it won't matter, because I'll be gone and people will think that Beorn and Ástríd cast me out when they discovered the truth. They will be exonerated in the eyes of Ribe folk.

Egill always said I'd regret taking in the monk. He's doing his best to make it so. I don't like the idea of regret. It's stupid to wish you'd done otherwise. You can't change the past. All you can do is learn from your actions, so you make good decisions in the future.

Besides, who can regret saving a life?

I find a small boat, and I paddle across the river. I wish I could leave the boat in the open on the far shore, so that the owner will see it and get someone to ferry him across to fetch it. But then he'd figure out it was me who did it, and they'd know which way I'd gone. So I hide it in the scrub. It might not be found for days.

I know exactly where I'm going. I've known it since Beorn first talked about the big slave market: I'm going to Heiðabý. South and east of here, over the ridge. If Mel was sold as a slave, there's a good chance it happened in that town.

I don't know how far it is—several days at least. There's a path along the river that goes east, and if I walked on it, the going would be easier. But I'd risk meeting travelers who would know I came from Ribe; there's no other town around. And they would talk of me when they got to town. A girl alone is a phenomenon. People in Ribe would realize it was me. No one must know where I've gone—neither enemy nor friend.

So I note the wind direction. As the rising sun warms the land, winds go any direction. But at night, winds blow toward the sea, which is due west. Sailing with Beorn taught me that. Since it's night, I assume this wind is going west, and I head southeast across meadows, through beech forests.

If somehow the winds change course before sunrise, I can still know which way is east by following the slope of the land. Uphill means I'm moving away from the sea—eastward. It's only a slight incline right now, because I'm traveling on a diagonal, but it's there. The road we took from the north ran along a high ridge. If I keep going uphill, I'll find that road eventually.

I am aware that by listing all these cautions and all the things I know, I am trying to calm myself. I hate being vulnerable again. And I'm furious at Egill. And more furious at myself. How on earth could he have followed the cart close enough to hear Papi's words and my laughter without my sensing he was there? Inexcusable. The only way to be safe is to be constantly vigilant. I learned that at eight. Here I am, twelve. I have no excuse.

And I'm crazy at the fact that I'm leaving the four people I have come to love so tenderly. Grief hammers inside my head. But I knew I'd leave them in a few years. My mission nags at me. I must find Mel. We will go back to Eire, to the family that still aches for us. We'll go together. *Immalle.*

Still, I'm too young to be on my own yet. That means I have to find another family to worm my way into for a few years. With Beorn and Ástríd it happened by accident; I didn't design it. I don't know how to design such a thing. But I can learn. And I'll be in Heiðabý, at least; the right place to start looking for her once I'm old enough.

I took nothing with me but a pouch of food. I thought of taking the amber in Beorn's personal chest. I gave it to him as payment for Papi's upkeep, but now that Papi found bog iron, he has paid his own upkeep. So the amber should be mine again. But I couldn't talk with Beorn about that without him sensing that I needed the amber, and then he might have guessed I was planning on leaving.

And I couldn't simply take it; that might have left him feeling robbed. I want him to feel he gained from having me. I want the loss of me to sear him.

What a proud and an unchristian thought.

Papi didn't feel he had to justify his upkeep. He was prepared to be fed forever and do nothing in return. Before, I saw that as selfishness, but now I think it's humility.

I could never be that humble. That's why the only thing in my pouch is food. Cod: I caught it and preserved it with salt from seaweed I gathered. Cabbage: I planted, tended, and harvested it, then I rolled the leaves tight and buried them in sand for keeping. Onions: I stored them in hay in the animal room. I didn't take cheese, because Ástríd makes the cheese all by herself. I didn't take smoked ham, because Beorn does the smoking all by himself.

I should have. It would have been a gift to them to let them know they were taking care of me even far away. I cheated them of that small consolation. I'm mad at myself for being so stingy with them, so mean-spirited.

Good. Anger keeps me from being too afraid. I don't like walking alone at night. I don't like the unfamiliar sounds around me. It's undoubtedly just animals scurrying about, more frightened of me than I am of them. But still I hate it. Plants scrape at my ankles. Now and then branches smack my arms or face. A few times I stumble over big rocks because it's just so dark.

Gradually, though, the world around me assumes shape. The sun rises, setting a meadow of heather aflame. I cry at how glorious it is. Well, that's ridiculous. I'm too old to cry at something like that. It's just because I'm so anxious that seeing something beautiful overwhelmed me. I have to act sensible. Mature. It's morning. What can make things feel more normal?

Breakfast. Of course. I reach into my pouch and walk along eating cod and onion. I wipe my nose and mouth with grasses that I yank without stopping. Food cheers me up. I walk all morning, through the afternoon, all evening. Whenever I have an unobstructed view, I turn in a circle to spy first whatever can spy me. I pass a spring and slake my thirst with the sweetest water ever. Birds perch on top branches of shrubs. Their backs and wings are orange, their heads gray with a black mask over the eyes. I make a game of sighting them. They've come to breed. They must be disappointed at spring's tardiness, but they don't show it. Good for them.

I walk until I see a doe. That little kind that stands no taller than my waist, gold in the setting sun, with a gray face and a white rump patch. She should be in the forest, blending with ash and maple trunks. What made her venture out? She lifts her head and freezes at the sight of me. But she doesn't bark. Maybe she senses I'm no danger, or maybe there are no others nearby to warn. Her belly is round. I hope she doesn't birth out here, unprotected.

I walk and wonder if the doe watches, but I won't look back in case that alarms her. I walk until a giant flock of starlings blacks out the sun before settling for the night in the field around me. Hundreds of birds, thousands. All noisy. But noise feels good now, cozy. And I realize that stopping here, surrounded by the birds, is a good idea. I need to sleep somewhere or I'll be too stupid to take proper care of myself. And the birds are a perfect warning system if a predator comes.

It's early. Days have lengthened a lot since winter, but sunset still comes early enough that normally I wouldn't be tired. This isn't a normal day, though. Exhaustion sweeps over me the instant my bottom hits ground. I finish the onion and another corner of cod and stretch out, wrapped in my cloak. I miss Alof's sticky hands and hot breath, the new lankiness of Búri's arms and legs. The missing is so strong I feel bruised.

I should tell myself Irish stories. I remembered Cúchulainn when I was talking with Papi. Maybe I can remember others. But the only stories that come to me are Norse—rough and violent. And then I remember the story Ástríd loves best, about Thor's one gentle spot, his love for his dazzling wife Sif. Her golden hair tumbled all the way down her back. One day after she had washed that wavy hair, she fell asleep letting it dry in the air. The mischievous god Loki sheared it off. Sif wept inconsolably for her lost beauty. So Thor made sure Loki paid for that insult. But now, in this moment, I don't like the story anymore. It feels foolish, frivolous. Ástríd can think about the sadness of losing beautiful hair because she has a home with a family around her—the important things of life are solidly in place for her. But beautiful hair means nothing to me, because I have nothing.

I close my eyes. I am alone and defenseless, with nothing but my wits. Like Mel. Where is she sleeping tonight? My chest feels so heavy, it's a wonder I still breathe.

I wake with the birds, of course. Noisy, noisy. Another day of walking, eating only as much as necessary, drinking my fill, this time in a muddy wetlands—which is fine; it helps to make me appreciate the gift of clear streams. Contrasts are good.

Sometimes my fingertips feel Alof's and Búri's soft skin again, and my eyes leak.

I sleep under bushes this next night, without the comfort of birds. It's a restless night. Every noise makes me flinch.

Toward the middle of the third day I see people traveling across my line of sight. On horseback and with a wagon. That's the big country road for sure. At last. I would have easily reached the road a day ago if I'd taken the path. But now I'm much more south of where I would have been if I'd done that, so that's good. I watch: a man, another man, a third man. My heart clutches. I hear Ástríd warning me inside my head. I sink to my knees.

But they continue past. Out of sight.

Still, I remember now. When Mel and I rode the horse along the coast south of Downpatrick, the slave ship passed us. Then it came back, when we weren't suspecting.

I search for stones until I find the largest two that will fit in my fists. I run, looking around everywhere, everywhere. No one will come back and find me unsuspecting. No one will hunt me down easily.

When I get to the road, I cross it and run beyond until no one can spot me from the road. Then I turn south. The smell of ocean is strong. Seagulls scream. Even the air feels different; there's a closeness to it, whereas west of the ridge it felt open. It's like the sea pulls me, would swallow me. I see water in the distance. And that dot—is that a seal head?

I walk till night, then finish the cabbage, the last of my food. I curl under a bush and try to remember details of

Mel. It's hard. How soon will I forget those I've left behind in Ribe? Everyone I love, I lose. But I refuse to lose memories. I make lists of the way Mel walked tall and straight, the way Ástríd shakes her hair free at night, everything I can remember, everything I must remember. I fall asleep making lists.

Hunger wakes me early. It's raining gently, which means I can forage for wild roots in the soft earth, but not with these stones filling my hands. I set them down reluctantly, feeling as though I'm yielding my only defense. But there's a stick on the ground—a sturdy one. I can dig with it, and if anyone should approach me, I can swing it like a club.

The rain soaks me, but I don't care. My Irish bones need this familiarity. And I'm still hungry. A patch of wood sorrel beckons. I eat it on all fours like a beast. The sour taste brightens me. I look up. In the distance I see the tall ramparts of a big city. Heiðabý. Already.

The rain comes harder now. There's a stand of trees nearby. I run for it. A stream rushes through alders and oaks. I take shelter under a wide oak and squat by the trunk. My pouch is empty, my stomach is empty, and apparently my head is empty: I have no plan.

The rain goes on for hours, and the oak is no match for it. No tree would be a match for this deluge. The drops drive through the new leaves and splatter on my head and back.

When it finally stops, I walk along the stream, a soggy, sorry mess, dragging the stick beside me. It isn't sharp enough to spear fish with. It's stupid. I'm stupid.

The stick catches on something. How annoying. I yank. A rope comes with it. Muddy, sunk in the muck. And very old, by the looks of it. I pull, using the stick to dig it free. One end goes to the bottom of an alder trunk. The rope runs so deep under the ground, it must have been tied to the tree base years ago, and leaves piled up and turned to dirt, burying it deeper and deeper. I follow the rope in the other direction. It goes to the stream! My heart thumps. *Please, let it be a mussel rope. Please.* My mouth waters.

I tug on the rope, but it's heavy. Maybe it's snagged on something. I look around. I'd have to undress to go in that water. There's no one in sight. The way the trees and bushes are situated, I'm shielded from view except from someone directly across the stream. I couldn't be so unlucky that there would be a spy behind those trees right there, could I? Even Ástríd would tell me it's probably safe, and she's as cautious as people come.

Still, I fear being naked out in the open. But I'm soaked anyway, so why undress? I wade into the stream fully dressed. It's deeper than I expected. I can feel mussels on the rope. Lots.

The end of the rope still holds fast. I have to duck underwater to free it. It's attached to something. I feel carefully. Is that a buckle? I come up for breath; then I duck under and circle the object with both arms and carry it up and out to the bank.

A skin satchel. Pitted and discolored. I fight with the straps and finally unbuckle it. Black metal disks. All crusty. I bite one. The black flakes off one side, exposing silver. And inscriptions in a curling script. I find two stones and place a disk on one and hit it with the other. This disk is silver too, a stamp of a ship on it, with—I count them— nine shields, and a fish under the ship. Coins. This one's Norse. The first was Arab. I've seen them in Ribe.

This is a hoard.

In Eire, if a rich man knew an enemy was coming, he'd bury his treasures so no one could steal them. Bogs are good for that. Here streams must serve the same purpose.

I use one mussel to open others, and I chew them greedily, touching the satchel every so often to assure myself it's real. I eat till I'm full. Then I gobble dandelion leaves and keep watching that satchel.

No one hides their wealth in a hoard month after month, let alone year after year. Whoever left this hoard here is dead. And he didn't tell anyone else about it before he died.

This money belongs to no one.

My amber would have sold for a lot of money. But there's a lot of money in this satchel. Far more than it takes to buy a slave girl. And far more than I can carry without drawing attention. Now all I have to do is find Mel.

I clean off a handful of coins and put them in my pouch. I rebuckle the satchel and make sure the rope is securely attached. I toss it into the stream and shove dirt over the rope. I stand back to survey the scene. No one would know. My hoard is safe.

CHAPTER FIFTEEN

I slept naked, covered with mud. It kept me almost snug. But the mud dried overnight, and I have to crack my way out now. I plunge into the stream and scrub myself clean. My clothes are stretched out over a bush. I washed them last night. They're slightly damp still, but that'll do. I run my fingers through my wet, curling hair and sit a moment to dry off.

Across the stream a hare nibbles in the weeds. For the first time in days, I am glad Ástríd is not near. She is expert at killing hares with a cast stone. Though a hare is delicious, this one seems slow and silly, and so I feel protective toward it.

From nowhere a polecat races out and bites the hare in the head. He drags it back where he came from. I see the burrow opening now. He dumps the hare inside. One back leg of the hare twitches. It's alive still! But crippled. The polecat pushes it with his snout till it's hidden. Then he races back to the stream for a swim. I understand now: He's storing that hare alive, for later. It's a brutal way to make sure your meat doesn't rot.

Shaken, I put on my clothes and tie my pouch to one of the brooches on my shoulder straps. I was hungry when I woke up, but that polecat put my appetite off.

I walk to the road, which curves as it approaches both the town and the sea, flanked by pastures with cattle, horses, sheep, goats. A round and small stone fort sits atop a hill outside the ditch that precedes the town ramparts. Beside the fort is a slim stone tower. I pass by the fort and tower and keep my eyes on the sea. There's an otter out there. What I thought was a seal a couple of days ago must have really been an otter. There's another one.

I'm smiling as I walk the plank over the ditch and through the town gates with nothing more than a wave of greeting from the guards, though I had prepared a whole story to tell if need be. I didn't live with a *skald* for years without learning how to tell tales. Still, I'm glad I wasn't put to the test. And I'm glad my smile is genuine. I love otters.

I keep walking steadily, so as not to give anyone the impression that I'm lost, or worse, on my own. Though Heiðabý is huge, I feel sure the inhabitants recognize one another, or at least have something in common that allows them to distinguish their own townsfolk from outsiders. People will sense I'm not one of them. But this is a trading town—the biggest trading town in the northern world, if Beorn is right—so they must be accustomed to strangers. They shouldn't bother me if I look like I know what I'm doing.

The ramparts I passed between circle the town, but for the edge on the sea. A stream cuts right through the center of it all. The houses have funny big supports on the outsides, as though the walls might buckle without them. The thatched gables face onto wood-paved streets that run diagonal to the stream, and most houses, no matter how small, have a fence around a plot in front or behind them. The side edges of the roofs nearly touch, so there are no side yards. If anyone keeps animals in town, I can't see them. More's the pity, since helping with animals would have been my most natural way of finding employment.

There are shops, though. Plenty. All on a wide street. Shops always need help.

There's a shop of men working leather. I'm good at sewing shoes, and it would be fun to learn to make horse harnesses, but I hate the stench of tanneries, so I hurry past.

Five men work at the smithy, slick with sweat, wearing nothing but trousers. Iron tongs, hammers, files, swords, spears, shears, harness buckles, ax heads—all are laid out front for inspection. Even spurs—which I'm proud to recognize. I'm a child of Eire, which has no spurs, but a child of Jutland, too. I know the Norse world.

I'd like to tell Egill that. I'm not just where I came from—I'm how I live day by day.

I have lost two families now. My skin goes gooseflesh at the thought. I am in trouble. But Egill's wrong: I will never be anyone's slave. And with any bit of luck, Mel will soon not be either. I touch my pouch—silver coins.

I pass a woodworking shop, with planes, gauges, bores. And men. Only men.

I turn up a road and pass a home with a porch out front and an open door. Inside women weave at two giant looms. Children play around their feet. The hearth is on the far wall. Beside the hearth is a huge soapstone pot with iron handles, and I can smell the porridge from here. It's funny that the big room of this house is at the end instead of the center. It's funny too that the hearth is on a wall instead of in the middle of the room. But maybe that's how it's done here. That's fine. Anything's fine with me. Anything will do.

Except I'm terrible at weaving.

I go back to the main road. Across from the smithy is a moneyer. I watch through the door. A man taps a die onto a strip of silver. He lifts the die and looks at me with a wink. Why, the imprint is the very ship with shields and fish on some of my coins! The man makes imprints all along the silver strip. Then he splits the coins off and uses a different die to imprint the other side. On the flip side of my Heiðabý coins is a deer flanked by a snake on the left, and a man on the right. But I don't stay to see what this man imprints on the flip side of the coins he's making, for it occurs to me that if this man makes the same kinds of coins I have in my pouch, someone could think I stole them from him. I hurry on.

I pass by the shop where men make quern stones for grinding grain. We use those in Ribe, but they were made somewhere else. Now I know where.

I hesitate by the potter's shop. I've never made pottery. Ástríd's always made our family's, and she loves doing it. So it can't be too boring. And even though the shops in Ribe employ only men to make ceramics, there's no reason why a girl couldn't work here.

"You could use a comb, pretty one."

I turn and look at the man in front of the next shop. He's Beorn's age and size, but his hair is trimmed neatly and his beard is cut in a smooth, careful curve along the jaw. Black makeup is smeared under his eyes as though he's dressed up for a celebration, but this is just an ordinary day. And he smells strongly—I can smell him from here—pungent but nice. He's wearing an oil I don't recognize. Maybe he needs a worker in his shop. I wonder what he makes.

"What else do you sell?" I ask.

"This is a specialty shop. Fine things. Come inside. Take a look." He steps to the side.

I walk past him into a tiny courtyard with an entrance mat, and from there into the shop. He's arranged a bench to catch light from the door, the courtyard, and a hole in the roof. A cloth hangs over the bench, with little grooming objects and jewelry displayed on it.

He lifts a necklace and holds it to the light. "Red glass beads. Manufactured right in town. They'd look perfect on you."

I hardly glance at the beads. There's nothing in this store that I could help make. Still, maybe he needs an assistant to sell things when he takes a break. I try to look agreeable. "You said you have a comb?"

He reaches under the cloth and brings out a bone-white object, the length of my hand, rectangular and slim, incised with reddish-brown diamond shapes. He hands it to me. It has a hole at one end with a strand of red thread attached to another object shaped like a key without any notches.

I look at him inquisitively.

"A nail pick. Of course."

At home— at Beorn's home—we pick our nails with green sticks. But I keep my face impassive. I want to ask how this rectangle can comb hair, when I see there's a separation down the front of it. I jiggle it. The separation grows. I stick in my thumbnail and push it apart. It's like a puzzle: The comb slides out. How delightful.

"Clever, don't you think? Antler, from our own Jutland deer. The miniature kind that you can't find anywhere else."

Does he know I'm gratified he's recognized me by my speech as living in Jutland? Am I that transparent? But I don't care what he thinks. He can't hurt me.

"Do you happen to need an assistant in the shop?" I ask. "Someone to mind things when you have errands?"

"Ah! Looking for a job, are you?" He shakes his head. "We shopkeepers help one another." He holds out his hand for the comb.

Too bad. But I'm running my finger along the teeth of the comb and thinking of Ástríd now. The night of the storm last autumn, when we waited to see if Beorn would ever make it home again, her long hair blanketed her arm all the way to the wrist. I'd love to give Ástríd a comb—this comb. And I certainly have far more money than I need, given that hoard. But I could never find a way to get the comb delivered all the way to Ribe. Still, my insides have gone warm and fluttery now. I really want this gift for her. "How much is it?"

The man purses his lips and scrutinizes me. "The

only things on you of value are the tortoiseshell-shaped brooches that hold up your outer shift. And now that I see them up close, I don't fancy them; they aren't fine quality. We make better ones of tin and bronze here in town."

"I have . . . a coin."

"It would take more than one Heiðabý coin to buy this comb. You'd need a coin plus a bit more silver, and you don't even have an arm ring to hack silver from."

"What about two coins?"

"For two coins you could have it, plus"—he takes a pair of copper tweezers off the bench—"these." He looks at me and blinks. His eyes settle on my pouch.

"I'll be back." I quickly walk out and then lean back through the door. "Two coins." I rush away down a side street. It's dangerous to open my pouch in front of anyone. But I don't see a place to be private anywhere. Except an outhouse. I go to the house with the weavers. "Please." I stand in the open doorway. "Please, may I relieve myself out back?"

A woman comes toward me so quickly, I fear at first that she'll knock me down. But she stops short and sniffs the air. "You're not bleeding, are you?"

"No."

She looks at me hard. "All right, then."

I go through the narrow passage between the houses

and around to the outhouse and slip two coins from my pouch in the dark. I tuck them in the side of one shoe. Then I hang the pouch so it falls inside my shift instead of outside.

I go back to the house. "Thank you."

They all look at me.

A boy child says, "Why are you still standing there?"

"Might you have some task I could do, in exchange for a bowl of that porridge?"

"Can you weave?" asks one woman.

"Badly."

"A ship can founder because of a sail that's badly woven. So, what can you do?"

"Farm. Take care of animals."

"That's boys' work."

"I could work on a boat—help out."

They all laugh. The woman who let me use the outhouse fills a bowl with porridge and hands it to me. "At least you have a sense of humor. This is payment for the laugh. Eat and be on your way."

I eat and give my thanks and return to the fine goods shop. The man stands outside, trying to lure a customer. I walk past them to the inside and dig the coins out of my shoe.

The shopkeeper follows me in. "An uncomfortable

place to carry one's money." He holds out his hand. I drop in the coins. The shopkeeper stares. He hands me back a coin. "Keep this one. It's from Heiðabý. This other is Arab. It's worth much more. I'll keep the Arab coin. You can have the toilet set for just this one." He smiles and gives me the set.

"And what else will you give me?" I say.

"What do you mean?"

"The Arab coin should buy more." The quickness of his smile told that.

"Come." He walks to the rear of the shop. On a work-bench he's set up a clamp that holds a small bit of antler. It's carved in the shape of a tiny spoon. He picks up an iron pin and makes punch marks in a curving pattern all up the spoon handle. The work is precise and slow. He unclamps it and hands it to me. "A perfect ear spoon."

"It's beautiful."

"Lucky for you that you said that. I'm pleased you appreciate my work. It's delicate work; it takes skill. So you get a prize." He puts the string of red glass beads over my head.

Probably the Arab coin paid for the beads, too. But that's all right. I'm happy. "Thank you. Tell me, why is an Arab coin worth more than a Heiðabý coin?"

"The whole world accepts Arab coins. But only the

north countries accept Heiðabý ones. Don't let that discourage you, though. Heiðabý coins are the only Norse coins, and there's prestige in that." He looks at me thoughtfully. "Wouldn't you want this carnelian pin? I'd give it to you for that Heiðabý coin." He holds out a reddish-brown stone with a fish carved on it. A coin with a fish, for a stone with a fish. This town likes fish.

"No, thank you." I make a show of slipping the Heiðabý coin into my shoe. Let him think that's the only place I carry money. Then I pull out my pouch and slide in the toilet set and put the pouch back inside my shift. I go out into the street again.

As quickly as my happiness came, it disappears. I've acted like a child, buying something frivolous. And I have no idea what to do next. In this town the best jobs are taken by boys. I turn around and re-enter the fine goods shop.

The shopkeeper is already positioning an antler in the clamp. He frowns. "You got your money's worth."

"Who gathers the antlers for you?"

"What?"

"Who goes around collecting the antlers when the deer shed them?"

"No one in particular. When boys bring them to me, I buy them."

"What if I supplied you with antlers? Would you give me a place to sleep?"

"Are you an orphan?"

"And food? Would you feed me?"

"If you're an orphan, where did you get those coins?"

"It was just a question. It meant nothing." I back fast out the door and race up a street, turn a corner, and keep running and turning corners until I'm sure he hasn't followed. I stop to let my heart quiet. Everything is wrong. It was a mistake to come here. And I haven't seen a marketplace yet. But Heiðabý is supposed to have huge marketplaces. Heiðabý has the biggest slave market in the Norse world. That's why I came.

Across the road is a sprawling building—like the others around it in most ways, but far larger. Larger than the king's house in Ribe. In the fenced-in area in front, a small child sits digging in the dirt. He's older than Alof, perhaps even older than Búri, though Búri is taller and more robust. Crawling toward him is a long gray thing; black zigzags cross its skin. It has a wide head and big red eyes with vertical black centers, like a goat. I've never seen a live snake before, but I know at once that's what this is.

CHAPTER SIXTEEN

I have no food on me. This is bad. Food would be a diversion. But then, I don't know what a snake eats. I have no stone in hand, no large stick. And I see nothing easy to grab and use to toss the snake away.

The child has still not noticed the snake. This is good at least. Animals can do their worst if a person acts their worst.

I walk through the opening in the gate swiftly and surely. Animals respond to confidence that doesn't seem aggressive. I am steady, calm. I walk past the child.

A woman screams. But my hand has already closed around the snake below his head. The woman is screaming and screaming, and now the child screams and people shout and run at us, which is all wrong, because this way I have nowhere safe to throw the snake.

I hold firm, but the snake writhes and fights and I can't believe how strong this short, stout fellow is. I move my other hand to grab him better, and he bites into the web between my thumb and index finger. In shock, I let go.

The snake hangs a moment by his fangs, and I'm lifting my hand high by my eyes and watching him as though this hand is not mine.

Then he drops. A sword flashes past and slices the snake in half. Blood spurts.

I stumble backward to get away from the sword, but someone's says, "She's falling. Catch her!" A man lifts me, one arm under my legs, one under my back. He carries me into the house. I am aware of everything, every detail, until I realize my hand is on fire. I look at it, amazed there are no flames shooting out. The two puncture wounds are black. My hand changes shape before my eyes; it blows up like an udder that needs to be milked, shiny and hot. I breathe loud. And now it's hard to breathe. My chest tightens. I try to roll out of this man's arms, but he holds me fast and there's nothing I can do; I'm sick all over him.

Then the men are gone and women wash me. When I lived in Eire, servants washed Mel and me. When I arrived all battered at Thora's door, she washed me. So I'm not afraid. I just wish I would stop coughing. I wish they would let me be. And finally they do. Finally. I sleep.

When I wake, I can't see. But then I realize it's because my eyes are shut. I can't open them. My hands move toward my face, but the bit one throbs hard, and I can't force my eyelids apart with just the other. I think of the god Loki, who writhed in pain when serpent venom dripped on his face. The giantess Skaði did that to punish him for a murder. His eyes must have puffed up too. What if I'm blind forever? A scream escapes me.

"What is it? What do you need?" The voice is breathless.

"I can't open my eyes."

"That's because of the *høggorm*—the serpent that bit you. It will go away. It was good he bit you and not Hakon."

I reach toward the woman and find her arm. "Is that the child's name, Hakon?"

"Yes. The king is named Hók. The sword he slew the serpent with is named Høking."

"The king?"

"You're in the king's home. You're the honored guest. The queen saw what you did. That serpent only made you sick, but it might have killed Hakon. I don't think the king could have endured losing another child. Certainly the queen couldn't have."

"Another? Did a snake kill another of their children?"

"Don't be daft. Killer serpents are rare. Their daughter died with the damp of winter rattling in her chest, gurgling phlegm. Hakon's their only child now. Go back to sleep."

"I'm not tired. Help me open my eyes."

"They'll open when the poison passes. Sleep. You'll be fine tomorrow."

I hear her walk away. I'm in a king's home. I was born in a king's home. And I was wrong a moment ago; I am sleepy. Very. I drift off.

I still can't open my eyes. What if I am blind forever, like the god Høð? Because he couldn't see, he was tricked into killing his own brother Bald. Hideous fate.

Something rustles. "Who's there?"

"Hakon's mother."

"The queen?"

"In this moment, all I am is Hakon's mother. I am grateful to you."

"Will you tell me the truth, then?"

"Of course."

"Will I really heal?"

She gives a little cry. "Tomorrow you'll be fine. Or maybe the next day."

I sigh in relief and feel my body sink deeper into the padding of blankets under me.

"You thought you might die, and yet you picked up the serpent. To save my son." The queen's voice breaks. "Thank you."

"It wasn't like that. I just did it. I'm good with animals. The bite surprised me."

"You're modest or honest or both." She sits beside me, and whatever I'm lying on swings. How strange! I feel her press against my side. "How old are you?"

"Twelve."

"My daughter would have been ten now if she had lived. Probably your size, though. You're diminutive, but I knew you were older. You're not as fair as she would have been. Still, you're pretty." I feel her pull on my curls. "I'm glad you're not coughing anymore. It terrified me. I imagined the world red. Blood can shock, it's so bright." She pats my chest.

I am thinking of the red blood of the severed snake, but that's not what she means, I know. She means a daughter, a dying daughter, coughing up blood. I work to suppress coughs. And tears.

"Do you tame animals?" she asks.

"Sort of. Like I said, I'm good with them."

"Better than good, I wager. The weavers told me you sought a job with animals. Or farming. Or boats even." She's quiet for a moment. "Did you come from Ribe?"

I swallow. "Why would you think that?"

"The way you talk. You sound like them."

I have no answer.

"I hear you're an orphan. With money you know nothing about. A mystery."

"Mysteries are scary. I'm not scary," I say quickly. "I'm just a girl without a home." I don't dare say more. She is Norse, and I know how Norse people feel about foreigners. It's best she believes I'm an orphan from Ribe—nothing mysterious about me. But she whimpers now. What did I say wrong? "What is your name, queen?"

"Tove. I am Queen Tove. And what is your name?"

"Alfhild."

The queen gasps. "I knew it. I had that strange sensation the moment your hand reached for the serpent. Then, when the weavers said you sought work on a boat, that confirmed you were special. You were sent to us. It's what the gods want."

"I don't know what the gods want. But I need to find work. Once my eyes open again."

"Høking, the sea king, he sent you."

Høking? "The woman in here before, she said the king's sword is named Høking."

"Yes. The usual name for a sword that belongs to a Hók. The king's father named him Hók so he would inherit the characteristics of the sea king Høking. He had aspirations for his infant son. He wanted him to become king of Heiðabý, and a king of Heiðabý must rule sea as well as land." The queen now touches my injured hand. "Does it hurt horribly?"

I shake my head slowly. Moving my neck hurts more than my hand.

"Would you tell me if it did?"

"I don't know."

She gives a quiet laugh. "You are the daughter of Høking, a princess of the sea."

I am the daughter of a king. But not that king. My throat closes in sadness. "I'm sorry, but—"

"Stop. Please. Listen to me. Alfkona is the name of Høking's daughter. A tiny girl, elflike. That's you. But you've been away from home so long, you mixed up your own name. Or maybe you changed it on purpose, because you had to fend for yourself, become a warrior. You had to enter *hild*—battles. So now we will call you Alfhild, because that's what feels natural to you. Either way, you are Høking's daughter. This I will tell the king. And you will not contradict me."

"But why?"

"Because you were sent here to become our daughter."

I am so sad for her. Oh, how much I need a family. But this queen may need more than I can give—she needs to be loved like a daughter loves a mother. I have no idea if I can love her that way. I have never lived with a woman who filled that role other than my real mother. I reach out for her with my good hand. "I can't stay."

Her hands close around mine. She sniffles.

"I must find my sister. I must go searching for her. Not now. But when I'm old enough. I have to."

"I understand." She sniffles again, and her hands rub mine. "That's years away. In the meantime, you're our daughter."

"I don't know if I can do that."

"I don't know either. But we can try."

PART THREE

SEARCHING

(FIFTEEN YEARS OLD)

CHAPTER SEVENTEEN

I have known Ragnhild for more than three years, almost the entire time I've lived as Queen Tove's daughter, so her behavior now is predictable. Still, it's annoying. I reach for the shoes in her arms.

Ragnhild clutches them tighter. "Our feet are tender after wearing shoes all winter."

"They'll toughen up." I flap my hand insistently. She shrinks away. I put my hands on my hips in exasperation. "They toughened up last summer and the summer before."

"Not fast." It's Thyra speaking now. She picks up her shoes too. "We go through weeks of pain, Princess. The scars on the bottom of your feet keep the skin thick, so you don't know. Why do all three of us have to go barefoot? It's only you who wants to."

I cross my arms at the chest. "The queen's servants are never this argumentative."

"The queen's servants are slaves," says Thyra.

Ragnhild sits on the floor and ties on her shoes.

This is what I get for hiring them. And it's more than

just arguing; they've grown bolder, pushing their wants over mine. When I first hired them, they tried to please. Now they act like sisters—belligerent ones! Thyra has taken her shoes off the suspended shelf and sits on my suspended bed. She rocks as she, also, ties on her shoes. I grab the shelf and stop its swinging. I stand behind the bed and stop its swinging too. Thyra doesn't even look at me. I shuffle in a circle. Then I give up. After all, it's better to be with people who choose to be with you rather than those who are forced to. "Don't call me princess outside."

"We never do." Ragnhild jumps to her feet. "Are you sure you don't want shoes?" She twists her mouth and looks me up and down.

"Ragnhild's right." Thyra assumes that knowing way she's adopted of late; it irks me. "If we both wear shoes and you don't, given how short you are, people will think you're our slave, despite the fact that you wear a shift and not just a blanket with a waist cord." She crosses her arms, mimicking me. "You know how men can be with slave women."

I blink. It's true. Most slaves stand a head or two shorter than free people, because they come from other lands. I sit on the bed beside Thyra and tie on my shoes. "Later we can go down to the beach and take our shoes off. You don't need tough skin for sand."

"I like digging my toes in the sand," says Thyra. "Good idea."

Out we troop, into the road, in our simple shifts, looking like poor girls despite our shoes, though Ragnhild and Thyra wear arm rings and I have four bracelets that tinkle against one another. Even poor people have jewelry, after all. Anyone who didn't know me already would assume all of us were servants in the king's big home.

We go to the market at the port. Traders have set up tents and arranged their goods for easy perusal. When they leave, others will come, all summer long and deep into autumn. The town stores sell flax combs and wool combs, spinning whorls and looms and weaving battens, wooden bowls and bronze basins, shears and knives, bronze brooches and strings and strings of glass beads—all made by locals. And they sell town specialties, like the wonderful beds that hang from the ceiling. But in this market, they sell everything from everywhere all over the world.

We wander through the soapstone cooking vessels from Nóreg and the colorful ceramics from who knows where. We tug at hides, pet wool cloaks, run our fingers over antler and gold buckles. We knock on wood planks and watch people weigh out salt.

My ears are always alert for the sounds of Gaelic, and

I'm always disappointed. If Irish traders come here, I have never been lucky enough to cross their path.

My eyes and ears are always alert for traces of an Irish monk, and I'm always disappointed again. If Beorn turned Papi out, I can't believe he managed to make it to Heiðabý, for I would have learned of his arrival. It would have been the talk of the town.

There has been no opportunity for me to send a message to Downpatrick, much less persuade someone to take me back there.

But that's not the only reason I frequent the marketplace. Nor even the most pressing reason. No, no, we three girls, Ragnhild and Thyra and I, we look at the slaves. We walk in and out of the lines of children standing for inspection. We linger at the women. We have to elbow through the Arabs to do it. Only the richest locals can afford to feed a slave. But the Arab merchants seem delighted to hand over their abundant jewelry and perfumes and coins to the Norse and Russian slave dealers, sometimes buying an entire harem.

Ragnhild and Thyra don't really know why we wander among the slaves. They never asked me, which is good, since I'd never tell.

Today I stop in front of one girl and look into her eyes closely and suddenly realize how stupid this is. I remind myself of the time that has passed—every passing season scores like a burn on my soul. I turned fifteen last autumn—the age Mel was when we were stolen. Mel is a woman by now. She turned twenty-two this spring. What must she look like now? Would I even recognize her?

I listen to the slave dealers talking, especially the Russian ones. They're the most numerous. I can't be sure if anything they say resembles the words of the wretched men who stole Mel and me; it was too long ago. But there's something in the sounds the Russian slave dealers make that grates and haunts. Every time I listen, I grow more convinced it was Russians who stole us.

In the faces of these people about to be sold, I see terror, anger, hatred. It's all I can do to keep from turning away in shame. But I have to look, to examine carefully. I have to plumb this faltering memory of mine for clues that can revitalize an image. Mel.

Mel was an extraordinary beauty. And the way we kept silent, that was unusual. If she kept that up, if she stayed hushed, then someone might well remember her for that trait alone.

And if I can't find her or news of her, then maybe I can find the Russian slave dealer who stole her. At night I search through my memories. I sometimes sit by the shore and let the salty air carry me backward in time.

It is essential to remember. These are the things I have managed to dredge up so far. They fed us boiled parsnips, salty, as though stored in salt. The main man ate cold roasted goat; the stink lingered on him. And his hands reeked of clay. He had a shout that was more bark than voice. There were nine crew members; I remember counting nine. One had a scar across his forehead that slashed through an eyebrow. One had a mustache. Or at least one had a mustache—maybe another did too. The ship had two sails. They used oil lamps that smelled rancid. It's not much. But given time, I'll remember more. The strangest things can make a memory flicker.

I walk through the market and try to appear interested in silk ribbons and richly inlaid bridle mounts, as though they are of equal import to me as slave girls are. I ask questions—random, disconnected questions—and I seal away information about where these traders have come from, the stops along the way, whether or not anyone remembers a mute slave girl. My motives must stay secret. Caution is now my firmest habit. Queen Tove loves me; I don't believe she would throw me out. But these people of Jutland never fully trust outsiders, so she must never guess I am Irish born. Besides, the queen lives with the king, a man who still regularly asks me for proof that I'm a sea princess, though we both know I'm not. A single silver coin is proof enough to last at least a moon, sometimes several. Yes, caution is the best guide.

My sister is not among the slaves today. Nor does any single slave dealer seem more familiar than any other. I am bereft. And grateful. Ignorance can foster hope.

A silver brooch on a patch of black cloth in front of a Norse jeweler catches my eye. The jewelry beside it is also silver, with gold wire in filigree patterns and amber studs and red glass—all of it from Eire. And usually stolen, since that's the Viking way when it comes to Eire. Irish goods are unmistakable. But this one brooch is Norse. It's a disc with ropy things entwined all over. I put my finger on a granule near the center and realize it serves as an eye, then trace down through the windings and writhings to find the whole animal, a snaky dragon. There are three of them, mouths agape, fearful yet beautiful. That seems appropriate, given that I hate snakes, for one threatened my little brother Hakon, and love snakes, for that same one tied me to the royal family. Plus, Beorn passed around the flask of dragon blood the first night I met him. Snaky dragons would be an emblem of the two families I have lived with and loved here in Jutland.

I turn to send Thyra home for money when a bell sounds. The bong of the huge iron bell is echoed by other bells all across our big, bustling city. People run in every direction, unsure whether to flee or gather. The cry goes up. *Hval*—whale! And now the splinters of people come together and flow down the bank of the fjord. Amazed cries mingle with laughter. Thyra and Ragnhild and I are caught in the current, but that's all right because I want to go. Visitors talk much about whales, but I've never seen one.

A ship appears in the distance. Oars dip together, then rise together, throwing shining spray. The men's shouts are ferocious, even from here. The crowd runs faster.

Ahead of the ship a long white streak appears in the clear waters. And, oh, there's another one. A third. How many more? The front one lifts its head, arcing backward gracefully. I didn't know whales were that flexible. This is not the dark-gray beast with the big dorsal fin, nor the long-snouted light-gray beast that is said to jump high. This is a small white beast with no fin and a bald rounded head. It's fully submerged again, but now I hear an underwater sound. They're squealing. Frightened. Good Lord, they sense their doom!

I stop, and people bash against me in their hurry. Once they're past, I go to the water's edge. I shouldn't look, but I want to know. I see everything from here. Men on the ship throw spears. Red stains the blue. Spears stand up in ragged rows as the whales drag them through the water, in crazy patterns of pain. The harbor reddens. A bloodbath.

I turn and run, not anywhere particular, just away from the harbor, away. The *sjøvættir*—sea spirits—failed today. They are supposed to guard these waters. They never should have let this little pod stray into this sea. They failed hideously, totally.

I run until I reach the city ramparts, then I race along inside them to the gates and out. I run all the way down to the beach, to the warming sands. The small waves are white-capped. Wind blows from the sea, making sand dance along the strand like a cloud that reaches to my knees. I go behind a dune and pant. I put my hands in my hair and hold my head. By now they will have pulled the beasts from the water. They will be slicing them up. There will be no more squeals of horror. My head is a giant lump of clay in my hands.

"Was it that bad?"

I turn quickly. The young man sits in a sand hollow, invisible except to someone standing right in front of him. His eyes are strange—the color of rain. The color of Eire's air in autumn. They look amused. "Wretched man," I say, "how can you act amused at butchery?"

"Butchery?" He holds up a slim white thing in his hand. It's a bone, for sure. "My musical skills have been insulted before, but never with that word."

My cheeks go hot. "What are we talking about?"

He scratches his cheek with one finger. "You tell first."

"They're killing whales in the harbor."

"Whales? In these warm waters?"

"Clearly you have the skin of a seal."

He laughs. "Ice floats all summer in the waters off Nóreg, the waters that whales love. They'd find this water hot. Even in winter, they wouldn't come this far south."

"They did."

"A mistake of nature."

"So what were you talking about?" I ask.

The man puts one end of the bone to his mouth and blows, running his fingers up and down holes on the top side of the bone. The sound is light and airy and whimsical. He stops and smiles, with teeth that say he's younger than I had assumed at first.

"I've never heard a bone flute before," I say.

"Really? I bought it here in Heiðabý just this morning. From a local." He holds it out to me. "It's an eagle wing bone."

I'd like to look at it, but I won't get that close. From where I stand, I could outrun this youth to the city gates if I had to. "Why do you northerners treat the whales so badly?"

"People kill the whales to eat, not for fun. It's not malicious."

"They were squealing."

"Oh. White whales then? The small ones?"

"Yes."

"Many creatures whimper when they're trapped. This is the way of the world."

And of course I know that. People kill animals to eat. And animals kill other animals to eat. And almost all creatures are smart enough to experience fear. I'm not an idiot. I hate it that he thinks I am. It's just that there are cruel ways to do things and uncruel ways. This might have been efficient, but it was cruel. The whales sounded pitiful and knowing.

And now I think of the spread of jewelry in the market—all those silver pieces from Eire. "Why do you northerners treat the Christians so badly?"

"What? What are you talking about?"

"You hate them. You invade their lands and rob their churches and monasteries."

"Some men do, yes—Viking men. Churches are where the wealth is. Again, this is the way of the world. It's business to them. No one hates the Christians."

"Some put wandering monks to death."

"If the monks do them harm, that may be just. If not, that's pointless." He tilts his head. "My turn to ask a question now. Why do you keep calling me a northerner?"

"You talked about the waters off Nóreg."

"Have you never heard of voyaging? I've gone far north. And east and west, too. All the same, I'm your countryman. I live in Jelling. It's north of here, yes, but not far. Still in Jutland. A girl like you, of course you've never gone anywhere you couldn't walk."

A girl like me? Well, I've been to Jelling. "That's not true!"

"So where have you traveled?"

I could bite my tongue. "I don't want to say."

He laughs. "Don't feel bad you haven't gone anywhere. Between family feuds and warring neighbors, just stepping outside is dangerous. Like the poets say, 'Let the man who opens a door be on the lookout for an enemy behind it.'"

"You sound worried. But when you play that flute, you sound carefree."

"What you heard was joy. But I'm never carefree. Where I live, pirates raid ships and coasts. There's a settlement of good people on the island Samsø, just off the coast from us. We helped them dig a canal across a neck of land so they could quickly send forces out to either sea—east or west— to keep pirates under control. And we patrol the coast."

"Princess!" Thyra comes running. She stops short when she sees the youth. Ragnhild, behind her, trips over her heels. They both stare.

"Farewell," I say to the youth.

"Wait." He stands and reaches into a pouch. "I've been

collecting these." He extracts a black capsule, the kind that holds shark eggs. "A mermaid purse. One for each of you."

Ragnhild steps forward, hand outstretched.

Thyra grabs her by the arm. "And what would you be expecting in return?"

The way she says it irks me; is she flirting with him?

"Nothing," says the youth. "I want nothing from you."

"Which is only fair," I say quickly. "Since anyone can gather these year round." I take a few steps toward town, then stop and look over my shoulder.

Ragnhild snatches a mermaid's purse from the youth. Thyra takes two more, but daintily. I am almost sure she's flirting. The girls catch up to me.

"Who was that?" asks Thyra.

"A voyager," I snap, and walk faster.

"Are you angry?" asks Thyra.

I don't answer. Thyra can flirt with whoever she chooses.

"I thought you were alone. I didn't see him at first. Otherwise I never would have called you princess."

"It's all right. I'm sure he thought you were joking."

"Then what is it?" asks Thyra. "I can see you're upset."

"How did you know where to look for me?"

"You always come this way when you go outside the ramparts," says Ragnhild.

Thyra reaches behind me over to Ragnhild, but I still see the pinch.

I stop short as it dawns on me. "Do you follow me?"

Ragnhild looks down and rubs at the pinched spot.

"I know you do," I say. "You gave it away. So you might as well tell all."

"It's not our fault." Ragnhild's eyes threaten tears. "The king told us to."

"And what have you seen?"

"You go down to the beach and walk. Then you disappear."

"Is that true?" I turn to Thyra. She's cleverer than Ragnhild. "What have you seen?"

"The same. You go into the woods. But we don't dare. Who knows what lives in the woods? So as far as we're concerned, you disappear."

"And what do you tell the king?"

"Simply that: You disappear."

"You tell him about the woods?"

"If we did, he'd make us follow you there. We say you go along the beach and the next we see of you is hours later, and your hair is soaked, as though you've been in the sea."

All right. That's no problem; the king can know that much. So long as he doesn't know about the hoard

I take coins from in order to appease him, all is fine.

I realize my hands are crossed over my chest. I let them drop. The youth's eyes shimmer before me, like magic. He is right. From now on I have to look ever more carefully when I open doors.

CHAPTER EIGHTEEN

"Hold it with both hands. That gives the best control." Though the words are encouraging, Earl's voice lacks sincerity. He has no confidence in Hakon—a position I understand. The boy has been engaged in military practice under Earl's instruction since his birthday, and so far shows no inclination toward any of the weapons.

Hakon, however, seems deaf to the tone of Earl's comment. He grips the sword with both hands, swells his chest with energy, and chops at the bush. He's merciless.

I gape. It is a terrible thing to see an eight-year-old destroy a bush, but he's so happy to be doing it, and it is such a surprise, I have to smile.

Satisfaction softens Earl's face. "Well, well, well. It looks like the sword is your weapon after all. We'll continue with it for the rest of the afternoon."

I step forward. "No, we need archery practice too. Like always."

Earl shrugs. "All right."

Thank heavens. I regularly urge Hakon forward in his

pitiful attempts at spear throwing—which can't be his fault, as the spears are longer than he is tall—and stake throwing, which actually can be his fault, as some of the stakes are short and should be manageable. I am constant in watching him hack with sword and ax—which are not real, since both sword and ax are made of wood—but which don't interest me because they require nothing but brute force. All this I do ostensibly out of a big sister's love. Though, indeed, Hakon is dear to me, the real reason for my dutiful behavior is that Earl allows me to be part of archery practice. So it is only fair that we should not skip it.

Archery matters. Battles lie ahead. Thorkild named me Alfhild—elf warrior—that day in the fishing boat. He did it out of fury. But over the years I've come to understand it was prescient. Rescuing Mel will not be easy; nothing in life is easy. I don't have the strength to hurl a spear, or the heart to swing an ax or sword into a body close by. But I could aim an arrow at a body that was far from me. I could be the fiery arrow my Irish name said I'd be. I lock my jaw and feel the nerves along it twitch. I can and will be ferocious in that way if I have to.

I watch a second bush get hacked to shreds, and a third.

Then we get our bows and shoot at targets. I'm good at this. I was good right from the first day, maybe out of motivation, but I'm getting better all the time. I can face one direction, then twirl around and shoot fast and hit the target behind me. I can walk along and hit a target without stopping. Today I walk faster and faster. Soon I'll be able to shoot as I run. Each time I hit a target, I feel more exonerated from my failure to meet my goal so far. *I'm sorry, Mel. I'm sorry it's taking me so long to grow up. But at least I've been getting ready. At least I'll be able to fight for you when I finally come find you.*

When archery practice ends, Earl takes Hakon off on a walk along the fjord with the shield in one hand and a stake in the other. Hakon's job is to understand the weight of the shield and learn how to move with it regardless of what obstacles Earl puts before him. The shields are made of wood, with leather covering and a reinforced iron edge. There's an iron plate—a boss—at the center, and across from it on the inside is the handgrip. The boss protects the hand. Since the shield stands higher than Hakon's waist, it is quite remarkable that he can stride along holding it. Usually I walk by his side just to celebrate this feat. But today I stay behind and continue target practice.

Only I'm no longer aiming at the prearranged targets. I select a leaf on a tree and shoot it. Then the leaf beside it. Then the one beside that. I spy a feather in the grasses. Maybe an eagle feather. Maybe the eagle whose bone became the flute in the youth's hands this morning. I shoot it. And there's a gray stone, the color of the youth's eyes. I shoot it. I am shooting at everything now, anything. I am shooting at my memory of the youth—the boy who said he wants nothing of me. I am shooting at the thought of the king asking my own servants to report my actions to him. I am shooting at whoever still holds my sister captive. And I am hitting everything I shoot at.

That feeling of conquest coats my lips as the afternoon passes, and it lingers as we dress to go to the great hall for a feast. I don the dress of a royal daughter now, with gold and silver brooches, and accept the limitations that clothing imposes on my behavior. Queen Tove smiles at me in approval. She manages to control her anxiety over my excursions in ordinary clothes so long as I maintain the proper demeanor when I'm dressed royally. She herself wears the hawk-plumage cloak I love so much.

"The evening is neither hot nor cool," I whisper to her as we walk. "Those feathers must feel perfect."

"Hawk plumage allows me to move with grace and authority among strangers."

"You always have grace and authority." This is true.

The queen smiles. "This kind of cloak is called a *valsham*, like what the goddess Freyja wears. It's especially good for traveling. It makes me feel strong, fearless."

"What a wonderful thing. Someday I want a feather cloak."

The queen takes my hand. "Tomorrow you can wrap it around yourself so that it forms a tent you are entirely enclosed within. Then shut your eyes and travel."

"Travel?"

"Inside yourself. The best kind of journey."

The queen mixes tales of gods and goddesses with the lives of humans. I know that, of course, for she sometimes asks me if I miss my true father—and I can sense she means both whoever that may be and specifically Høking, the sea king that she has claimed as father for me. So I should not be surprised at the mystical nature of her words now. But I am. I float on them. And I realize this is the second time today that I've been drawn into a conversation about voyaging. I feel mystical myself—like a visionary. Something is about to happen.

Outside the great hall, food is being baked in holes in the ground, packed around with heated stones. I expect meats and fish, like usual, but this smell is new. Something is carved already and arranged in overlapping slices on wooden trenchers. The pieces are cooked brownish purple at the edges and pink in the middle. My cheeks go slack; it's whale, of course. That's why every earthen oven has the same contents. And, of course, it is the right thing to eat; so much slaughter must not be allowed to come to naught. Yet this knowledge brings no consolation. I am standing on the bank of the fjord again. I am seeing the white beasts bathed in their own blood. Something shreds inside me. I put my hand over my mouth and nose—I refuse to taste these smells—and walk past the coals into the hall.

The walls of this hall are lined with woven wood— wicker. I'd never seen wicker before coming to this city. Small tables and four-legged stools clutter the room. Stools I knew—we had them in Eire. But I'd never seen them in Jutland before. Right now I am so grateful for wicker walls and stools and tables. I can love this hall, regardless of what those around me are nibbling off the tip of their knives. I can pretend I am alone here.

Except I'm not alone. I'm surrounded by crushing crowds. The music is loud, and it pulls me past the gaming boards and the people laughing in little groups. The spirit is infectious; I'm getting happy again too, when the servant Gorm hands me a glass container full of purple liquid.

I stare at it. We drink beer and milk and fruit juices and water from wood cups, and horns sometimes too. We drink *mjød*—mead—often from small silver vessels. But we rarely drink anything from glasses. I hold it gingerly to my nose and breathe the aroma. "What is this?"

"Wine. One of the guests brought it. He brought the glasses, too. They're imported."

"Where from?"

"Ask him." Gorm points toward the other side of the room. "He's with the king."

I can't see past all the people, but I'm intrigued by this drink. Grapes for wine don't grow in Jutland, and importing fruit means half of it is spoiled before it gets here, so what's the point? But once last year I sniffed deep of red wine in the king's cup. It smelled exotic. I dip my tongue tip in it now. It tastes exotic. I drink it all down and work my way over to the king.

When suddenly here he is, in front of me, the youth I've been imagining ever since this morning. He watches me approach. His eyes are liquid.

"Princess, indeed," he says. "The princess of the curly hair."

"Have you met my Alfhild?" says King Hók, looking quizzically from the youth to me.

"Only briefly." The youth clasps my forearm. "I am Alf."

"How strange. I've never met a man with a truncated form of my own name."

"Nor have I met a woman with an elongated form of mine. Do you like the wine?"

"Yes."

"Have another glass." He takes my empty glass and hands me an already full glass from a round tray on the floor beside him.

I drink it down.

Alf laughs. "Wine is to be sipped."

My head spins. I totter.

The king puts his arm around my waist from behind. "We're not accustomed to this drink." He pulls me to him.

I would normally protest; I'm not a child. But given how unsteady I am on my feet right now, I lean into him with gratitude.

The king and this Alf talk on and on. People sing and dance. Someone announces a *skald* has come. Who? I look around, and from nowhere appears a large man, hairy-looking from behind. I panic: Beorn has come to Heiðabý at last. I will be exposed. And then I realize that I have nothing to fear for or from him anymore. No one will connect me to Beorn. I am the king's daughter now—I can stay the king's daughter forever, or at least as long as the hoard holds out. Nothing is to prevent Beorn and me from simply talking a moment.

I remember the sound of Beorn's voice so well, I can almost hear it at this moment, hear the care in it. He can tell me news of Ástríd. I can finally give him the antler comb I bought for her—a luxury beyond her dreams. I can learn what Búri and Alof's latest triumphs are. I break away from the king and push my way past everyone and grab Beorn by the arm, my heart nearly bursting with love.

The big man turns. It isn't Beorn. Of course not. The

look on his face changes from a question to a leer.

From behind the giant, the man Torel appears. He takes this giant by the arm and speaks to him of some business deal. Torel is among the richest traders in town. So this giant isn't the *skald* at all; he's come to make business.

I back away, with the crowd closing in front of me, blocking off the image of the giant and Torel. I have the sensation that I'm sinking backward into water, until it all becomes solid and I'm flush against a wall. Nothing is right. All I want is to leave. I have never missed my family in Ribe more. Not a night passes that I don't think of Ástríd, that I don't think of Búri. Sometimes I fear I've merged Ástríd and Mel in my dreams. And I know I've merged Búri and Hakon, though the two boys have every right to be distinct. My arms ache for Alof. My heart can hardly beat.

"Are you all right?" Alf stands before me.

"No."

"Can I help?"

Would that he could. "Are you trustworthy?"

"I believe myself to be."

"Do you travel often?"

"Yes."

"Do you ever travel to Ribe?"

"Once a year, at least."

"Will you deliver something for someone?"

"Yes."

"At what price?"

Alf moves to lean his back against the wall, so we are standing side by side, looking into the room. If he says he wants nothing from me, just as he wanted nothing from we three girls for the mermaid purses, I will stamp on his foot. "If you had not just drunk wine, I would have asked a price."

I remember Egill wanting a kiss. My lips curl. "What price?"

"It doesn't matter now. I can't ask, the state you're in."

"It does matter. What price?"

"A truth."

"What do you mean?"

"I want to know something you believe—something you hold true."

"I feel challenged by the price, and dulled by the wine. Everything takes so much effort."

Alf nods. "And if it doesn't take effort, perhaps it's not worth doing. Thank you for this piece of wisdom."

"Wisdom? It was a description of my present state. Wisdom. Do you fancy yourself a soothsayer? I thought you chased fun and pirates."

"Your words smart."

"Do they really?"

"Does everything have to be a challenge with you?"

"You bring it out in me."

He sighs. "So what is it you want me to deliver to Ribe?"

"Come."

I lead him as steadily as I can back to our home, then leave him at the front gate while I dig through my personal chest of belongings. When I come back outside, he's gone. I step through the gate and look up and down the road. Bleak. The whole world seems bleak and horrid. I sit on the ground. Who cares if dirt stains my clothes? Who cares? Who cares? My head drops backward, and my hand goes to my throat. My eyes feel like they are glass beads that will fall backward through my brain. I want a reason, an excuse, to howl in grief. The heavens are empty.

"Have you got it?" And here he is, sitting on the ground beside me.

"I thought you had gone."

"I wanted you to think that."

"But why?"

"To see if you'd be sad."

"You're tricky."

"Perhaps."

"Not tricky enough, though. You don't know why I was sad—whether for lack of you or for lack of a messenger."

"Do you know why you're sad?"

The question wavers in the air. It swirls now. It could make me shiver if I let it. "You haven't earned an answer to that one." I empty my hand into his. "A toilet set. For Ástríd, wife of Beorn, mother of Búri and Alof. And maybe others by now."

"Beorn the *skald*? He used to come through Jelling every year when I was a boy. Then he got married and came no more. Is Ástríd your sister?"

"Not by blood."

"Those can be the best kind."

"Don't say that. Don't ever say that!" I grab hold of his arm and throw my weight on him to help me get to my feet. "When will you deliver it to Ribe?"

"I'll leave soon."

"When?"

"Tomorrow. Yes, tomorrow, in fact. I had other plans, but plans are meant to be changed."

This feels too good to be true. I turn in a circle. "There is no moon."

"No stars, either." But he's looking up at me, not at the sky.

"Heaven is empty."

"No. Just full of clouds."

"They're filling my head."

"Then I'll bid you good night."

CHAPTER NINETEEN

"Sit down, Alfhild."

I sit on the bench built into the side wall of the main room. Queen Tove stands beside King Hók. Her face gives nothing away. That alone is enough to worry me. Has something gone wrong? I want her smile. I long for it.

"We've had a marriage request for you."

My cheeks go hot. I stare at my hands in my lap. When he says no more, I look up.

The king smiles. "King Valdemar."

I have recovered from my inebriation of last night. Yet it seems the king speaks gibberish. "Who?"

"He's king of the Gautar."

The queen steps forward. "Gøtaland is across the water from here—and a little north. They speak the same language we do. Or nearly."

I clutch the sides of my shift. "I don't even know him."

"He saw you last night," says the king. "He says you caught him by the arm."

The giant. I remember his teeth.

"Did you?" asks the queen.

"Yes," I say.

Queen Tove raises her eyebrows. "Does that mean you fancy him?"

"It would be a good alliance," says the king. "Uniting our area with—"

"I don't fancy him. I don't fancy anyone." I say the second sentence more loudly, and even to my ears it feels false.

"You're of a good age to marry," says the king.

I stare at him. A father cannot force a daughter to marry, not even if he is a king—he knows that. He would not violate that.

"Age is not the only factor," says the queen.

"But a request denied requires the most tactful of answers. You are sure, Alfhild?" The king's voice has softened, at last.

I nod. He leaves. The queen looks at me hesitantly. "I didn't expect this," I say. "Please believe me. You know I have something important to do before I marry. I must find my sister. I told you that when I first came. We never talk of it, but you must remember."

"I never forget. This just happened. Like the king said, it's your age."

"I have no interest in suitors."

"Don't fret over it, Alfhild. The king will give Valdemar

your answer, and that will be the end of it." She touches the side of my arm. "Wait here." She leaves and comes back a moment later with the hawk-plumage cloak dangling from her hands. She drapes it around me. "Travel inside your head, daughter. Inside your heart. Anywhere you need to go. And Alfhild . . ." Her voice drops to a whisper. "Don't leave me for real travels. Not yet. Go far, far, far, right here, in this cloak. I won't let anyone come into this room till mealtime." She leaves again.

I grab the sides with each hand and raise my arms to close the cloak over my head. The feathers are many enough and thick enough to shut out the light, but the cloak is still practically weightless, which, strangely, makes me feel weightless. I bring my legs up on the bench and cross them. I am now entirely within this cloak. It is a good place to retreat to.

But I'm not supposed to retreat. I'm supposed to travel. That's what the queen, my queen, my mother, told me to do. Travel inside myself. I close my eyes.

Gold. Something shiny and gold with a black center. Hawk eyes. I sense them on me. They see the air go in and out of my lungs. They ride the thick slowness of my blood. They poke at my heavy bones, poke and poke to make them hollow—hollow as a flute. They inspect the hairs of my head, of my body, and lengthen them, fray them, fan them out into feathers. They are my eyes, and I am flying high over the land, over the sea. I soar on the wind currents. I drink the clouds.

My land, my sea, my wind, my clouds.

I alight on the top of an enormous tree. Oh, yes, this tree is Yggdrasill, where the gods hold daily assembly, and I am the eagle who perches there, so high that I have knowledge of the whole world.

Jutland might as well be the whole world. It has been my home for seven of my fifteen years. By now this language feels more mine than any other does. The habits of these people no longer surprise me. Probably the habits of people in Eire would, in fact. Even the gods of these people make sense to me now. Christian stories belong to another time, another life.

I could let go of that other life completely. I could give myself fully to this land. I don't have to be the eagle that sits on the top of Yggdrasill, I don't have to be anything fancy. I could be a simple hawk. Here. Happy. I could dive around another hawk, sweep across the skies, and plummet together with him, talons intertwined. I could build a nest.

Especially if my husband had eyes the color of rain. That realization pins me to this life like knives through flesh. I would have to rip away parts of me to escape it.

But that other life—the lost and distant life—isn't

simply a matter of language and habits and gods. In that life I was a real daughter and a real sister. My parents and brother, they may not need me, though I know their hearts are sore. What Papi told was enough to convince me of that. But Mel, she may need me. She may have a life that nicks at her soul.

No soul can endure that forever. It will come to bits; it will disappear. The real sister in me has no choice.

I have waited all these years to grow up. Now is the time to act. That giant man, let him fester if that's his choice. That rain man, let him dissipate, leaving me dry as rock.

I lean back against the side of the room, lower my arms, and open my eyes. I am spent.

"What did you do to that man?" King Hók strides back and forth in front of me.

"Nothing. I told you."

"Tell me again."

"I thought he might be the *skald* everyone said had arrived—and I knew a *skald* once. So I reached for his arm. To make him turn."

"You touched him! That was your mistake! That's what convinced him!"

"On his arm. Only on his arm."

"What did you say?"

"Nothing. Not a single word."

"He says your face spoke passion."

"I cannot answer for what someone says my face speaks."

Queen Tove pulls on her fingers. "Alfhild has never been the least flirtatious. She cannot be held responsible for how this stranger interprets her action."

The king stops pacing and looks at me. He slaps a fist into a palm. "We have to seal you away."

"Seal me away?" My cheeks turn icy.

"We'll use the high tower beside the fort. There's only one entrance. We'll dig a wide pit in front of that entrance and add a door that drops down to form a bridge over the pit for when you want someone to enter."

The queen shakes her head uncertainly. "Bridge, pit . . . What are you talking about?"

"Vipers. It was a viper who brought Alfhild to us. Vipers will help us keep her. A pit full of vipers."

"What vipers? We keep no vipers."

"I'll pay high sums. The word will get out. Arabs charm snakes—Arabs will bring them."

"That will take too much time," says the queen. "The word would have to travel with them all the way to their home countries before they could come back with snakes. But this Valdemar is breathing down our necks now."

"Then we'll use our own vipers. There are snakes to be

caught in the north countries if you search. I'll pay exorbitantly. We'll fill the pit. No one will get to Alfhild."

I stop gnawing on my fist. "What will I do locked in a tower?"

"Be safe. And keep us safe. King Valdemar has threatened war if he cannot have you, and the way he talks, I believe him."

"But, King," says the queen, "how can putting Alfhild in a tower save us from war?"

"I'll announce where she is. I'll declare that I will prevent no man from entering her chamber. The vipers will stop him, not me."

"That's good," says the queen. "He can't declare war if you make it clear that he can try to enter the tower."

"What if he brings arrows and simply shoots the vipers dead?" I say.

"That will be against the rules. No arrows shot at the vipers unless you are inside the pit with them. No large rocks, either. Yes. I'll announce that."

"What if he has no fear of a viper pit?" I say.

"Have you heard of Ragnar Lodbrok?" asks the king.

"No."

"He was a Norseman. Years ago they captured him in Saxland. They threw him in a viper pit, and he died screaming."

"This Valdemar will know the story," says the queen. "It will stop him. Everyone knows the story."

I didn't. The king and queen look at me, but none of us say it.

I shake my head. "He could still try. After all, I didn't die from the viper bite."

"But a single bite made you very sick," said the queen. "He'd get many bites."

"He'd recover and try again," I say. "He could try and try until he succeeds. No. I have to leave."

The queen gasps. "What? You can't leave me yet. No."

"I have to." I had already realized it was time for me to go in search of Mel anyway—I realized that when I wrapped myself inside the hawk-plumage cloak today. It would appear that three years is all I'll ever get of family life. Three years with Ástríd, three years with Queen Tove.

"No!" King Hók shakes his head vehemently. "We're not going to lose you because of this wretched King Valdemar. You're going nowhere except into that tower until the danger has passed. Listen to this rule: If a man should try to get you out of the tower, and if he should fail, he must yield to me and I will immediately decapitate him and impale his head on a stake for all to see. I will announce that, as well."

"What a hideous threat!" I say.

"Let's hope King Valdemar agrees."

CHAPTER TWENTY

My father, the king, is a *dróttinn*, a military leader. He has many men who will come at his call, ready to fight for him—his *hempægar*. He also has an older man, his *þegn*, who has sworn loyalty to him at all costs. And he has a younger man, his *dreng*, who has also sworn loyalty at all costs. My father, the king, is the leader of so many warriors.

Yet it is the middle of the night and I am high in this tower and King Valdemar stands below, on the far side of the viper pit, calling up to me, and not a single one of these loyal souls is guarding me. Do they think evil sleeps at night? Are they daft?

"You can hear me, I know that. Show yourself!"

I go to the window, aware of being framed in the softest glow of the new moon. I hold my hair out above my head and screech like a hawk. "Go away, giant."

"What!" He laughs. "That's what I saw in you, that spirit! You'll be mine."

I sink back into the shadows. "Never."

"Don't be foolish. I am a legendary lover."

"You disgust me."

No answer. It was an ugly thing to say—but he deserves it. He should let me be.

"Tell me, Princess Alfhild," he calls at last, "how dear do you hold your brother Hakon?"

I rush to the window again. I can't see anyone else with this giant. But the boy could be hidden somewhere nearby. "Where is he?"

"Deep in dreams. But I can fetch him here within the hour. They say last time you saved him from a viper bite. Could you save him from . . . let me see . . . six snakes in this pit? But, oh yes, I forgot . . . now only three." He laughs. "Could you save him from three cobra bites?"

Cobras. The call for snakes produced three vipers from northern countries on the very first day. But then no more. I felt relieved; three seemed too few to "fill" a pit. Surely the king would change his plan, and I wouldn't have to be locked in this clammy tower. But on the third day an Arab ship bearing three cobras happened to stop in Heiðabý. The cobras were each in separate cages, beside cages of scorpions and skinks and beavers. It turns out nearly every part of a cobra is useful in medicine, especially mixed with crushed scorpions or skink blood or beaver testicles—or so the Arabs would have the world believe. The captain planned to sell them to surgeons but was only too happy to unload all three at once. And so, it turned out I was cursed, after all. The cobras went into the pit—for a moment there were a total of six snakes—and promptly ate the three vipers, as the fascinated townsfolk looked on. But that didn't matter: Three cobras were plenty to fill a pit.

"Answer me, Princess. Could you save your brother?"

"If that is your threat, then you don't fight fair. So you deserve whatever you get. Indeed, if that is your threat, I will let fall the door now. You can march over the bridge-door into this tower. You can take me away."

"Do it!"

"And then . . ."

He waits. Finally he says, "And then what?"

"I will soon get my chance. Perhaps immediately. Perhaps tonight."

"What do you mean?"

"I will kill you." I keep the shake from my voice and speak slowly, clearly. "Not with a quick knife stab. Not with a push off a cliff. Not with anything you can foresee and take precautions against. I will use a slow method. It will hurt. The pain will grow. From the center of your skull. From the center of your belly. From the center of your groin. Excruciating, incessant. You'll be like the god Bald, dying from the mistletoe arrow his brother shot—writhing. You will wish you were dead long before you breathe your last."

My voice shimmers in the air a moment. Then silence.

At last he says, "You have an ugly way with words."

I hold my tongue.

"What slow method?"

"There are many at my disposal. But I have already chosen the most vicious one. A toxin . . . from the sea. It liquidates you, from the inside out."

"They say you are a sea king's daughter really."

"Which is why I am immune. But you are not, nor ever will be."

"I don't believe you," he says. I hold my tongue again. He shakes a fist at me, then drops it. "Bah! You're more trouble than you're worth." And I remember Thorkild, saying those very words, time after time. King Valdemar walks a few steps off, then turns to face me again. "Word has gotten around. Did you know that? Has anyone told you? I've made you famous. Your beauty is the talk of the known world. Brave lads from all over have sworn to give a try at winning you. And these are lads who never looked in your eyes, so they don't know what fire burns within you." He clears his throat with a growly sound. "They will listen to your ugly words and think a pretty little thing like you must have been told to say them. They won't believe them. They will storm the tower. One of them will get you. Or maybe all of them." He laughs. I can hear him laughing long after his shape has melded into the night.

If Valdemar's words are true and other men come, I won't have to say my hateful lies again, for I cannot believe there are others who would stoop to threatening Prince Hakon. So they will stand at the edge of the pit and try to think of ways to get across it. As they stand there, they will hear the rumors: If you cut a cobra in half, you wind up with two. If you throw rocks on a cobra, it will change into a monster and crush you. And the worst rumor of all: Cobras always get revenge. Men will listen, and then they will leave. Alive.

So Valdemar is wrong: I will not be made into a victim, nor a monster. No one can do that to me. No one can turn my life into a tale for *skalds* to tell.

Besides, the king will release me now; Valdemar has gone home.

I sleep fitfully.

The king does not release me, for Valdemar did not lie. Over the next few days three men take the challenge, and I am obliged to stay in the tower while they do. The king has announced that every attempt must be made solo. Townspeople come for the show.

The first solo man arrived dragging a tree trunk long enough to span the pit and land on the bit of dirt in front of the tower door. Anyone could see that easily. It was wide, so he would not fall off. He seemed to have solved the matter of the snakes. But once he crossed the pit, how would he scale the tower? The only window is at the top, in my room.

I almost called out that question to him. Why not save him useless effort? But calling out would have meant I'd need to drop the robe that I held muffling my face. I will allow none of them to see me. That was the lesson I learned from Valdemar: I will allow no one to claim that my beauty brought their downfall. Their downfall is their own cursed fault.

And I am not a beauty, anyway. I will learn to spit fire if they continue to use a maiden's virtue against her.

So I kept quiet, like all the other spectators, waiting to see what this man would do after he crossed the pit.

But no one got to see his plan, because once the tree trunk was pushed out midway over the pit, the front tip dropped in. Of course! No man could hold steady a great trunk suspended in the air like that. The man hauled it out, straining with loud groans. Sweat dripped in his eyes. Or I think it must have, for something blinded him to the cobra that clung to the trunk. The cobra opened its hood, hissed, and struck. The man spun, round and round, astonishment on his face, and fell backward, soundless, into the pit, taking the snake with him. It happened in the space of seconds. No one dared fetch out his body.

That the snake came out with the tree trunk was a fluke. Who is responsible for a fluke? Who is responsible for a spinning corpse? But I wouldn't even pose those questions. I couldn't. I couldn't think.

The second solo man dragged a *krage*—a tree trunk again, but now the branches were lopped off a short distance from the base, so, propped up, it made a kind of ladder. The kind they used in the pit house I lived in with Thora and Thorkild and the others.

This man clearly intended to solve both problems at once with that *krage*: getting over the pit and arriving at my window. But all of us spectators were alerted to the dangers of weight now. How on earth did he expect to get that *krage* into position for climbing? Besides, it was too short. It would reach only halfway up the wall. Was his mind deficient?

The man had a long rope tied around the upper end of the *krage*, looped around the highest branch-footholds. When he had dragged the *krage* to the edge of the viper pit, he stopped. Then he took the other end of that long rope and ran with it in a huge circle that encompassed both pit and tower, back to his starting point. He then pulled on the rope until it went taut, from the upper end of the *krage*, straight to the tower and around it, and back to the *krage*. He stood there and pulled on the rope.

It was ingenious—almost. Something was wrong

with the plan, though I couldn't grasp what yet. I chewed on his folly.

The man leaned all his considerable weight against the drag of the rope and managed to get that *krage* across the viper pit. But now the tip of it was at the side of the tower, not the middle. The more he pulled, the more the *krage* went along the side of the tower, farther and farther from the man's aim. Nothing could make it go up the wall.

Good Lord. I wanted to scream to him to run. To annul the attempt, say it was a joke, halfhearted. Queen Tove stood beside King Hók, and I watched her shoulders curl forward in defeat. We could not allow our poor king to have to behead this man, this fool. The king would put a good face on it if the man left now. He'd laugh and call off the whole thing. He could give some stupid gift to whatever men had spent their money to travel here for the challenge and just send them all home again. I didn't really need to stay in the tower anymore. This whole nightmare could end.

The man didn't try to laugh it off, though. Perhaps he was of limited imagination. In a rage, he shouted curses, threw down the rope, and raced over the *krage*, as the crowd gasped. Then he jumped from the *krage* to the tiny plot of earth in front of the door and stood there, staring up the wall at me. But I had no answers for him. I didn't invite these attempts. I had no plan to offer. If he didn't know enough to leap back on that *krage* immediately and run for his life, it was not my doing.

He reached out toward the *krage* with both arms. What? The whole crowd moved forward to try to understand what he was doing. He managed to snag one of the truncated branches, and he pushed it upward, leaning out, as though to wedge himself under the tip of the *krage* in order to push that tip up the wall. The *krage* slipped out of his hands and the entire thing swung sideways, the point of contact on the far side of the pit acting as a pivot. The *krage* thumped into the pit and knocked the man with it.

Another fluke.

But somehow a little more predictable than the last. Someone somewhere was a little more culpable. Who?

Sleepless nights, though I am not lonely anymore. Ragnhild and Thyra came to bed down with me. Queen Tove came to rub my back and moan into my neck. But we didn't speak. Some horrors are unmentionable.

Today makes a full week that I have been in this tower, and the third solo man stands at the other side of the pit and waves to me. Solo man one and solo man two had names, which I refused to hear. This man has a name as well. But I don't want to know it. He is doomed. And none of this is my doing. The world has gone crazy.

He stands there and waves like a lunatic.

Suddenly I wave back and lower my robe from before my face. "Go home," I call. "Live."

"Wait right there for me," he calls back. "Nothing can kill me."

This I'm not prepared for. What can he mean? Clearly he must mean nothing—nonsense—for he told me to wait here. Where would I go?

He opens a satchel and pulls out armor. A *hjálm*—an iron helmet. A *byrnja*—a shirt of mail. He puts them on, and I imagine their weight. It's as though the helmet pushes my head down into my neck, the mail shirt pushes my shoulders down down into my chest. All of me feels forced toward the ground. I know this is how he feels, for I have put on a helmet myself. I have donned mail myself. I wanted to know the parts of battle in that near and intimate way. Earl, little Hakon's trainer in the ways of warriors, has allowed me this. Earl has taught me so much, always incidentally— an accident of the fact that I stand beside Hakon with my eyes and ears open. I know to be brave. Be ready. Don't set your heart on a specific tactic; look for opportunities. Use the element of surprise. Attack at night when others are complacent enough to sleep. Use everything you've got.

Does this third solo man know these things? Does he know anything?

He opens a jug and takes a swig, then holds the jug

high to me. "*Bjór!*" *Bjór* is a fermented cider, rare and magi-cal. I've seen only one person drink it ever, and he drank it from a silver vessel tiny as a thumb tip, because it's so pow-erful. The man lifts his ax. He walks to the edge of the pit and shakes his ax over his head. For a moment I think he'd be better off with a sword—for I don't believe the rumor that a snake sliced in half equals two—but then I realize I am thinking in the fog of that *bjór*, just as he must be. Ax or sword—who cares?—both are futile. There are three snakes—he can't attack all three at once. And his legs, his face, his feet—all these are vulnerable, even if the iron shields the rest. Surely he will see that. His desire to sur-vive will make him cease before he begins. His belief in the magic potion cannot be so strong as to annihilate all sense.

But he doesn't retreat. He rocks from foot to foot.

"Go home!" My voice is a shriek. I cannot bear one more death. I will have nothing to do with marriage ever if there is one more death.

He jumps into the pit.

Snakes strike. Stupid crazy mystic.

I grab the window ledge, but I cannot hold myself. I fall to the floor of this room, this prison, and press my cheek to the cold hardness and wish my mind senseless.

CHAPTER TWENTY-ONE

The very worst has happened. He has come back to town: Alf. Alf of the eyes the color of rain—though I have not seen them again; it is only my memory that tells me this, and who can trust the memory of a girl who has witnessed the horrors of the past week?

He apparently traveled by sea to Ribe, going all the way north around the tip of Jutland, then all the way south again. Given how short the land journey is, that was not a sensible act if speed had been his first concern. But he is a seafaring man, so the boat was his natural means. And speed dictated his actions only insofar as he didn't stop at any towns along the way. He and his crew camped at the mouths of rivers at night. They walked upstream to fill up their water barrels. They built fires and roasted fish on long iron forks. They woke early, went to bed late. They were quick about it.

My mind knows all. I see him at the helm, steering. His eyes intent. His hand pats the toilet set in his pouch, his precious trust, determined to deliver it to Ástríd. This innocent man.

Then he lands at Ribe. All that time at sea meant he didn't learn the news—the absurd quest of Valdemar and the princess in the tower. He knew nothing until he arrived in Ribe six days later, to news of two morons dead in the snake pit. The third was yet to come, yet to die.

Perhaps it was Beorn himself who informed Alf. An atrocious thought. Please, let that not be so. Please don't let the finest man I've known in this country be the one to have planted the seed that will ultimately grow to my grief.

Alf wore this news close, like skin. He told his crew to sail back to Heiðabý on their own and meet him the following week—and he ran across the land, without sleep, without pause, back to this town, my town, in a single day.

I see him run. I hear his feet pound the earth. I feel his heart throb.

Ah, it sears, how I see this man. This innocent man.

Then he arrives in the king's home.

All this Queen Tove tells me. And more: Alf has returned for one purpose. He will take the challenge. Tomorrow.

I will not accept this grief. "No!" I have been clutching the queen's hands ever since she spoke his name. "No!" I shout. "He will not take the challenge. I will not allow this."

The queen's face lightens for the first time since Valdemar intruded into our lives. "Your distraught response can mean only one thing: You will accept him as a husband without the challenge. I knew it. I knew you cared for him. I glimpsed the two of you at the feast that night. I saw it in your body."

"I accept no one as a husband."

The queen looks stricken. "You have the right to refuse a particular suitor. But surely not the right to refuse all. It's a duty to procreate. Do you not understand?"

"The horror of this tower has changed me. Forever. I will have nothing more to do with this tower, nothing more to do with men who tell me what I have to do. I'm going out right now."

"Listen to me, Alfhild."

"There's nothing left to say."

"Listen to me!"

"I'm leaving." I open the door of the tower room.

"You can't."

I stand at the top of the stairs. "Send this suitor home. Pay him. End it."

"Things have changed." The queen's voice is heavy as an anchor. "This Valdemar business has brought new fame to Heiðabý."

"Infamy, you mean. Three men died horrible deaths for no reason."

"People come here now who wouldn't have come before, and they spend money. The town grows rich. It is said that Heiðabý girls are more beautiful than others; they are made in the image of the stunning goddess Freyja. The wealthy men of town are getting marriage proposistions for their daughters that are better than what they hoped for before. The king's name has become a household word in much of the northern world." The queen sinks to the floor and looks up at me. "Many are coming to see Alf take the challenge. The king would be glad—all of us would be glad—if you'd simply marry him. No one wants more needless deaths." The queen puts her palms on her cheeks, and her face shows again a small glimmer of hope. "The king would turn it into a grand marriage celebration. I could make all the plans. It would become a legend. A happy tale. That would be even better for the town's business than this infernal cobra pit."

I see eyes the color of rain. An innocent man.

But I also see a girl in a boat. Fifteen years old. Her mouth is gagged. Her hands are tied behind her back unless it's time to eat. She was my sister. Whoever she is today, she is still my sister. I'm shaking my head violently.

"You can avoid his death, Alfhild—I know you want to. A marriage would do that in an instant. But we cannot have everyone come with expectations and give them no show whatsoever. The king will not allow you to simply call it all off and go back to life as it was."

"Then I won't go back to life as it was. I will run away."

"Oh, girl, my girl. The king anticipated this. After what you said about leaving—just going away—it wasn't hard to figure you might try to do that. The king has posted men inside the bottom door. They will not let you leave."

I look into this queen's face.

A tear rolls down her cheek. She stands with difficulty, as though this conversation has aged her years and years. She walks to me and stops. "Forgive me."

"Do you control him?"

"No."

"Then there is nothing to forgive. But promise me something," I say, speaking the words without the thought fully formed yet.

"What?"

"After tomorrow, whatever happens, I will need to do something. You know I need to do something. I've told you that from the very first."

"Yes, I know."

"And I will need your help."

"How?"

"Promise me your help. No matter what."

Her eyes plead. But then she swallows, and I watch her neck lengthen with determination. "I will help you, even if it incurs the king's wrath." Her shoes slap the stone steps as she descends the stairs. Gone.

I pace. I have no thoughts. Just feet, which can do naught but follow circles. Perhaps I'll trace so many circles in the stone that the floor will fall through and crush the men who guard the door below.

I cannot avoid thought forever. I cannot afford to avoid it even until tomorrow. I must find a plan. The queen is ready to help me—I must find a plan that will work.

Ragnhild and Thyra appear at my door.

I stop and stand in the very center of the room. "Have you heard?"

"Yes." It is Thyra.

I'm grateful she doesn't bother to feign ignorance and ask what I'm talking about. "Your face is strained," I say.

"And yours is wasted, Princess."

"Did my father talk with you?"

"You know he did."

"Did he send you here with a mission?"

"Of course," says Thyra. "We are to talk you into marrying Alf before the challenge."

"Do you intend to do that?"

"So far as I can see, you do what you please, Princess."

"But it's not just that," says Ragnhild. "You must have a reason for your hesitation. You always have reasons. So we have agreed between us not to argue with you."

"I appreciate that." I touch my head. The hair is still there. It still curls. It has no right to do that. Nothing ordinary should be happening anymore. "Thyra, have you ever loved a man?"

"No."

"It must be a pitifully painful thing, don't you think?"

"I can't guess."

"It is," says Ragnhild very quietly. "It is pitiful. It is painful."

The tremor in her voice steals my breath. When I can speak again, I ask, "Who have you loved?"

"Igor."

"Igor, the slave?"

"And it is not past." Ragnhild's cheeks are blotchy red. "Don't talk of it in the past. I love him."

Thyra takes Ragnhild's hand. "I feared as much."

"Does he not love you in return?" I ask.

"He adores me."

Ragnhild is adored. She is simple, but honest and sweet. She works hard. Why shouldn't she be adored? "Then what's the problem? A free person can marry a slave."

"But their child then becomes the property of the slave's owner. Igor will not allow any child of his to be a slave. He will never marry."

"What if my father were to free him?"

"He won't do that. I asked. And he forbade me to prevail upon you for help. He says you are stubborn in your vehemence against slavery, and if I ask you for help, he will sell Igor to an Arab and buy someone else to replace him. Then I'll never see Igor again."

I am helpless. "The king can be harsh."

"All men can be." Thyra sniffs and pulls herself up to her full height. "I learned that long ago. It's why I willingly left my last post to be employed by you—a girl. It's best to enjoy what you can of life, with or without a man on each occasion, but always on your own two feet."

"I can hardly believe my ears." I take the hands of these two girls, and we form a closed circle. "You were hired three years ago—and all this time, we have never talked like this. It's as though we didn't know each other at all."

"I know things about you," says Thyra. "You love Alf. Admit it."

"I don't know what love is."

"Do you think about him all the time?" asks Ragnhild. "Do your insides fold over and over when you're near him?"

I look down.

"It doesn't matter what the king wants," says Thyra. "You want Alf. Marry him because you want to, not because the king wants you to. Don't let your stubbornness make a fool of you."

"It's not that. Nothing like that," I say.

"Then what is it?" asks Thyra. "Tell us."

Ragnhild moves her hand up my forearm. "We've been honest with you. And you could hurt us if you wanted to. But we trust you."

"I have something I must do." I swallow, and my ears pop with held-in tears. "I think about Alf, it's true. But I won't know what I want in the long term until I've done something else first. I've already waited too long to do it."

Thyra comes closer. We all clasp forearms now—the circle shrinks. "What must you do?" she asks.

"Find someone—a woman. She may need rescue."

"Who?"

"My sister."

"Oh, you have a sister!" Ragnhild squeezes my arm. "But Alf could help you find her."

"Maybe. Maybe he could. Probably. But then I'd be beholden to him. And you know how it is. When you work with someone at something, when you share a goal, you grow closer. He'd want to marry me even more. But I don't know what I'll want after I find her. I might want to stay with her."

"Well, that's no problem," says Ragnhild. "She could come live with you."

"Except she might want to live somewhere else . . . somewhere else entirely."

Thyra's brow furrows. "Where?"

"Írland." They stare at me. "Eire," I say in my old tongue. "It's the land where we were born."

"Ayyyy." Thyra drops her head and swings it side to side. "This is a mess."

"If Alf takes the challenge," says Ragnhild, "he'll die."

"So I have to stop him."

"You have to do more than that," says Thyra. "You have to get out of this tower. I've listened to them talking. The king won't let you free unless you marry Alf."

"There's got to be a way." I shiver. We move into a hug. "The King doesn't control everything. He can't."

CHAPTER TWENTY-TWO

Alf stands on the other side of the cobra pit. He is handsome. I haven't really allowed myself to think about him that way till now. But I am on the verge of tragedy—there's no point holding back. Tragedy cannot be cheated; it calls for complete surrender, it calls for extravagance. The man is beautiful.

"Don't be an idiot," I call.

"Good advice," he calls back.

"Three men have died," I call. "Their bodies stank so bad soldiers finally fished them out with hooks."

"I know this."

"Go home. Please."

"Will you come home with me?" He squints against the sun. "Will you be my wife?"

A dream existence. "Perhaps in some life. Not in this one."

"Can you explain that to me?"

"I doubt it."

"Try, Alfhild."

239

Alfhild. It isn't even my real name. "You know nothing about me."

"That's what marriage is for. To learn each other."

It's a good answer. But an easy answer in the abstract. Alas. "I cannot explain myself to you. Not yet, at least."

"Do you love another?"

"No."

"Do you love me?"

"How can I know? I am inexperienced at this."

"As am I. I may love you already. And in any case, I believe I can grow to love you. Do you believe you can grow to love me?"

"My answer is irrelevant."

"Humor me, please. Answer."

"Yes."

"All right, then." He opens the satchel on the ground beside him.

I think of the third solo man, who opened his satchel and put on a helmet and a mail shirt and jumped to his death. "Please," I cry out. "Please, please do not do this. I will not marry you. Believe me."

"This is what you think now. Perhaps you'll change your mind by the time I stand beside you in that room. In any case, I must take my chance. No other option makes sense to me."

Sense? There is no sense in a world in which one man can completely unhinge the life of a girl simply because lust overcame him. A world in which that girl's father then makes decisions about her whole life based on money. A world in which people steal people and bring them to other lands. I could scream and scream. But no one would listen.

"Would you rather die or have a broken heart?" I call.

"They are the same to me." Alf takes a smaller satchel out of the big one. He carries it to one end of the pit and shakes it upside down. The carcasses of rats tumble down into the pit. They are each so bloated, the tight skin shines. I see wide stitches of string holding together their bellies. How very odd. I'm fascinated against my will. Alf goes to the big satchel and takes out an enormous jug. Then he pours a glistening red stream over the rat carcasses.

The cobras wind with determined speed—after all, they haven't eaten anything all week; cobras don't eat people, as we all know now. Their tongues flicker, tasting the scent. It's so strong, I can imagine swooning. They open their hoods and mouths gigantically wide and strike. Slowly, ever so slowly, rats disappear down cobra throats. Each snake gorges on multiple rats.

Alf pulls two axes out of the satchel. He throws them into the other end of the pit. And he jumps in, hits the ground, and rolls. I scream. He doesn't look up at me. He collects the axes and stares at the snakes. None of them gives evidence of knowing he's there.

He chops at the side of the pit that is in front of the ground before the door. He chops an indentation here, another above it and to the side, another above that and to the other side. He chops now high over his head.

"A snake," I shout.

He turns. A cobra moves toward him, but awkwardly; it is a lumpy rope of rat. Alf aims the ax and throws hard. It cuts the snake in two. I stare to see if, against all reason, the rumor might possibly be true. The two halves of the snake twitch, but they don't move forward. And what's that? A huge shard of glass sticks out from one half of the snake.

Alf takes a step and halts, then another, his eyes on the two remaining snakes. He makes his way like that to the thrown ax and fetches it. Then he races back to the place where he's been chopping.

He looks at the two snakes one more time. Then he tosses an ax up onto the ground in front of the door. The crowd gasps. He tosses the second ax up. The crowd gasps. I am swallowing and swallowing. My eyes go to those snakes.

Alf puts his hands into the holds he has chopped and begins to climb the wall.

A cobra moves away from the remains of the heap of rats. It winds toward Alf.

Alf climbs the wall. The holds crumble under his feet and hands.

The snake stops and flinches. Then it winds closer.

"Faster," I call. "Climb faster!"

Alf's hands are over the edge of the pit now, but his feet search for the holds.

The snake is directly under Alf.

"Faster!"

He kicks a hold with the tip of his boot. Then another.

The snake opens its hood and jaws. It strikes and falls sickly to the side with a series of spasms.

Alf stands on the earth in front of the door. He wipes sweat from his brow and leans, hands on his knees, looking back into the pit. Now he looks up at me. "Thank you for cheering me on."

"Take your axes and go back."

"And have my head impaled on a stake?" Alf smiles. "I seek a better end to this tale."

"Don't talk crazy. Go back, Alf. Live. Please. I want you to live."

"That's all the encouragement I need." Alf throws an ax at the bridge-door. It wedges in firmly, a half-arm's length above his head.

"Are you daft? It would take you days to chop down that bridge-door."

"I have no intention of chopping it down, for then how could we walk together across it over the pit once I win you?" He grabs the other ax in his left hand. With his right, he reaches up to the ax that's embedded in the door and pulls himself up with that one arm. He swings the other ax into the door higher up and then hangs by only the left hand. He works the first ax free, then swings it hard. It embeds even higher. He climbs the door like that, hanging from the axes by his arms. At any point, an ax head could give way. He would fall backward onto the ground, perhaps into the pit. At best he would be badly broken. And who dares think of the best?

But the ax heads bite firm.

In the pit, the two snakes move as though in death throes. I imagine their insides sliced with every muscle twitch. Glass-filled rats. The man is brilliant. Insane, but brilliant.

Alf is at the top of the door now. It astonishes me that he's made it this far. How can his arms be that strong? But axes can't bite into stone. What now? Oh, good Lord, what now? He cannot descend by the same method he used in climbing. He is lost!

He hangs from an ax by his left hand and reaches into

the pouch that dangles around his neck. He pulls out a dirk. A broken dirk, short and stubby, but the jagged edge glints sharp. He closes a fist around the handle and jams it between two stones. Then he hangs by the right hand from that dirk and pulls a second dirk out of his pouch. Equally broken. He climbs the wall like that. It's slower going than with the axes, because the dirk handles are so short. But at least the stones offer him footholds, so he's not swinging free.

When he is just below the window, he stops. The window ledge is one continuous slab of stone. No dirk could penetrate it.

He clings there, a hand on each dirk. His feet in narrow holds. "Help me."

Without thought, I reach both hands out.

"No! Get away from the window. Move to the side." He talks in bursts between breaths. Blood vessels stand out on his forehead. I back off. "I'm throwing in a dirk. Use it to pin one end of your cloak to the wood floor of your room and toss the other end of the cloak over the window."

A dirk comes flying through the window. It lands with a clunk on the stone floor. Everything in this room is stone! What can I do? The only wood surface is the door. And it's farther from the window than my cloak is long.

He's hanging there. Exhausted. Heart and bones.

I pin one end of my cloak to the door at the height equal to the bottom of the window. I take off my outer shift and use a strap brooch to fasten one end of it to the other end of the cloak. It is still not long enough. I take off my under shift and use the other strap brooch to fasten one end of it to the other end of the outer shift. The remaining end of the under shift now just barely reaches to the center of the window ledge.

I lean my head out the window. "Reach your hand to the center of the window ledge. You'll feel the cloth."

His hand fumbles. I place the cloth in it. He pulls. Then his other hand is reaching up and pulling. His head appears over the window ledge.

The under shift rips. No! I lunge for his arm.

But he has already clasped a hand over the inside lip of the window ledge. He pulls himself over and slides in onto the floor. The skin of his chest has been scraped away.

I turn my back and cry. He's safe. He will live.

I hear his footsteps cross the room. Then my cloak descends around my nakedness.

"Thank you," he says. I listen to the drag and sough of his rough breathing. "Will you marry me?"

I sob into my cloak.

CHAPTER TWENTY-THREE

The king and his men are in the great hall, feasting. It is a celebration of Alf's success. The queen is there as well. But she kept true to her word; she did me the favor I asked today. Then she dressed herself beautifully, put on her hawk-plumage cloak, and left.

Thyra and Ragnhild have also done their parts: Women are gathering in the large room of the king's home. They look at me sideways as they enter. Their skepticism is natural. I am the king and queen's adopted child—I might well assume the right to order them around. And of late I am the girl in the tower; men died trying to win me. Who knows what evil might lurk in such a heart? And, perhaps most worrisome of all, I am the girl who has kept herself hidden away since the valiant Alf stormed the tower yesterday. What could I be thinking? My mental powers are called into question.

The women sit on the floor. Twelve of them, including Thyra and Ragnhild. Some work in this household. Others, I don't know. They are friends of Thyra and Ragnhild.

I get to my knees. The very action catches them by surprise—their eyes shift around the room, as though spies might jump out at any moment. They expected me to walk in their midst royally, making declarations, perhaps? I open my hands to them. "Some of you are slaves." I look around at the faces, some dark, some scarred, all thin. "Some are free women, but servants." I nod. Only a few of them dare to nod back. "Many of you—maybe all—find few choices in daily life. Maybe you foresee marriage, maybe not. But whether or not to marry and who to marry, for many of you—maybe for all—will not be your choice." I nod again. They stare at me, unblinking. "Choice. It is a mighty thing, choice. How to pass your day, your life. Who to bed with, or not. Choice." They are still staring. "I want choice. I demand it. I am taking that right—by force." I lower my voice. "And if you come with me, you will have that right too. You will choose how to pass your day, how to live your life."

The women look at one another. They speak only with their eyes, but so many conversations are going on. One woman, the older slave Unn, shakes a hand, open-fingered, toward me. "What do you mean, come with you? Where are you going?"

"I cannot tell you."

A small murmuring of distrust runs through the group.

Thyra gets to her knees. "Speak, Alfhild." There is a gasp as the women realize Thyra has called me by name without saying my title first. "Tell them why you cannot say where you are going. If you don't trust them, how can they trust you?"

I hadn't planned on this. I would have shared with the women, once we were away. But beforehand, it's dangerous. I don't want those who stay behind to lead pursuers to our trail. Thyra's reasoning makes sense, though. "I cannot say where because I do not know. I have to find my sister." I swallow the lump of grief in my throat and force myself to say it: "She was stolen by a ship. I think a Russian slave ship. I'm sure of it."

Their faces open. I see the sadness they carry. How many of them were stolen? But others must have been sold into slavery by their parents. That has to be worse.

"Your sister?" says one woman, a little older than me. Her face is not open; it is shrewd and hard. She is a servant to Queen Tove. Her name is Ingun. "You have lived here a long time. We never heard talk of a sister."

"It was seven years ago."

"Seven years?" Ingun looks at me as though I'm void of reason. "Why, anything could have happened to her by now. She could be anywhere."

"Exactly," I say. "So if you come with me, you may wander far."

"How will wandering with you mean we have choice?" It is the slave Unn again. She is bold and tenacious. That's what I need in my companions. I must win her.

"I will pay wages. Everyone gets the same pay. You can choose to leave anytime."

"Where will you get the money to pay wages?" asks Ingun.

"I have money." I look around, my eyes seeking and holding the eyes of each of them in turn. "It is not stolen. It belongs to no one else. This is truth. I will pay you, I swear."

"But I'm a slave," says Unn. "No law protects a run-away slave. If I am caught, your father, the king, can have me put to death. And he will. I have no doubt. I have lived here twenty-three years, serving both king and queen, and the king and queen before them."

I've thought about this, at least, thank heavens. "We can send word back to Heiðabý about each of you. The rumor will be whatever you want. It can be that you were lost at sea. Or died of illness. Or that I forced you to come and you've escaped and are on your way home. It can be a secret message to the people you love who need to know you are well. It's up to you. Think about that one thing: It's up to you. Everything will be up to you. In a new place, with money in your pouch, what becomes of you will be your choice."

"What do you mean, 'lost at sea'?" asks a girl I don't know. From her clothes and skin, she is a slave. "You said that. You said the message can be we were 'lost at sea.'"

"Can I know your name?"

She presses her lips together, and I see her fight fear. "I want to hear about the sea."

"I am Alfhild." I look at her and try to radiate gentleness. "Your name. Please?"

"Jofrid."

"Jofrid. A good Norse name. And Unn is a good Norse name. All of you go by good Norse names. As do I. But"—I fold my hands in front of my chest—"we may go by other names inside our heads. Those people, those other girls and women with those foreign names locked inside us, they need choice."

"That may be," says Unn. "But Jofrid is right; tell us about the sea."

"The only way to follow the path of a Russian slave ship is by sea. Right?" I look around, appealing to them for agreement. They just look back at me. "There's a boat waiting for us. It will be our home."

"I know nothing about boats," says the servant Matilda.

"You'll learn."

"And just who is going to teach me?"

"Me," I say.

"You know how to manage a boat?"

"I do."

"That's hard to believe. But even if it's true, what will happen to the boat at first, when none of the rest of us knows a thing about it?"

"Maybe we need some men," says Ragnhild quickly. She's at my side. I hear her heavy breathing. "I can think of one who might come."

"No men." I shake my head hard. "If women leave, they may chase us, but they will give up quickly. If men leave, they will hunt us down relentlessly."

"Then we're back to my question," says Matilda. "How can we think of setting out with only one person who knows about boats?"

"I know about boats," says Jofrid. "So we'll be starting with two of us knowing how to do things."

I rub my hands together as hope rises in my chest. This may really happen. "Within days all of us will learn every detail of managing a boat."

Matilda stares. She shakes her head. "I can't even swim."

"You'll learn that, too."

"I can teach you that," says Thyra.

"What about food?" asks Matilda. "We have to eat; we're not like the god Óðinn."

"Ah!" Grima, the slave of Queen Tove, slaps her hand to her chest in sudden realization. "The boat is well stocked for at least ten days."

"How do you know this?" It is the king's slave Osk.

"I just know." She looks down. "Believe me."

"And the king knows nothing about this?" asks Osk.

"Nothing," I say.

"Just how did you get a boat?"

I look from face to face. "You don't need to know that. None of you. And it's better if you don't."

"Better for you?"

"Just better," I say.

"And what's supposed to happen to us once you do find your sister?"

"That's up to you. You will be free women. You will decide."

"Free women." Osk shakes her head. She stands. She looks hard at Grima. She has clearly figured out that the queen had Grima stock the boat with food. She sees it all as treachery. My heart beats erratically. It was a mistake to invite all the women household slaves and servants. Of course some of them would be loyal. Of course. I stuff the back of my hand in my mouth. What an idiot I am. What will happen to Queen Tove now?

Osk looks at me at last. "What do we need to bring?"

I fall forward on hands and knees in grateful relief. "A cloak for sleeping under. It gets cold at night on water. An extra shift if you have one. A pouch. And whatever else you want. An ax if you can get your hands on one. A dirk. But don't invite suspicion. Don't carry anything you can't account for should someone ask."

"If we had men with us, they could bring axes and no one would question them," says Ragnhild. "I know one who speaks Russian. That would help if we're going after a Russian slave dealer. That would help us, Alfhild."

"I can speak with Russians," says Osk.

Ragnhild's face crumples.

"Ragnhild." I put my arm around her. "When we are finished, you'll have money enough to buy a slave. Whatever slave you want. We can send someone to buy him for you, and then the two of you can go wherever you want together. We can't risk the lives of all of us because of any one person's needs."

Ragnhild wipes tears away. "I know. I was just being stupid. But I know."

"Hurry, everyone. Tell no one. Meet me by the fjord bank where they slaughtered the whales. If you don't show up, we'll leave without you. We have to put as much distance as possible between us and town by the end of the evening's feast. We cannot wait."

"With luck," says Jofrid, "they will all fall into drunken stupors till morning, and then wake with pounding heads and be unaware of our absence till midday."

"I've never counted on luck in my life," says Ingun. "Don't make me start now. Race, everyone. Race."

PART FOUR

THE HUNT

(SUMMER, FIFTEEN YEARS OLD)

CHAPTER TWENTY-FOUR

Over the past seven nights and days, the landscape has changed from flat grasslands to hills to more meadows and now to low rolling hills. We have sailed under full wind. If any among us has misgivings, we don't voice them. Maybe we're simply too busy for misgivings—learning the new tasks of sailing, staying alert to both land and sea, surviving.

We turned out to be only nine in the end: Ragnhild and Thyra, Unn, Ingun, Grima, Jofrid, Matilda, Osk, and me. All of them were part of the king and queen's household except Jofrid. The four women who said nothing at our meeting never appeared at the fjord bank. None was part of the royal household, so there's no reason for anyone to suspect they might have information about us. If they simply continued to say nothing, no one in Heiðabý would know anything about us beyond the fact that a boat went missing.

But even if those women did talk, it's clear the kings' men must have gone looking in the wrong places. Perhaps they followed the coast to the north, or went to nearby islands, or crossed the sea to Skáney. We, instead, went south and then east—east and east and east. That's the direction the Russians come from, after all. We hug the shoreline, attentive to small settlements. They hold nothing for us—no one in a small settlement could afford a slave, at least not a beautiful, full-grown slave woman as Mel was seven years ago. But once we get to a big town, we'll stop and look around. I'll knock on every door and look in the face of every slave woman if I have to. I'll find my sister.

We anchor only in isolated bays with no signs of people. We swim there, which turns out to be decent bathing, since the water of this sea is barely salty. If there's a creek that empties into the bay, we fill up on fresh water. We always fish when we stop. And for the past two days we have relaxed enough for me to go off hunting with Grima, who is new to bow and arrow. We brought back hares to roast on sticks over open fires.

We never anchor for long. The wind is our friend, but I know what a fickle friend she can be. So we make use of her day and night. There has been a growing moon, and that helps us steer safely at night—or as safely as anyone can at night.

Four ships have passed us, all in daylight. But all were going the opposite direction, and all traveled farther from shore than we did. Still, each time we passed one, we then headed straight north—out to sea—and once we were far out there, we took down our sails and drifted for a while, hoping to be less than a speck on the horizon should the ship have decided to come back and take a second look at a boat full of women.

At night, though, no one passes us. The wisdom is that it's foolhardy to sail close to shore at night unless you know every outcropping of boulders, every underwater reef. But we have to be foolhardy—it's that or increase the risk of being caught.

Ingun is at the helm tonight. The others lie on the open deck. An overlapping spread of cloaks covers them. They sleep hard and deep, the sleep of the exhausted.

I stand at the prow and look ahead. The wet air laps my face. The wood of the gunwale eases against me. Even the floor of the ship presses up at me. That's how I feel these days, as though the world touches me instead of me touching it. That's how I have felt since Alf slid into the tower room. He thunked on the floor. Every day that *thunk* assails my ears. The smell of his sweat invades my nostrils. The bulk of him clouds my eyes.

I rub my eyes now, to rid it of that bulk. No use: There is still something big ahead—bigger than a rock, given the distance it's at. I strain forward. It's a dwelling. And then another. There are many along the coast ahead. Many! Finally.

"Osk! Unn!" I wake them with a hand on their shoulders. "Lower the sail."

Ingun has already pulled up the rudder and is waking the others.

We peer through the dark. "There's a city ahead," I say. "It has to be Trusø, no?"

"It couldn't be anything else." Osk cups her neck with both hands and rubs. "I knew we were close. It's the biggest city along this shore. The huge river Vistula runs through Vendland and empties into a large lake called Estmere. From the east comes the river Elbing; it flows into Estmere too. The city is on the bank. Traders bring amber from the Baltic Sea and travel the Vistula to the south."

"Traders bring slaves, too," I say. "Right?" But I know it's right. I've listened carefully in the Heiðabý slave market. I know it. Still, she has to confirm it. "Right?"

"Yes." Osk hugs herself now. "I was captured somewhere along the Vistula. I was brought north. We passed a few days in Trusø. I was ten years old."

Ten. That's two years older than I was when the slave dealers stole me. I touch Osk's shoulder and speak firmly. "We passed a small creek a little while ago. Let's turn back and anchor there. Out of sight from the sea. We can sleep the rest of the night, and then tomorrow we can go into town by foot."

Thyra squeezes my forearm. "If anyone's still following us, that will give them a chance to catch up."

"They're not following us," I say with conviction.

"How do you know?"

"Tonight, as you slept, Ingun was at the helm. The king would be astonished to see that. Osk and Unn just lowered the sail, fast and efficient as men. The king would never recognize them doing that. All of you can take to the oars and row like mad. No one back in Heiðabý would believe we could do that. No one knows any of us have knowledge of sailing. They probably figure we have foundered and rest on the bottom of the sea by now." I touch her hand. "I don't think they're following us."

Grima pokes her face in mine. "But if they are?"

"Does anyone have a better idea?"

"I do." Ingun leans forward. "Let's sail past the harbor to the next creek on the east side of the city. If anyone's following our ship—anyone from Heiðabý—they will surely stop at Trusø. This way there's no chance they'll see our boat. And if we go carefully, very, very carefully, tomorrow, when we approach the city, we'll see them before they see us."

We don't even discuss it. We simply raise the sail, and

soon we are past the town and sliding into a small bay sur-rounded by forest. It's ideal. No one could see us from the water unless they fully entered the bay. We anchor near a stretch of beach in water shallow enough that we'll be able to jump overboard when we want and wade to shore easily. Everyone settles down to sleep again.

"Leave the guarding to me tonight, Alfhild," says Matilda. She stands and goes to her personal chest to sit. From there she can swivel to get a view in every direction. "I don't want to go into town tomorrow anyway. I'm afraid of these Slavs. In the morning, I'll go on land and crawl under a bush and sleep the day away."

I hesitate. Then, "Thank you." And I'm dead asleep in an instant.

In the morning Matilda finds a thick bush, and Ingun stays with her. After all, someone needs to guard her as she sleeps. They are Norse—servants, not slaves—perhaps this has made a special bond, for they are close friends. Nevertheless, it makes me nervous to leave Ingun behind. Ingun is smart. We'd be safer if she came with us.

We walk in two groups. The lead group has four—Ragnhild, Unn, Jofrid, and me. The other group—Thyra, Osk, and Grima—follows close enough to come at a call for help but far enough to escape if something horrible happens to the first group. Since Ragnhild and Thyra are clearly Norse, if need be they can behave as though the others in their group are their slaves. We have only two axes, one per group: Osk and Unn carry them. We have two bows, one per group: Grima and I carry them. All have dirks we can pull out quickly.

It feels strange to walk as groups on land after all those days at sea. Slow and clumsy. As though we're sick. We head inland, with the plan of turning west and following the river into town, so that no one will know we came by boat. It just seems sensible. Or it did when we first decided it. Now, as we walk, it seems stupid. If we didn't come by boat, how else could we have come?

I wish Ingun was with us.

We step around broken branches on the ground and I think of Hakon, obliterating that bush with his wooden sword. I imagine him gripping a stick tight and marching with us. Búri, too. For an instant I can smile. My little brothers are with me in spirit. I pick up a stick and hand it to Ragnhild. I hand another to Jofrid.

After a long while, my group comes out of the forest onto a dirt road. We turn west along the road.

We come to a pile of clothes, men's clothes, in the center of the road. How odd.

"Let's take them," says Ragnhild.

We look around. The second group emerges from

the woods way back along the road. We wave to them to retreat into the woods again. Then we snatch the heap of clothes and run back among the trees. We race, hidden by foliage, until we find the other group.

"What are you doing?" says Thyra. "We're supposed to stay separate."

"Look what we found." Ragnhild dumps her load on the ground. We all do. "Men's clothes. We can put them on and pretend we're men."

I think of my Ástríd—how she wore men's clothes and pretended to be Randolf and it worked—it actually worked with people she was living with day after day. I think of Mel and me, dressed as peasant boys on the Russian slave ship.

"What do you mean, found them?" asks Grima. "We're not thieves."

"They were sitting in a pile in the road."

Grima's eyes are troubled. "That doesn't sound right. Why would anyone leave clothes in the road?"

"You're right." Jofrid looks at Ragnhild and Unn and me. "We have to return them."

Osk hits her forehead with her palm. "Hide!" She lies flat in the undergrowth. "Fast. I don't know how much time we have. Lie down. Keep your eyes on the road."

We hide and wait. The rumble of horses' hooves comes

from the east. I have the urge to run. What have I done to these women? We could all get killed. But none of us bolts.

Men go galloping by.

When the last horse has passed and we hear no more hoofbeats, Osk rolls onto her back. "Those clothes belong to a dead man. He will be burned today. So this morning they put his belongings in five heaps along the road into town. The men on horses were waiting outside town, and at a signal, they raced for the heaps. The biggest heap, with the most valuable stuff, is the farthest away from town, so the man on the fastest horse will reach it first and gets to keep it. Then each heap is less valuable, as you get closer to town."

"So these clothes are no one's anymore?" says Grima. "We can keep them?"

"Yes." Osk sifts through the pile of clothes now. "But if we wear them into town, people might recognize them. Especially this shirt—see the nice stitching? And this hat. It's a city, yes, but people know things about one another. I don't think any of it is safe to wear here, really."

"Unn," I say, "you and Jofrid carry this stuff back to the boat. And take your ax with you, just in case."

"I want to help," says Jofrid.

"You're still the best one with the boat," I say. "You can have everything prepared for a quick getaway if need be.

Really, Jofrid. These clothes are a treasure. Like Ragnhild said, we can dress as men. We won't have to worry every time we pass a ship of men. They'll pay us no attention." I gather up the clothes as I talk. "We can't just leave the clothes here to fetch later. People will realize that one of the heaps went missing, so they'll come searching. Please."

Jofrid nods.

I hand the clothes to Unn and face Jofrid. "First, let's trade clothes, you and me. So I clearly look like a slave."

We do that. Then Jofrid and Unn scoop up the clothes and disappear into the forest.

We have one ax now, and Osk carries it. And two bows. And the two sticks. We run through the trees toward town. Once we're close enough to smell burning, we go out onto the road. Ragnhild and Thyra link arms and walk in front. Osk and Grima and I follow, as slaves should, our weapons showing.

The funeral pyre is in front of a house. The body is already consumed in flames, but I can see pieces of iron puncturing the flickers: swords. I bet the dead man's ax was burned with him too. Probably all his weapons and tools. What a waste.

Beyond the pyre, people feast out in the open. The air is smoke and honey. People swill down mead as though it's milk.

We continue along the road, holding ourselves tall out of respect for the funeral. A man notices us and follows. He runs a bit to catch up and says something to Ragnhild. Osk whispers in her ear. Ragnhild steps back, and Osk says something to the man in a nasty tone. He laughs, but his eyes dart around and he walks back to the crowd.

We walk a bit more when Osk says, "Look. There's a woman alone over there. See her, gathering wood?" The woman is well off the road. "Let's go talk to her. Find out what we can."

So we go to the woman and Osk has a conversation with her, while we help gather sticks at the edge of the forest. The conversation is slow going. Osk speaks haltingly. The woman answers just as haltingly.

I keep staring at the woman's feet. She wears no shoes. Most of her toes have rings on them. She has silver earrings with hanging balls, too—but that's not special; everyone wears earrings. I've never seen toe rings before, though. They couldn't possibly be comfortable. And what happens to her when she needs to run?

The man appears again. Mead stains his beard. He says something to Osk. She stares at him. Then she says something back. The man comes up to Ragnhild and Thyra. He speaks his language as he gestures—touching around his neck and up his arms enthusiastically.

"He has jewelry to sell you, my mistresses," says Osk to Ragnhild and Thyra. Her eyes glitter. Something's going on. She nods.

Thyra looks hard at Osk. Then she nods back.

Osk says something to the man.

The man walks down the road we came on, past the funeral pyre. He checks over his shoulder that we're following. And we are; Osk is urging us on.

I don't understand anything. But it's just him against the five of us. We'll be all right.

The man cuts off the road and leads us along a path to a house. We follow him inside. Then he lays bowls on the floor. Ordinary bowls. Osk shakes her head and points at a wooden chest. The man looks surprised, but he opens the chest and puts his clothes on the floor.

Osk nods. She steps beside him and opens a hand to Thyra and Ragnhild, as though offering them. As though they're for sale. Prickles go up the back of my neck. The man steps toward Thyra, a stupid look of lust on his face. Osk conks him on the back of the head with the butt end of her ax.

The man falls unconscious.

"What just happened?" asks Ragnhild. She wrings her hands.

"He wanted to buy you two," says Osk. "He figured we slaves would easily betray our owners, isolated from the men as he saw we were. So he decided to lure you here with the promise of jewelry. Look at the junk he offered. Clearly he figured the rest of us, being slaves, had no idea what a woman should cost. An opportunist." She pushes him with her foot. "This should teach him a lesson. A man who buys women deserves to be robbed." She looks at me. "I know what we want to know, Alfhild. The woman told me. So let's take this man's clothes and get out of here fast. Because I'm almost entirely sure friends of his will show up soon. It's only because they're all drunk that they haven't staggered in here yet."

We raid his larder and run.

CHAPTER TWENTY-FIVE

We are dressed as men. All of us. Some have cut their hair off—like Ástríd did when she was playing Randolf—but some have simply tucked it under a hat. That's what I've done, braiding it first. I remember Alf calling me the princess of the curly hair. My curls stay, though tamed by the braid, for I am still that girl, though I am many other things as well.

We are only eight now. Osk helped us until the very last minute, but then she jumped off the ship. The idea of leaving again when she was so close to home was too much for her to bear. She will follow the Vistula River on foot till she finds the village where she was born. There may yet be people there who remember her. She had two brothers, three sisters, once upon a time. I couldn't blame her, of course. I have a brother, I have a sister.

But no. In a way, I have three brothers—Nuada and Búri and Hakon—and three sisters—Mel and Ástríd and Alof. No, I could not blame Osk one bit.

When I tried to pay her, she said being carried home

was payment enough. But she took an ax. I've lived with the Norse so long, I feel helpless without an ax. So only one ax for the remaining eight of us appalled me. But I didn't let on; Osk has her rights.

This morning I am scanning the sea. Osk told what she learned from the woman we helped to gather wood. Some women and children stolen from the giant islands to the west of Jutland—one of which is my Eire land—are sold as slaves in Heiðabý, yes, and many others are sold in Birka, across the Baltic Sea on the east coast of the Swedes' land. Most, though, are taken by boat down the Vistula River. Then the boat is portaged across land and around waterfalls—how many, the woman didn't know—to another river that empties into the great sea in the south. That's where the enormous city of Miklagard lies; that's where the largest slave market in the world is. Girls sold there can wind up in Africa, Asia, anywhere.

According to the woman, Miklagard is the most dangerous city in the world. She says that's partly because it's the center of Christianity, what she called a warring religion that wants to conquer the world. I'm glad I couldn't understand her language, or I might have been tempted to argue with her and ruin everything for all of us. I may not pray to Jesus anymore, but I still remember the preachings of the Christians.

I had heard of Miklagard before. The slave dealers in Heiðabý talked about going there via rivers. I just didn't know that the rivers were discontinuous. As Osk said all this, my throat thickened with disappointment. We could never portage our boat. We could never get to Miklagard. We are but eight women, strong and smart, but weaker than men.

So I hatch a plan. We will haunt the Baltic Sea. We will visit the Birka slave market often. We will stop every ship we pass and find out if they have anything of value to tell us. We will do this all summer. And if nothing comes of it, when the weather turns cold, I will pay all these women and say farewell, and I will travel alone, however I can, to Miklagard.

Have I taken leave of my senses? It would seem so. An Irish girl stolen seven years ago—who on earth would remember her? But they might. They might remember a mute beauty, with skin like alabaster and brown hair that catches the light in so many ways that it's sometimes night dark and sometimes day light and sometimes a mix—and, oh! I realize now why I love Queen Tove's hawk-plumage cloak so much: Its colors mimic Mel's hair.

So someone will remember. Someone has to. Mel was unique. Mel is unique.

But even if someone did, could I track her down?

Could I really make it to the ends of the earth? The only answer is: I have to try. I have money to buy her freedom. I will try.

And I have to make sure I don't get robbed blind along the way.

And there! I see it, the first ship we have passed since we made our new pact. "Get alert," I call. "Starboard!"

But Grima, at the helm for her first time, has already spotted the ship and steers straight for it. The wind is against us. The other women have taken their places on the wooden chests and pushed their oars through the holes and row with all their might. Everyone knows what to do, as though we're practiced at it, which we are not. Gratitude makes me falter for a moment. But then I run to the prow and hold my bow ready.

The ship clearly sees us, and I fear they will take flight. After all, ships don't approach each other on the high seas. They won't know all we seek is information.

But the ship turns and sails toward us. Good.

Except it comes fast. We are on a collision course! Are they insane?

I know nothing about flagging down another ship. And less about a ship that's aimed for us. "Pull in your oars!"

The other ship arrives at our side and throws two

huge ropes across. "Grab hold," shouts a man. "Grab hold because we're coming aboard. It's that or we sink you."

What on earth? But Thyra already has one of the ropes. Ingun takes the other. The men pull hand over hand on their end of the ropes until our ships are side by side. They take the ends from Thyra and Ingun and loop them through oar holes on our ship and bind the two ships together at stern and bow, so we form one big floating platform.

I'm counting the men. Four. All I see is four men on this boat, and it's bigger than ours. I can't make sense of this.

The shouter climbs into our boat, brandishing a sword. "Who's in charge?"

I feel eyes on me. But Ingun says, "Who's in charge on your boat?" Her voice is bold as anything, and it sounds manly.

"Me."

"That's not true!" A second man climbs into our boat. He has a sword as well, but at least he keeps his in the scabbard.

I turn to the second man, pointedly ignoring the shouter. "Are you the captain?"

He twists his mouth.

"I need information. About slave ships."

"We don't know anything about slave ships," says a third man, standing in the other boat. "And we don't have a captain. We lost him and nearly all of our crew off the coast of Borgundarholm two days ago."

I feel light-headed. Storms wreak havoc with sailors. We women haven't discussed that. What must be going through my crew's minds? "Borgundarholm?" I ask weakly.

"You know. Off Skáney. It was one hell of a battle. Rivaled the legendary battle of Brávellir, I tell you."

A battle. I grip the gunwale to steady myself. That is worse than if it was a storm.

"Look here." Grima fits an arrow into her bow and stands like an archer, as though she'll shoot that man through the heart. It's not much of a distance; she might be able to, even with her poor aim. She looks fierce. I'm stunned. "What kind of battle?" she shouts.

"What kind do you think? We're pirates."

The two men onboard our ship look at us with disgust, as though we should have known. But there's a falseness to their swagger. The other man on their ship simply looks defeated. And I'm starting to understand the situation now: Without their captain, they're lost. They have no idea what to do next. Even boarding our ship wasn't really their idea. We set out after them—they simply responded.

Thyra climbs on a wooden chest, places her feet wide

apart, and puts her fists on her hips. She's the tallest of us, as tall as most men. "You've met your match, and better," she says. "A sword won't do any good to you if an arrow pierces your heart. So put that sword away before you cause trouble."

These women are bluffers. And good at it.

The shouter lifts his chin a moment. Then he sheathes his sword.

Good Lord. These women are great at bluffing. Magnificent.

I point at Grima. "Keep watch over the two here." I point at Ingun. She's the second tallest. "Grab your ax." Ingun doesn't have an ax. She doesn't even blink, though. She picks up my ax. "We're coming aboard," I say to the two men in the pirate ship. "Stand at the middle, hands on the mast."

The two men actually move to the mast. But I mustn't get complacent—they could have knives at the ready. Ingun and I climb into the other boat. Two against two doesn't feel good, though. I gesture to Jofrid. She practically leaps into the other boat with us.

Jofrid and I search through their belongings while Ingun stands with ax raised. I pick up an iron fork for roasting meat and thump it against my palm. I count six axes, and that's just what I can see lying about the deck. Jofrid and I exchange glances. She nods.

"All right," I say. "Here's what's going to happen." Everyone looks at me—men and women alike. "For the moment, you all stay where you are. Stand still, while my crew comes into this boat." I look at the women. "Gather your cloaks and anything else you want, and come across. And you"—I point at Ragnhild—"bring my cloak and the old skin satchel in my personal chest. You"—I point at Grima—"bring my bow and arrows."

"I'll bring your cloak," calls Matilda to Ingun. "Anything else?"

Ingun shakes her head.

"And I'll bring yours," Unn calls to Jofrid.

The shouter grabs his sword handle and looks around, confused. But he doesn't draw his sword. His face lights up. "Good thinking. We can be one big crew. Hurry up, men."

But the women need no encouragement; they're already climbing into the pirate ship.

"You two," I say to the men at the mast. "Go into the other ship. Look around for what's useful."

The two men quickly climb into our boat.

I look at Jofrid and Ingun and nod. They untie us from the other boat.

"Hey!" shouts the sword man.

But I have my arrow in place. "Don't move or I'll shoot. And I'm accurate. We're exchanging boats."

"What! You can't take our ship," says the shouter.

"Use your brain, if you have one," I say. "The four of you couldn't manage this big boat in a storm. You're better off with ours, and even that will be hard for you."

"No! Joining forces is a better idea. You can be the captain. I have no taste for it, and you're good at it. Eight of you, four of us, we can beat anyone."

"You'd just be in our way." I wipe at my nose with the back of my hand like I always saw Beorn do. It seems a manly gesture. "If you head due south, you'll wind up in Trusø."

"Trusø? Who the hell wants to go to Trusø? They don't even speak Norse there."

"You're right." I look around at the women. "Does anyone have a message they'd like these good men to carry back to Heiðabý?"

"Heiðabý's far away!"

"Seven days, if the wind is with you."

"Tell the queen that Grima drowned," says Grima. "But that she said good things about her, even as she went under."

"Matilda drowned too," says Matilda. "She couldn't even swim in the first place."

"And tell Igor that Ragnhild loves him," says Ragnhild. I look around. "Is that all?"

"For now, it seems," says Thyra.

The shouter stands glaring at us as the boats drift apart. "Why should we deliver any messages at all?"

"Because if you don't, we'll tell every ship that passes how you let a boat full of women outwit you."

"Women!"

Matilda and Ingun already have the sail up. Grima is back at the helm. We are off and away.

CHAPTER TWENTY-SIX

"Pirates? Incompetents, I'd say." Ingun passes out loaves of stale bread. She chomps, rips off a piece, and smiles as she chews. "But at least they had bread."

"I wish you hadn't told them we were women," says Thyra. "Imagine how surprised they would have been when all they found in our wooden chests were shifts!"

We're all laughing.

"Look at this stuff," says Unn. "Iron plates for baking flat bread. Grill pans and griddles. All these wooden vats of pickled foods. They must set up a regular hearth whenever they stop on land. Why, they're more domestic than we are!"

"I feel bad about leaving them with just the two swords and no other tools," says Jofrid. "It's going to be a hungry ride back to Heiðabý."

"They probably had dirks on them," says Unn. "Right?"

"And they have our fishing nets," says Matilda.

"Don't feel too sorry for them," says Ingun. "They were dishonorable cowards."

"What do you mean?" I ask.

"Nothing's ruined on this ship. There are twelve chests, for twelve men, and they're all full. The food vats are full. Only weapons are missing." She holds out a hand, as if reasoning with us. "Each man had a sword, an ax, a spear, and a shield to start with. Some of them had to have bow and arrows, too. What's left of all that are seven axes, four shields, one bow. The pirates must have jumped on another ship—to commandeer it, like they tried to do with us, carrying with them most of their weapons. And all took shields, of course. But the other ship's crew fought and they were winning, so the four cowards jumped back on their ship, with their shields, and whatever weapons they still had. They escaped when they saw their captain and crew members had died."

"Or worse," says Matilda. She moves closer to Ingun. "Maybe they escaped when they saw they'd be defeated, and left their fellow crew members to die. They should be condemned to freezing Hel."

We're all silent a moment.

"Well, good," says Ragnhild at last. "I can sleep guilt free."

"Me too," says Matilda. "And I'm going to laugh a bit more, remembering what Alfhild said: 'You let a boat full of women outwit you.'"

"It should become our parting call with pirates," says Jofrid.

"Well, I, for one, hope we never meet up with pirates again," says Ragnhild.

The sails are down, and we're anchored in an island's bay. I bet it's that Borgundarholm the pirates talked about, because it rises a great height—*borg*—from the sea, like a mountain of rock. We haven't seen any settlements on this side of the island, but it's a big island, and the settlements are probably on the coast that faces Skáney, anyway.

Skáney. That's where Ástríd was stolen from. But she wouldn't envy me being close to it now; she wouldn't want to go home. Her home is with Beorn.

I pull my knees up to my chest and hug them. What if we really do find Mel, and she feels like Ástríd and doesn't want to go home? She might not. She might love the people she lives with. But she is almost certainly a slave. She'll want her freedom; at the very least, she'll want that. She deserves to choose where and how she lives. So it isn't pointless that I've brought these women away from home and that we're out on a sea full of pirates with nothing to protect us but our own wits. It can't be pointless.

Mel. *What do you look like now, sister? Your hair should still be the same—and those highlights are special. Your nose, I'll recognize your nose. The color of your eyes. But your mouth . . .*

oh, a person's mouth can change with experience. A mouth can grow grim and taut. But Mel, I promise you, if only you'll smile at me, I'll know you. I will definitely know you.

The sun sets later these days. I look at the burning orange ball and the scudding clouds, and my head empties. The women are bedding down. It's Unn's turn to stand guard, and she's pushed a wooden chest against the mast and taken her post. Grima calls out in her sleep and turns over swiftly, with the sound of cloth tearing. I remember my under shift tearing when Alf climbed into the tower room. I reached for him—I threw myself across his back and grabbed under his arms—I pulled with all my might. For a split second, I felt the weight of him. The heft. The heft of that man in these hands. My palms tingle.

In the morning we bathe and eat fish Unn cooks and then decide to skirt the island and travel north, staying close to the coast of Skáney. The very first day we set sail, I taught everyone Beorn's rule of staying within sight of land. So when we left Trusø and headed out into the open sea and were out of sight of land for an entire day and night before meeting up with the pirates and then the whole rest of that day, we were so tense we breathed shallow. We gave a whoop of joy at finally spying Borgundarholm. We won't easily give up sight of land again.

We have been sailing for a few hours when we see the first ship. It's traveling south, and even closer to the coast than we are. And it has two sails. This is the first ship we've seen so far that has two sails. I go cold.

The Russian slave ship that stole Mel and me had two sails. Probably all Russian slave ships do. Maybe all Russian trading ships do. I don't know. In my time at Heiðabý I stayed away from the foreign ship dock. Deep in me nestled the fear of being snatched again. It was crazy, for if a slave ship left and a local girl went missing, I have no doubt the king would have sent a ship in pursuit. The slave dealers had to know that too. But the fears you learn as a child are different; they stay, no matter what.

I stare at the ship.

"Well?" asks Grima, standing at the helm again. "Who's going to lift the flags?"

"I will," says Jofrid. "All the rest of you are taller than me—everyone but Grima and Unn—and Unn's sleeping. So you'll look more impressive holding the axes and bow until we find out if they're friendly." She grabs the two white flags we've made from the shifts that Matilda gathered from our old ship at the last minute. Jofrid stands at the bow and waves the flags.

Grima steers us. She likes steering. She likes using the bow and arrow, too. She seems to revel in every opportunity this new life offers her. And her skills are getting sharp. I send her an encouraging smile, but she doesn't even notice.

The wind is in our favor, so the rest of us can grab axes. I put a bow and arrows beside Grima's feet just in case, and another bow and arrows beside Unn, who is still asleep. I have no idea if she's a decent archer, so I put an ax beside her too. I grab my own bow. I wish we had spears, but we're lucky there's something in everyone's hands.

We go straight for the ship, flapping those flags. Then we take down the sails, and they pull in their oars. It seems peaceful enough, so far.

"We'll throw across ropes," I yell.

Jofrid scrambles with the rope at the aft, and Unn has woken and holds the rope at the forward. They toss them across. The men in the other ship loop them through oar holes so Jofrid and Unn can bind us together.

"What's the problem?" asks a mustached man in heavily accented Norse. I am sure I've never seen him before. The other men are looking at us, but it's clear that one is the captain. I count five. Five men to our eight women. All of them perfect strangers. But the thing that's driving me insane, the thing that's screaming in my head, is that they have a woman and two children gagged with hands bound in the center of the ship.

"Are they for sale?" I ask.

The man's eyes widen. "What price could you offer?"

"How much are you asking?"

"I normally trade in Miklagard. I get the highest prices."

"You go all the way to Miklagard with a crew of five to sell just three slaves?"

"Of course not. I pick up the rest of my crew in Gotland. That's where I'm headed as soon as I finish a little business here. Then we'll pick up more slaves along the way and take a full ship of slaves to Miklagard."

Gotland. Everybody talks about the big island of Gotland. It dominates Baltic trade these days. It has the best natural harbors, especially for boats that ride shallow, like ours.

"Miklagard is far away," I say. "Anyone could get sick and die by the time you get down there. A dead slave goes for nothing, if I'm not mistaken."

The captain nods. "You still haven't told me what you're offering."

I have no idea what to offer.

"The woman isn't a beauty," says Thyra with authority. "And the children are too small to be useful yet."

The captain nods. "A price?"

"I need information first," I say. "I'm looking for a slave

girl. I want to know where she is now. She was taken from Írland years ago. Seven . . . I think."

The captain frowns. "Lots of girls are taken from Írland every year. Who could possibly know about a particular girl?"

"She's special. A beauty."

"Lots of girls are beauties."

"A mute."

The captain blinks. "I heard talk of a mute. Probably drowned in a bog by now."

"What! Why do you say that?"

"Well, she was a witch, right? You're talking about the famous witch."

The witch? Did Mel make them believe she was a witch? I shrug.

The captain shakes his head. "A dealer took her all the way to Miklagard . . ."

My heart cracks.

". . . but she had cast such a spell over him, he didn't sell her there. He took her back up north and finally managed to break free of her."

"What do you mean 'break free'?"

"He gave her up—sold her. Finally."

"Where? What city?"

"I don't know that. But someone in Birka might know."

"Thank you," I say.

I look at Unn and Grima. They were slaves—they've got to be thinking what I'm thinking. In an instant we all three hold up our bows with arrows fitted into the bowstrings.

"What?" The captain steps backward, and his men quickly grab spears. "What do you think you're doing?"

"If any of your men hurls a weapon, we will all three shoot at you. Only at you, Captain. And we don't miss. You'll be dead."

"My men will throw their spears and you'll be dead."

"That doesn't affect my point. I assume you don't want to die, captain. You will die if anything goes wrong. That is a certainty. Tell one of your men to gather the spears from all the others and hand them over to us."

"And if I don't?"

"Then we will kill you. Precisely you."

"Without our spears, you can kill all of us."

"But we won't. We will take the woman and the children and the spears. You will leave. Alive. All of you."

"How do I know you'll keep your end of the bargain?"

"We always do."

"You're stealing our slaves."

"You stole them in the first place."

"You're pirates. There's no believing pirates."

"You're slave dealers. What's your point again?"

The captain clenches his fists over and over.

"We'll keep our end of the bargain," I say. "You keep yours. Tell one of your men to give us the spears. Don't give the order in words. No tricks, Captain. Just point at a man."

Finally the captain jerks his chin toward one of his men. The man gathers the spears and stands at the side of the ship.

Matilda moves toward him, but Ingun catches her by the arm. She pulls Matilda with her, and they retreat toward the aft of the ship, out of reach of the men. "Drop them into our boat," says Ingun.

The man looks back at the captain. The captain nods. The man drops the spears into our boat.

"Now the slaves," I say.

The man goes to the woman and jerks her along by the arm. Her eyes are terrified. She stops at the side of the ship. The children stay behind.

"The children, too."

The man goes back and yanks the two children, one by each hand. They stand beside the woman.

"Get back," I say to the man. "Go all the way to the other side of the ship and stay there."

He steps back.

Jofrid helps the woman into our boat. She reaches for a child, but the children just stand there, crying now. The side of the boat is too high for them to climb over, and they're too blinded with fear to be trusted to act reasonably if one of us reaches across for them. They need to be lifted over. I know that. I'm telling myself that. But I'm looking at the children, and they're so small. Five years old maybe. The age little Alof is now. I remember that terror—I remember, and I was three years older than they are.

My eyes go back to the captain. He's looking at me oddly. He takes a step forward.

"Pay attention," says Ingun to the captain. She's still standing near the aft, but her voice carries strong. "Tell one of your men—a different one—to lift the children and drop them into our boat. One by one. Remember, if he does anything wrong, you'll be dead."

The captain jerks his head at a different man.

The man picks up a child and throws him into our boat. The child's cry of pain is muffled by the gag, and I fear he's choking. Jofrid's already on him, cutting away the gag.

"Carefully!" I shout at the man. I look at the gasping child, then back at the captain.

In that instant the captain lunges and grabs the second

child. He clutches him to his chest. "You won't shoot me now, will you?" He puffs himself up, all triumphant. "You won't risk killing the child. You have affection for him. I see it in your eyes. Ha! Now I'm in charge." He barks orders at two of his men in Russian.

The men run to the bow and stern and struggle to undo the ropes that bind us together.

"Throw back our spears!" shouts the captain. "And the woman and the boy!"

Ingun swings her ax. It cuts through the wrist of the man across from her, one of those who were fiddling with the ropes. It lodges in the gunwale of their ship. He's screaming. Blood's squirting.

"No!" shouts the captain.

"No one move!" screams Grima, pointing her arrow at the man closest to the wounded man, who now writhes on the deck, curled around his missing hand.

"You broke your part of the bargain, Captain," says Ingun, wresting her ax free. "We are as good with axes as with bows. Carefully drop that boy into our ship, or we will chop off pieces of your men until you do." Her face and the tunic over her shirt are splattered with blood; in this moment I believe her.

The captain drops the child into our boat.

"Now step back."

The captain steps back.

Jofrid and Unn have already looped the ropes onto our deck. Jofrid goes to the helm. Matilda and Ragnhild lift the sail.

"Stealing women and children is wrong," shouts Ingun. She waves the bloody ax over her head. "Next time we catch you at it, you all lose a hand."

"You're not long for this world," says the captain. "Once word gets around, everyone will want to kill you."

"How will word get around?" calls back Ingun. "Are you going to announce to the world that you let a boat full of women outwit you?"

"Women!" shouts the man who handed over the spears. He races to his wooden chest and digs out an ax.

We are already sailing away, but he throws it hard. It spins in the air and hits Ragnhild in the shoulder—not the head end, but the butt end. The blow sends her over the side of the ship. Thyra immediately jumps in after her.

We've got the sail down and are rowing back, and Grima and Unn and I stand with our arrows aimed at the slave ship. But the ship is rowing away.

Thyra shouts from the water. "I can't see her!" And we're all scanning the water.

"There!" Jofrid dives in. She comes up with an arm around Ragnhild's chest.

We manage to get us all onboard again. Sopping and injured.

"We were lucky," says Jofrid.

"I don't count on luck," says Ingun. "I told you. Luck can't hold. We need to think it through ahead of time. We need a plan for every contingency."

"Right," says Thyra. "But we did good today, thanks to you. We're on our way to making the reputation we want."

"And what reputation is that?" I ask.

"Terrors," says Thyra.

"Anything less and they will, indeed, come after us," says Ingun.

CHAPTER TWENTY-SEVEN

I'm rolling the last of the boiled goose eggs between my palms and sitting on the deck with my back against the mast. The ship is anchored in a sheltered lagoon between the shore and a belt of enormous rocks that rise from the water like gigantic gray whales. The rocks make the ship invisible from the sea. That means, for the moment, we do not have to stay alert. The feeling is rare. And somehow empty. I'm at a loss.

My crewmates, all but Unn, have gone off to accompany Tofa home, on foot. Tofa is the woman the Russian slave dealers stole. She lives in a small settlement not far to the south of Birka, which will be our next stop.

Unn is in the forest hunting. She knows little about archery. So standing with the arrow fitted into the bowstring and pretending to have her sights on the captain of the slave ship unnerved her. When we finally left without her having been called upon to shoot, she collapsed in a weak heap of gratitude. She has decided to become an expert marksman. I gave her a lesson this morning, and then she took off on her own to practice, swearing to bring back the evening meal. It will be a feat if she accomplishes it, for the forest to our south and west is nearly impenetrable—unlike the airy open woods of Jutland. She'd have to be very close to a target to have a clean shot.

The children, Bolli and Sigurd, are gone. Tofa turned out not to be related to the boys, nor did she know them in the least. But she had been captured by the slave ship first, and so she saw where they were taken from. We returned them to their families yesterday and stayed for a feast that lasted far into the night.

Their settlement consisted of nothing more than a hall plus perhaps ten small dwellings for families, and huts and pit houses for metalworking. And wells, so many wells you'd think they were afraid of dying of thirst. Maybe it doesn't rain here the way it does in Jutland. The important point, though, is that they were self-sufficient. They had skis to cross snow, they had sledges to carry goods, they had horses for long-distance travel. But they could survive just fine all on their own if they needed to. Trading wasn't necessary.

That's where the boiled goose eggs came from—that settlement. Bolli's mother gave us a satchel of them and flat breads for travel. I peel and eat the egg slowly. The yolk is sunshine itself, but it cannot cheer me. I close my eyes.

A man lost his hand, just like my brother Nuada lost his hand: an ax swung by a Norse person chopped it off. This is something about the Norse that I will never understand, this chopping off of hands and feet. It is a common punishment leveled at outlaws, particularly slaves. Though I had never seen it done before, I have seen more than one slave with a missing hand. Ingun dealt with that slave dealer just as an owner would deal with a wayward slave. She said it served him right; it was just.

Logically, I see the justice. But I hate it. Especially since it was my fault. I let myself respond to the children's plight in a wrong way. I was caught in the quicksand of their misery. Because I thought of Alof. And, I have to admit, because for that moment, their misery became mine. I was eight. I was terrified.

I remember the training sessions that Earl gave little Hakon on military practice. Never think about things that make you frightened or sad—think only about things that make you angry and fierce. Those are rules of battle. They're as important as the rule: Go easy at the start of the battle to see how bad it will be, then use everything you've got only if you need to. They're as important as the rule: Spare the enemy's ship, because it's valuable to acquire—just like their weapons—so make them jump overboard rather than burn it. Burn their land if you have to, but not their ship.

All the rules matter. What goes on in your head is as important as what goes on with your weapons. Warriors win because they know they will.

I didn't act properly as a warrior, and it cost that man his hand. And it could have cost Ragnhild her life—for the crew might not have been so furious at us if we hadn't mutilated one of them, so she might not have wound up in the water, only barely conscious.

Ingun and I talked privately this morning. She said what matters with an enemy is acting decisive. She said I am the first in command and I must never forget it—because the rest of us depend on it. I promised never to hesitate again.

How does one keep a promise like that?

I am furious with myself. If someone else had displayed such weakness, I'd have wanted to send her home. I must keep my promise to Ingun. We have a mission. And to be successful, we must become the terrors of the Baltic, as Thyra said.

Mel was not sold in Miklagard. Mel was sold somewhere up here, on this sea, if she's the famous witch. And I'm almost sure she is. Why? I don't know. Maybe just because I have to have something that keeps hope alive—and this is the only thing so far.

So we'll go to Birka and find out what we need to

know. Then we'll rescue Mel. I turn my face to the early evening sun and hope the warmth will heal whatever there is to heal within me. I am not eight anymore. I will never be powerless again.

And Beorn and Ástríd will protect Alof. They will protect Búri. Queen Tove and King Hók will protect Hakon. The children I love are safe.

A low sound comes to me. Regular. I sit up and open my eyes. Unmistakable. It's the steady, vigorous pull of oars. I grab my bow and fit an arrow in the string. The sound comes from my left. It stops, and I hear the splash of an anchor. But the rocks block my view of the ship. Men talk. It isn't Norse. Someone's crying. I hear shuffling. Then a scream. A man yelling. Laughter.

A memory is jogged—something hideous. I go hot. Sick. It's all a confusion, but at the same time too familiar.

I have to know.

I could climb the mast, but I wouldn't be able to find a good perch up there. And I doubt I can scale the rock beside me. Plus, from the top of that rock I'd be an easy target, nowhere to hide.

A man grunts, and others grunt in encouragement. A woman weeps.

I remember Mel and another woman herding the children away from a weeping woman while the men closed around her. Mel wouldn't let our eyes meet. She didn't want me to know. But I did. And I do now. I cannot simply do nothing.

I take off my shoes. I'm more surefooted without them. I fill my quiver and sling it over my shoulder. I hang the bow across my chest. I carry one arrow in my teeth. I sit on the gunwale, swing my legs around, and jump from the boat to the side of the rock. I grab hold, but the side is steep and without crags; my feet find no purchase. I slide, face mashing against the rock, barnacles just below the surface scraping me bloody, down, down with a splash.

Did they hear? But there's no choice of action at this point anyway.

The arrow is still firmly in my teeth.

I swim soundlessly to the far side of the rock, away from the weeping woman and the grunting men. My hands and eyes search. The waves on this side sweep me against the rock and batter me against sharp edges. But there's a little ledge here. I manage to climb onto it. Then from there to a spiny ridge. Finally to the top. I flatten myself onto my belly and shimmy to the edge closest to the boat.

Two sails. At one end of the ship, five men guard a group of women and children. At the other end, two men grunt appreciatively while a man savages a weeping woman.

I take the arrow from my teeth. I fit it into the bowstring. No one would fault me for meting out justice to a
villain in the act. Or they wouldn't if the victim were a free
woman. But I don't have a clear shot of the man on top of
the woman. It kills me to wait, but I must.

Now the men laugh. The lout climbs off the woman
and searches for his trousers. One of the two watching
men drops his trousers and takes his place on top of the
woman.

I aim and shoot.

The man reaching for his trousers screams and claws
at the arrow stuck in his shoulder.

The second watching man looks around and spies me
and points with a shout, moving just enough to give a clear
shot.

I aim and shoot.

The man on top of the woman now screams and pulls
at the arrow stuck in his rear.

A spear flies at me. I don't bother to duck; it doesn't
even come close. Slave dealers are not warriors. I am learning that quickly.

"Put your captives on the shore and leave," I shout.

Two spears fly at me. A man is pulling up the anchor.

"Drop that anchor or I will shoot you."

He continues pulling.

I aim and shoot. The arrow lodges in his arm, sticking out on both sides. The air is nothing but screams now.

"Shut up!" I shriek. "Put the captives on the shore and leave!"

"They're our slaves," shouts one of the uninjured men.

"No longer."

"Are you alone?"

"All your captives—on the shore—now!"

"You're alone!" A spear flies at me.

I have to duck this one. I aim. "Time is up. If you don't put those captives on the shore now, I'll shoot you. All of you. It will be easy."

The five uninjured men toss slaves into the water. Gagged and bound!

I aim and shoot. A man screams, with an arrow embedded in his ribs.

"Jump in and save them," I scream. "If any of them drown, we'll hunt you down and kill you all!" And I drop my bow and dive into the water.

The sea is clear and the sun comes brightly through the water, and I have my hands on a child in an instant. I swim with her to shore and drag her onto the pebbled beach and run back into the surf, expecting a spear to pierce me at any second.

To my amazement, three men are dragging women

onto the beach. I don't understand. I am without a weapon now. I am in easy range. They could kill me and leave.

"Fast!" comes the shout. It's Unn, standing on the shore with her arrow aimed. "We will kill you—all of you—if a single captive dies!"

The crew race back to the surf and jump in. We are all searching for the fifth one they threw in—a child.

"You," shouts Unn to the one man onboard who isn't injured. "Jump in and help!"

The man looks panicked. He mimes swimming and shakes his head.

A man in the water shouts. He hauls the body of a child onto the shore.

"Now the rest of the captives onboard," shouts Unn to the nonswimmer. "Unbind and ungag them. Then get them to shore. If anyone drowns, you die."

The man unbinds and ungags women and children. One child climbs over the side, jumps in, and swims to shore. The man hands the others over the side of the ship to the men waiting in the water. They bring the slaves to shore.

Unn stands with arrow ready while the slaves on the shore are caring for one another. One woman holds the body of a girl upside down while another slaps her on the back. It's chaos, but no one cries or screams. No one but the wounded men onboard.

"Leave," I shout.

The crew in the water climb the hanging rope into their ship and pull up the anchor.

One of the crew members points at me. "You're the women pirates!"

And I realize my hat is gone; my braid hangs over my shoulder.

"You cut off a man's hand. The medicine woman in Birka talked of it. You stole that ship's slaves too. But you don't have red hair. You're supposed to be the red maidens."

Red hair? How did that start? "I'm the exception," I say.

"The women pirates! You're like the wild women, the *valkyrja*, who fly over battle scenes, choosing who will get to go up to Valhøll and who will die ingloriously."

Die? We've never killed anyone. But the more frightful our reputation is, the better off we'll be. "The terrors," I shout. "Get out of here. Give up the slave trade."

CHAPTER TWENTY-EIGHT

It's late August, and we've been hunting for news of Mel constantly. The slave market at Birka closes this week. Already the days are colder than winter nights in Jutland. We have come to this market every two weeks all summer long. This is the last time.

Birka feels funny to me, as though it should be familiar. The Christian monk Ansgar, the same one who came to Ribe years ago and whose church was eventually burned to the ground, also came to Birka. He lasted only six months there. Nevertheless, I feel I should sense his Christian steps in the earth under my feet. But I don't. This is a totally Norse city.

Thyra, Matilda, and Sibbe, our latest crew member, walk ahead of me. Whenever we come to Birka, four women go into town. Two vary. A third is always someone with a local accent, who can speak for the rest of us without drawing suspicion. The fourth is me, since I'm the only one who could recognize Mel or the Russian crew that stole us. Which is a fancy, no matter how much I wish it weren't; I don't know if I could recognize either. My sister could look more like my mother by now—and I haven't been able to imagine my mother's face for years. When I try, it merges with Queen Tove's.

The rest of the crew stay with the ship, which we harbor in an inlet to the north of town, so we can come into the market on foot, looking no different from the women in town or those who travel here from nearby settlements. Today I wear a long woolen shift that ties at the neck with a drawstring, and a shorter outer shift on top, dyed pine green. Huge cast-bronze and tortoiseshell buckles the size of my hand fasten my shoulder straps. Jet beads are strung between the two buckles, and they make a nice heavy thump against my chest as I stride along. Suspended from one buckle are a key and shears. They give me a domestic look that announce I belong to a family who might be near, so don't disturb me. I don't wear a cloak, because I always want to be ready to move fast. Thyra, Matilda, and Sibbe are dressed similarly, but in different colors with different beads. We resemble the leaves on the trees these days—a variegated flutter. Combs, knives, needles, keys dangle from them as well. These disguises have come to us as gifts from the families of the women and children we've rescued this summer. We also now have a goat, Cadla, who nibbles toes in a friendly way. It is marvelous to have a steady source of milk. Cadla is on the boat this morning, naturally.

Our cheeks are ruddy and weathered from being in the wind on the water day after day—but that could as easily be taken as evidence of working the farm fields. Ástríd and I were ruddy in our life together back in Ribe, after all. Our gaze is steady and direct, though we try not to appear challenging. Given the rough nature of the Birka traders, a challenge from a female could incite lust, despite the fact that we wear our hair braided like married women. And a man's lust is at best irrelevant to us and at worst an impediment.

By staying close to shore, we have repeatedly come in contact with slave ships. We have become pirates, indeed, but the only cargo we steal are slaves. It wasn't planned that way—it just happened. We wanted the safety of being close to shore, and slave ships trawl close to shore. They spy children or a woman alone on land, anchor at the next bend, and send back crew to capture them. Every time we meet one that already has captives, we take the slaves, warn the crew off the slave trade, and then cripple the ship. Usually by shredding their sails. We have two swords now, and Sibbe and Hrodny have become expert with them. When a crew has to row back to Birka with shredded sails, they become the target of jeers—beaten by women! It's an extra humiliation for us to savor—an extra way of warding them off the slave trade. It's as though we were fated to this work.

But in fact, probably we have not diverted anyone from the trade. We learned that lesson the first time we met a slave ship with a crew we had already tangled with once before. They had more weapons and additional crew, but none of them were any better at wielding those weapons. After all, you don't have to be good at fighting when your normal opponents are lone women or children. Slave ships don't even have to protect against pirates; no pirates other than us would choose to deal with the complications of human cargo over ordinary goods. So somehow these crew members hadn't realized it wasn't just a matter of having weapons, but of knowing how to use them. I asked the captain why he didn't take up another trade. He said the slave trade was all he knew. Inflexible moron.

Last week, though, we met a ship that had hired two warriors to come along. Archers, both. If it weren't for their haste in exposing their weapons, we might not have realized till too late. As it was, Unn and Hrodny and I made the others lie flat on the deck, and we shot the two warriors in the shoulder and threatened to make the rest of the crew jump overboard if they didn't hand over the slaves with no more trouble.

We haven't met a ship since, but it's clear that the easy days, such as they were, are past: Slave ships will have more and better protection from now on.

But the slave season in the Baltic is nearly over anyway. Two nights ago we came across a little pond upstream from the shore that was icing up. Ships that trade only locally are disappearing into storage in the boathouses—they have winter boathouses here, unlike in Jutland, because the weather gets so harsh. Ships that trade over far distances are heading across the open water to Trusø now; the trade will migrate south for the winter.

And I'm sick of this, truth be told. Every time we rescue slaves, we have to get them back home, and some of their homes are across the sea to the east. The Russians have no compunction about stealing and selling into slavery their own Slav women and children. We can spend a whole week returning them; once we even spent ten days. It is important work, but it's not what I'm here to do. So I actually rejoice inside when a slave decides to join us rather than return home, even though that usually means her home life was an abomination.

We now number fourteen. We are skilled and strong. But, good Lord, what a mess our routine has become. I have to change this. I know that. But I have no idea how.

The Birka market is nearly empty because it's mealtime. This way there will be fewer people to stop us from carrying out our rescue plan for Mel, fewer witnesses, if in fact we ever do get the chance to go through with it, which looks more doubtful every day. Sometimes I think half my women are still with me out of loyalty. The other half, because any alternative open to them is hateful. No one really thinks we'll find a trace of Mel.

Something has to change. And something will, of course. Winter is almost upon us.

Frustration speeds my steps through the market, when I suddenly halt. A slave dealer has set up a tent with a rug on the ground in front. It's set back from the rest of the market, as though the dealer thinks his goods are special. Three women sit there, hair combed, faces washed. They are tied by the waist to a single rope. They are on display, like jewelry. The slave dealer stands off to the side, his back to us, talking with a customer, but it's the women that interest me. They're young and pretty, and they're murmuring.

In the language of Eire.

I'm sure of it. I have to strain to hear over the loud rush of blood in my ears, but I am totally sure of it. One of them tells the other that she's so grateful for the fish and goat after a week of nothing but boiled parsnips. She runs a finger through the now empty bowl beside her and licks it. That's what she said, those exact words: boiled parsnips.

Boiled parsnips are what they fed us on the slave ship seven years ago.

I wander away from my companions and closer to the girls—because that's what they are, really—girls my age. Fifteen years old, maybe sixteen. The girls stop talking. Like wary birds. How quickly people learn the way of animals when they become the hunted, the captured.

"What do you want?" comes from behind me. That voice, that accent.

I turn to look at the slave dealer. It's him. Older and heavier, but him. I sway on my feet. My stomach threatens to pitch. He smells of goat like he did years before. Yes, yes, the girls were just talking about goat, so that might have influenced me, but still I could swear it's him. I force myself to step closer and take a whiff. Clay. He reeks of it. The slave dealer seven years ago reeked of clay. I catch one hand in the other behind my back to stop the trembles. I look at him with as blank a face as I can manage.

"You're not a customer. So get away from my beauties."

"How much do they cost?"

He raises a thick eyebrow. "One mark of silver. Each."

"That's a lot for girls from Írland."

He scratches his throat, and I can tell he wants to know how I found out where they came from. But all he says is, "So?"

"Is that what you got for the witch?"

"What are you talking about?"

"You know. Years ago. Seven years. The mute. She came from Írland too."

His face goes slack. "Aist?"

Aist? Is that what he called Mel? I don't remember him giving her a name.

The man leans toward me. "The one with the large gold ring on a leather strap?"

Oh, good Lord, I'm right. It really is him. He's talking about that gold teething ring Mother gave Melkorka from when she was little, to carry it with us so that we could prove we were royal children if we needed to. The ring that was supposed to be part of keeping us safe. But nothing could have kept us safe from this animal. I fall back a step.

His eyes narrow. "She had hair the color of yours. But loose and curling."

"Where is she now?" It's Sibbe speaking. She presses against me from one side and Thyra presses from the other and Matilda stands with her arms crossed at the chest in a belligerent pose.

"Who wants to know?"

"Alfhild," says Sibbe. "And what is your name?"

"Gilli."

"We'll pay," I say.

The monster looks across us, then settles his eyes on me. "Are you Alfhild?"

"Yes."

"You remind me of a little girl. A wild one. She jumped into the water and disappeared. Along with a boy. I thought they both died."

"The boy might have."

He runs his tongue across his teeth, then picks a bit of meat from the top ones. "She was bought by the Norseman Hoskuld. He took her to Iceland."

He says the name funny, but I recognize it: Ísland. The very name turns my skin to gooseflesh. "Why?"

"She's his concubine. In that desolate place, they need all the comforts they can get. Besides, she was too beautiful for anything else."

My fingernails dig into my palms. "Have you heard news of her since?"

"Nothing." He holds out a hand. "Pay me."

I look at Sibbe. We have rehearsed this, but it can't go the way we rehearsed. These girls are Irish. They won't trust Norsewomen. We have to change roles. And Sibbe, though she's been with us only a month, has a natural tendency to lead. Will she take the risk? "Pay him, please."

"Of course," says Sibbe. "But Thyra must come with me into the tent. I don't want to be alone in there."

Thyra nods.

Gilli frowns. "Pay me out here."

"I carry my money in a private place," says Sibbe. "On my person."

A touch of color goes up Gilli's cheeks. Men are so easy. "Well, you're not going into my tent alone." He walks to the tent and lifts the flap. "After you."

Sibbe and Thyra disappear into the tent, with Gilli.

"I'll take you back to Eire if that's what you want," I say to the girls in Gaelic.

"What? Who are you?"

"There's no time to explain. You'll be safe with us. Are you coming?"

Matilda has already cut the rope.

The girls look at one another—good, they're united.

We run straight into the forest, the five of us.

A scream comes from the tent. Screams and screams.

CHAPTER TWENTY-NINE

Back in Birka the town is having horse races on the beach. Then there will be horse fighting, which is as dangerous for the spectators as it is for the competitors, and demonstrations of fighting with weapons. It's the summer games—and all of it is ending soon. Swimming races are already long over, as are boating races. We can't hear any of the commotion, because we are now far from town, out in the sea, going south with the wind. But I know what's happening. The same thing happens in Heiðabý when summer ends.

Jofrid is at the helm, which means there is not much for me to do as first in command; I can give up control. I press my forehead against the mast and close my eyes. My sister is with a Viking named Hoskuld—she's his concubine—in a country so inhospitable it is called Ísland. But Eire must be our first stop. The three Irish girls have been promised delivery home, and I keep promises.

Mel. Sometimes I have felt as though I made up my whole history—a tall tale that a *skald* like Beorn might tell. The only one who knew it was true was me, and that alone made it suspect. But now Gilli confirmed it. He confirmed that I jumped into the water and a boy jumped too. He confirmed that Mel exists.

She lives in Ísland.

She is a concubine.

Someone throws an arm around me. In surprised gratitude, I turn to find Sibbe there. We lean into the wind.

Sibbe and Thyra played their parts perfectly. They waited until they felt sure we were far, and then they set to screaming as though Gilli were murdering them. A trader nearby came to see what was up, and the girls accused Gilli of molesting them. The trader, a Norseman, was disgusted; in his eyes Gilli was a dirty Russian and Sibbe and Thyra were fine Norse girls. Such an attack couldn't be allowed. An argument commenced; other traders were drawn into it. Sibbe and Thyra escaped in the confusion.

We are gone. Free. And I have the information I've been searching for all these months . . . no, all these years. What now?

I pull away from Sibbe. "What now?"

"Let's put the question to everyone," she says.

And so, when we harbor the ship for the night, we have a talk. It is so much like my idea of a *þing* assembly that I cannot help but think how very Norse I have become. I've grown up in Norse country.

The discussion is brief.

Everyone is ready to go to Eire. No one is ready to go to Ísland.

The first voyage—to Eire—requires travel that can be largely close to land, with perhaps at most a single day at any given time totally at sea. And though my crew cannot talk with the Irish girls we rescued from Gilli's clutches, the physical presence of them is compelling; they want to see these girls get home safely. Besides, Jofrid would scold anyone who suggested we go back on a promise—and no one wants to be scolded by Jofrid.

The second voyage—to Ísland—requires days if not weeks of sea travel after leaving Eire. And all that long time without land in sight. With storms that can flip a boat. In a season where the sky could dump snow at any moment. All for a woman, Mel, who is nothing but an idea to them.

So we make a pact. And I pay everyone from hoard coins—all but the Irish girls.

We will go to Eire now. Before winter sets in. We will return the girls to their homes. And we will winter with their families. We are all able; we can contribute in useful ways to the life of their ringforts.

Then, early next spring, the ship—this ship that has

become so much a part of me—will return to the Baltic. The crew will gradually disperse, choosing where to live. Perhaps Heiðabý, Ribe, Birka. These are the names that come up. Big cities seem safest for maintaining control over their own lives. No one wants to work in a small settlement for the rich farmer who makes them do all the heavy labor. In a city some of them can pool their resources and maybe set up a shop. Maybe even become traders. Ha! They know so much about trading by now. And I will sell this boat and take a job on one of the giant seafaring ships to Ísland. If I disguise myself as a man, someone's sure to take me on.

It is a fair plan.

Then we eat fish and plums, the first plums of the season, yellowish inside, with deep pink staining the flesh around the pit. I suck on the pits till it hurts the roof of my mouth, all sweet and hard together. The hunt for news of Mel is finally over, and I have these women to thank for that. What a marvel they have become. They navigate by sun and stars. They know the tides and currents and the migratory patterns of birds. They wield swords and axes, and so many of them are superb archers now—all of them as good as Skaði, the hunter giant. They have done everything I could have hoped for. And all of them are proud of themselves for it, not just Grima—all of them revel in their new skills. I will miss them terribly.

I wrap a silk scarf around my neck, red with gold embroidery. It could be from China. Or Byzantium. Everything can be bought at Birka. Everyone can be bought at Birka.

Just as in Heiðabý.

This is the way of the world. I think of the man who taught me that phrase.

Ragnhild is on duty tonight. She stares at the moon.

I watch the black lapping of the waves. It is insistent, so regular, so normal—it is the way of the world. Everything is the way of the world. I feel without power. I move beside Ragnhild. "Will you go back to him?" I whisper.

She doesn't ask who. "I never had any other plan."

She is so free in her passion—so clean and wonderful. I stuff my mouth with the back of my hand. Alf. Good Lord, my thighs tremble. I feel like a *draug*—a ghost—as though I've seen my own death and it's too late. Inside my chest, something shatters.

But something else is whole and right. I realize I love this boat. The very ship itself. It is slender and flexible. The keel is made from a single timber, so it moves with the water. The overlapping planks are riveted together perfectly. The sail is huge and strong. The rudder is just the right size to steer us properly. The mast, seated in a huge block of timber, couldn't be knocked over by any-thing. This is a perfect boat for travel to Eire. And next spring, after the others have left, I will board another wonderful boat for travel to Ísland. I have become a woman of the sea.

I may have given up Alf, but I will find my sister.

CHAPTER THIRTY

We sail for days without seeing other boats. Local traders have stopped for the season. Long-distance traders are crossing the Baltic Sea southward, migrating like birds.

At night the women talk of setting up home on an island. It began with an offhand comment by Jofrid. But others joined in. Why not pick an island that no one else wants—a rocky crag? That way, no one will suspect women live there. No one will bother them.

They can take sand from the beach and kelp from the sea, and form layers—sand, kelp, sand, kelp—filling the largest indentations in the rocky top, until weather does its magic on the layers and turns it into fertile earth. They can grow what they need. The deepest indentations can be sealed somehow to hold rainwater. They'll make ponds that way. There are hundreds of islands off Jutland, where the weather is so much milder than in Skáney. They'll find the right one, and then they can live independently of the rest of the world. Women alone. Free. They fall into one another's arms in joy. They can be as independent of the world as that child Bolli's settlement is. And if they want, they can trade, but have someplace to retire all winter. They have choices now.

Their dreams jab me, for I cannot share them. I cannot even envy them.

One night, as we eat a wild boar that Unn killed for us, I listen to the animal's skin. It is so thick, you hear it as it tears. It says something secret, about the hollow under one's neck, the private folds behind one's knees, the fact that we all die, sooner rather than later. It drives me crazy. I am fifteen, nearly sixteen. The skin of my life is tearing.

Rain comes. We've been at sea in rain before, of course. But this one goes quickly from a gentle patter to sleet. So we stop at the first settlement we see. It is on a hill, across a fjord, just around the west tip of Skáney.

We eat with the people, who welcome us heartily as the traders we present ourselves to be—traders who have already sold everything. That makes sense to them, for it's the end of a work season for them, too. They've been fishers all summer. The bay is rich in cod, plaice, flounder, herring. But they've spent the past day packing their belongings into wagons. They are moving inland for winter, where the firewood and the game are plentiful. They are cheerful and hospitable.

Then the stories begin. They tell tales of the ghosts

who haunt this place. I thought I knew all about them. But their ghosts are from the sea, and they can turn themselves into trolls, with a dreadful stench, or into seals that lead you astray at sea; you only realize what they are when you throw a spear and it bounces off them.

After stories we're all more comfortable, more intimate. And now they warn us about the notorious women pirates, red-haired devils who kill without a second's pause. They tell us that the kings of the Dan people, including all of Jutland, have banded together to send out ships of warriors to track them down and kill them. They think this is a good thing. They don't talk about the women and children slaves that these pirate women have returned to their homes—they know nothing of this. And I suddenly realize no one knows the truth about us except the families of those women and children.

They talk about pirates in general—how the whole system they count on for survival will collapse if pirates are allowed to prevail. They tell of pirates who get enraged at ships that are empty, having already sold their goods, and torture the crew out of spite, even kill them. They hate pirates. And they hate these women pirates most fiercely of all—as though the fact that they are women makes it unnatural and therefore far worse.

We sit there in our male disguises and listen impassively. I am glad no one of our crew speaks up, no one gives in to the urge to set them straight about what the women pirates have done. After all, then they'd wonder how we knew.

We tell them we are sailing to Írland. They laugh, thinking it is a joke, thinking we are saying we are going to raid monasteries and burn farms, which would make us even greater terrors than the women pirates. But I explain that we are giving passage home to the three Irish women (an explanation their faces tell me I quickly have to revise), in exchange, of course, for considerable silver, since they are all three princesses (at which their faces tell me I have gone too far) or, rather, one is a princess; the others are servants.

Once I stop blathering and they realize we are serious, they are full of advice. They tell us to go up the west coast of Skáney till we reach the point where the forests are so thick, no light penetrates the trees. Then we are to cross the sea westward to Jutland and cut through a giant fjord at the north that will spill us out on the other side into the North Sea. They say this will shorten our journey by two days, maybe even three, depending on the winds.

I know about that fjord, of course. That's where Gilli cut through seven years ago—the Limfjord, where I jumped overboard and lived for that spring and summer and part of autumn till Beorn whisked me away with Ástríd and my little egg Búri.

"But won't the passage from Skáney to Jutland be long at that point? Won't we be out of sight of land?"

"For a couple of days," says a man. "But to long-distance traders like you, what does it matter?" The way he says it, the thrust of his chin, puts me on alert. He finds us suspect, though he can't be onto us or they'd all be attacking.

"This ship is new to us," I lie. "For safety's sake, we want to keep within sight of land whenever possible."

So they tell us to go north only half a day, and then we'll see the largest island of the Dan people to the west. It's called Selund, because it has so many seals, but good ones—not shape-shifters. We can go west there and follow the northern coastline of Selund until we see another island of reasonable size to our west and a little north. That's Samsø. We are to go up the east coast of Samsø and cut through a passage that will let us out on the island's west coast and within sight of the mainland of Jutland. From there we can go north to the fjord that cuts across Jutland and will allow us to come out on the North Sea. After that, they can't help. Only one of them has ever traveled outside Skáney, and that one never went beyond Jutland.

I've been only half listening since the first mention of

Samsø. I know a man who uses the channel in that island when he goes after pirate ships. I see his eyes. I toss and turn all night.

Before dawn, Ingun wakes us. "Shhhh. No talking. We have to leave quickly."

We act without question. Within minutes we have everything we brought on land with us. We sneak onto our ship and Ingun tells us "North," so we set sail northward.

Once we're far from the settlement, Ingun tells her tale. She was relieving herself in the night, when she saw a man from the settlement jump off our boat and then get into another boat—a small one—and sail away south. "He was spying," she says.

And, of course, in our personal chests now are the women's clothing that families have given us—the clothing we wore on our excursions into Birka.

"Was he the tall one, missing a finger?" asks Jofrid.

The man who questioned why we wanted to stay within sight of land lacked a finger.

"Who could see his hand in the night?" answers Ingun. "But he was tall."

"I bet he was the one who grabbed at my tunic."

"What happened, Jofrid?"

"I was walking to our ship after the evening meal, to bring fresh water to Cadla and grasses to eat, when he appeared out of nowhere. I jabbed him in the ribs and he took off."

"Why didn't you say anything to us?"

"I didn't think much about it. You know. He could have been a *fuðflogi*, hopeful that a ship of men would bring him love for a night. I felt sorry for him; it can't be easy in these little settlements to find what you need."

"Maybe he was trying to see if you were a woman. You're the smallest of us—the easiest to target."

"Ah," says Unn. "He knocked my hat off. I thought it was clumsiness—but maybe he was checking my hair. Thank heavens mine is cut off."

"And not red," says Matilda, our redhead.

"All right," I say. "Let's assume he found us out. He went south. So I agree with Ingun, let's continue north. We just have to be extra alert."

We set up four lookout posts, one to each direction. Within the hour a fishing boat appears in a cove, but we simply head out farther from land and it stays there, possibly without even seeing us.

By midmorning we reach the point where we can see Selund to the west. We cross over and hug the north shore of the island. Within a few hours a fjord splits the land. The terrain is flat, so one can see long distances. There's no evidence of a settlement. We enter into an enormous bay, a perfect harbor, and anchor.

"I've never been hunted before," says Sibbe.

"That's because you were a servant, not a slave," says Unn.

"It's an awful feeling," says Matilda.

Ingun picks up an ax. "They'll be looking for us by day. So let's stock up with whatever we need so we can travel at night. What do you say?" She lifts the ax. "I'll get firewood so we can warm ourselves at night."

We fan out in pairs. Drifa and I hunt with bows and arrows. She's as good as I am. We quickly roust a pair of greylag geese and take them both down. I'm carrying the brace when we hear something behind us on the water. In one swift movement, Drifa turns and shoots. Then she gasps. I look. She's hit a swan!

In Eire it is unlucky to kill a swan or crane. Drifa was stolen from a country the Norse call Finlandi. I can see from her face that she also shares this belief. We feel cursed. The big bird struggles. It is wrong to leave it suffering. And the curse is already on us. I shoot a second arrow. The bird sinks.

"Fish will eat it," I say. Drifa says nothing. I see a muscle in her cheek twitch.

We start back toward the ship when I see a stone statue of a woman seated on a throne. She wears a long shift, an apron, four bead necklaces, a neck ring, a strange hat that flattens out to the sides like wings, and a wide cloak. She's flanked by a bird on each armrest. Above the back of her chair extend the heads of two dogs. Those must be Óðinn's greedy wolves, Geri and Freki. I'm guessing the goddess is Frigg—for she has the right to sit on her husband's throne.

Is this a good omen, to balance the bad? A boy bursts out from behind the statue and runs away as if for his life. There's a settlement in that direction, for sure.

We race to our boat, whooping the alarm call we've agreed on. Everyone clatters onboard. I count, to be sure, as Sibbe pulls up the anchor—twelve! I look around. "Unn!" I shout. "Grima!"

A ship rounds the bend. They can't help but see us.

Ragnhild and Thyra have our sail up already.

We go. We go without Unn and Grima. I feel insane.

That ship follows. It's bigger than us. But the wind is with us, so we're faster. The first shower of arrows comes.

"Lie flat," I scream.

"But we have to steer," says Jofrid from the helm.

"You and I will take turns. No one else will stand." I run for the helm and push Jofrid flat as the second shower of arrows comes.

Jofrid pops up in front of me. "Don't be stupid. I'll watch the rear. When they pull back the bowstrings, we'll both dive for the deck. Dive!"

This time some of the arrows are on fire. One passes through the sail, and instantly it's aflame. Cadla the goat bleat-screams.

Everyone's on their feet now, dunking buckets on ropes into the sea and splashing the sail. The flame is doused quickly.

The next rain of arrows falls short. We're out of range now. We're flying.

CHAPTER THIRTY-ONE

We speed along the northern coast of Selund, not a boat or house in sight. Ragnhild hugs Hrodny, who is crying out for Grima. Grima and Hrodny had become nearly inseparable.

"They'll be all right," says Ingun. "Unn and Grima will follow the plan."

If anyone got stranded, the plan was to claim a slave ship had snatched you, and then the women pirates had attacked and taken you. For some of us that was even the truth. If you were caught with weapons, that was because the women pirates had forced you to hunt.

Hrodny swipes at her tears. "We have to go back for them."

"That ship isn't far behind," says Ingun. "We couldn't return without passing them. Besides, who knows what forces might have amassed back in that fjord. Maybe the settlement there was large—it has to be somewhat large to have a ship that size."

"Let's discuss it," says Hrodny, looking around. "We need to discuss it."

"Once we're sure the ship has given up following," I say.

Hrodny glares at me. But she moves to the rear of the ship and looks backward.

The land to our port side is all tufted saxifrage, white and red and yellow. It could be spring, it's so colorful. But I imagine the grass on each little spur of land under my feet, and I know it's tough and old. Winter is close. The sky changes, even as I'm thinking this. Clouds come in from the north.

We scramble to put on cloaks when, all at once, the land ends. This is a finger of land—a long peninsula that juts out westward.

"Ship!" shouts Hrodny.

Up along the southern edge of that finger peninsula comes a ship. It can't have come from the settlement with the statue. There was no inlet in the peninsula the whole way—no passage for anyone to cut across. So this is a second boat, coming from some other community. How they got the message from one community to another so fast is anyone's guess. But they knew we'd stick to the coast. Our habits must be general knowledge.

Without hesitation, Jofrid steers us west, out to sea. No one speaks. They fill quivers and check bowstrings. They set out axes and swords. They line up shields. I watch the sea behind us. The ship that follows grows smaller. We are fast. *Please, let us be fast enough.*

Rain comes. The air goes cold with it. The wind picks up. The sky darkens. It starts high up and stains gradually lower and lower to the sea, now dark as charred wood. Thunder rumbles. A jagged spear of lightning splinters the sky ahead, making the world bright for the briefest instant. The waves grow, higher than I've ever seen them before. They spit white froth. We race at tremendous speed, rising and slapping down wildly.

"Tie yourselves!" I shout.

Everyone has a rope in her personal chest, and we're all tying them around our waists and through an oar hole. But the rope does little to reassure. It's insane to be out at sea in this. I'm sure both the boats chasing us have turned back.

The axes have disappeared back into the chests. The swords, too. The bows are tied to the mast, the quivers of arrows are in the chests. Every loose thing has been battened down. Cadla skitters across the wet deck, bleating piteously, till I catch her and make a harness of rope under her front legs and across her shoulders and tie her to the mast too. She hushes, but her crazy narrow slits of eyes say her silence is because she's given up.

The rain turns to ice pebbles that pock our hands and face, our only exposed parts. Thunder booms. A shaft of lightning goes straight down, from heaven to sea, directly in front of our boat. A wave breaks over us. Should we take down the sail? I have no idea.

I will not let us die at sea. There has to be land around here somewhere. These waters are littered with islets. More thunder; more lightning. "There!" I point port side. Something looms out there. It has to be land. It can't be just a storm cloud. "Do you see it?"

Jofrid calls for help. She and Ingun together pull the rudder and they turn us, but too fast. The ship lists to port so hard it rides on its side. Chests tumble into the sea. People tumble out. But the ship rights itself and we're going toward that looming thing, and those of us still onboard pull in the ropes of Ingun and Drifa and Ragnhild and Cadla the goat, hoisting them in. No one cries, no one screams. We are all pretending to be solid.

Lightning cracks behind us, so close I can smell it.

I should have reefed the sails long ago—before the winds howled.

And it is an island! It is, it is! We steer straight for it, but there's no ready harbor on this side, so we head west around it to the south side, and there's still no harbor, but at least the island protects us from the wind gusts and the worst of the waves. We lower the sail and secure it with ropes and brace ourselves. *Please, please let there be no reefs here.*

We bob for I don't know how long, listening to the trees

of the island rustle and break and fall with crashes. And then, as quickly as it started, the storm stops. The wind ceases. The waves dissipate. The sun returns. Gulls circle as though no sky could be more lovely. Dolphins jump and one breaches, playing in delight. I can't remember seeing dolphins in the Baltic before. It feels like a dream.

I call to Hrodny, "Do you still want us to discuss going back for Unn and Grima?"

Hrodny looks around. Few meet her gaze. "Does anyone know the name of that settlement?"

"I can't be sure," says Sibbe. "But the only settlement I've heard of on the north side of Selund is Hleiðra."

"All right," says Hrodny. "For now, let's try to get somewhere with all of us alive. Then I'll leave you. I'll find a way back to them."

Jofrid has taken the helm again. Her arms shake with exhaustion, but she doesn't complain. There's little sunlight left before nightfall. Still, she heads the boat west and slightly north. Out to sea. After all, this island is too small to have a fresh water source.

We do an inventory. We have six axes left, two swords, five shields, three bows, but not even a single quiver of arrows. Most of our food is gone. The rest of my hoard is gone.

The sea was greedy. But at least it wasn't monstrous: We are alive.

We spread out our clothes to dry. We undo our braids, those of us with long hair, and let our locks dry. We are alive.

Dusk falls. That's when we notice a fire. It must be Samsø island. The fire is above the horizon—on a cliff, for sure. We travel up the east side of the island. From what I see through the gloom, the land is softly rolling. The wind soughs through grasses.

Soon we see a second fire—high up again. But I don't see cliffs or even hills. It's as though someone has built a tower and made a fire at the top. How strange.

We hug the coast and travel around a hook, out into the sea, and then we head north once more. And there's the opening at last! The canal that the people of Samsø and the people of Jelling built together so they could fend off pirates better. We enter the waterway. It's lined with wood on both sides. We lower the sails and fit the four oars we have left into the oarlocks.

That's when the sky lights up. At first I think it's lightning again. But it's fire—torches! A ship bears down on us from ahead. Another comes up from the rear.

We scramble into our clothes and jam on helmets. I grab a sword, and then, on second thought, I hand it to Sibbe. She and Hrodny are both better than me, and Hrodny already has the other sword. I am without a weapon. I grab a rope.

Men come aboard, shouting threats. Everything is happening quickly. Chaotically. I see Drifa get thrown into the water. She's a good swimmer—but I don't know if she was wounded. I see Ingun pinned to the ground with an ax raised above her. These are real warriors. We have lost before we've begun. The air fills with screams.

I have to pick one point and focus on it. Sibbe—she's right there in front of me. She fights with another swordsman. He smashes the sword from her hand. It comes sliding across the deck. He chases her to the mast. I pick up the sword and go after him. He turns at the last moment and knocks the sword from my hand in one blow.

He has eyes the color of rain. He raises his sword to me. I am suspended in those eyes.

"No!" Thyra races to my side and pulls off my helmet. My curls fall to my shoulders.

"Alfhild," he says with awe. His sword is still aimed.

I shake my head.

"You are a pirate? Alfhild, my Alfhild?"

"I am Brigid."

"Brigid?"

"I was hidden before. But I'm Brigid inside."

He nods as if in a dream. "Brigid then."

My eyes leave his and travel to the tip of that sword, pointed at my chest. "Don't kill us."

Alf shouts, "Stop! Weapons down. Everyone!"

The screaming stops. The chasing ceases. I feel eyes on us.

He lowers his sword.

"We're not pirates, Alf. Not really."

"Tell me."

"We steal only slaves that were stolen from their homes. And we return them to their homes. If they want to go." I remember the rumors about red-haired devils. "We've never killed anyone. We've wounded, but only in defense of ourselves or the slaves."

"Strange behavior." His cool eyes cloud, then clear. His chest heaves. "But not criminal. Slave dealers don't own the people they stole. No, they don't. You are not pirates, real or fake."

"So we are free to leave?"

I see his Adam's apple rise and fall in a swallow. "Where will you go?"

"Írland. I have to return three girls. And I think . . ." Breathing is so hard. "I think I might just visit my parents and brother."

"You are Irish?"

Am I? "Born Irish, raised Dan."

"I hear Írland's beauty is magical." Those rain eyes hold me. "I'd like to go."

I'm shivering so hard I can barely talk. "Then I'll travel on to Ísland. My sister is a slave there."

Alf blinks. "Your sister. A sister is important."

"I have to go."

"My ship is better than yours for such a journey."

"Are you offering to go with me?" Offering what I have never allowed myself to ask for.

"I didn't want to love you, Brigid. Brigid, my Brigid."

He says my name with such sweet acceptance, I could laugh or cry. But I just stare at him.

"After you turned down my offer of marriage, my life was punctured. Joyless. No, I didn't want to love you. I wanted to forget you. But now I see I have no choice."

Nor did I want to love him. Nor do I have a choice. "Put out your hands."

Alf slides his sword into its scabbard and extends his hands, palm up.

I drop my fists into them. "Heart and bones. These are mine. Now yours."

Alf closes his hands around mine.

PART FIVE

HOME

(AUTUMN, TURNING SIXTEEN
YEARS OLD)

CHAPTER THIRTY-TWO

Mother and Father. And, oh, my brother. *Máthir, athir, bráthir.* I have not yet seen them. It was my plan to go directly to Írland. Those three slaves . . . no, those three good Irish girls . . . they needed to be brought home immediately. Then we could winter in Eire, and as soon as spring came, we'd head out for Ísland.

Alf agreed. He said, "I'd follow you to Hel and back." He said, "I'd fight armies for you." He said, "I'd slay Níðhögg, the worst dragon of them all, for you." He wore nothing but smiles.

Until he heard the rest of my plan. I told him I feared that if I became with child I would not be able to do whatever it took to rescue Mel, and therefore I could not marry him until after I had found her.

So Alf lost no time in persuading me of a new plan. I smile now as I think about how persuasive this man Alf can be and how much I respond to him, so that his new plan swiftly became mine as well. Next spring was too long for him to wait. So we paid all the women in my crew enough money to go on to the lives they chose, just as I had promised them. Alf paid another boat's captain to take the three Irish girls back home, and he hired a crew to take us—him and me—to Ísland immediately, before the weather turned.

The next four days were a flurry of gathering provisions and checking rigging. Then we set sail. Ten days later—only two weeks after we'd made the new plan—we arrived in Ísland.

After all my fruitless searching, suddenly everything became easy. Everyone knew of Hoskuld, the Viking chieftain; everyone knew of Melkorka, his mysterious concubine. She lives on land south of Salmon River, in a rolling dale called Melkorka-stead—named for her, despite the fact that she's a slave. Her wonderful son abides with her, while Hoskuld lives separately, with his wife and their children. She is still beautiful. Though the label of "slave" has worn on her, she is still strong. That's what they say.

I am walking across grasses now toward Melkorka's home. Alf walks behind, at a distance, as I've asked him to. Mel's home is made of wood, not stones with a turf roof, like the houses in the village on the coast where we landed. We've been told about that wood; everyone talks about it. It's from logs brought all the way across the ocean from

Nóreg, for the trees here are few and small, and nothing is as strong as Norse trees anyway.

There is no one outside the house. No activity. I see not a single window, so I have no idea whether the house is empty or not. But it's the middle of the day; maybe they are resting inside. *Let that be so. Please, Mel, please be home.*

But I can wait. I can circle this house. I can run around it so many times my feet dig a moat even in this rocky land. Seven and a half years I've been yearning for this moment. I can wait a little longer.

I am but five boat lengths from the front door when a woman comes outside. She squints into the sun. I walk faster. I lope. We stare at each other. She drops the basket in her arms.

"Mel," I call.

She's shaking her head. Her brown hair catches the light, dark and bright and mixed, like the hawk-plumage of Queen Tove's cloak.

"Mel," I cry.

And we're hugging. "Brigid," she says hoarsely into my hair. "Oh, Brigid."

CHAPTER THIRTY-THREE

The sight of those river rapids makes my heart pump extra hard; they are fast and ferocious. I remember the night I jumped off the Russian slave ship into icy water. This water can hardly be warmer. The combination of speed and cold terrifies me—my skin grows taut. The boy Óláf, my nephew—my nephew!—is six, two years younger and weaker than I was that night, and he has promised me I'll love his swimming hole. Are they crazy? My fingers close in fear around Melkorka's hand—my Mel—my sister. The three of us, together.

"I'm happy too," she says, squeezing back in her misunderstanding, and nearly shouting to be heard above the noise of the rushing water we walk alongside of. "My little sister, alive, alive—especially that—but also all grown up. After the wild child you were, to see you now . . . it makes me very happy."

"I wasn't wild."

"You were. You ran through mud and got your clothes filthy—but mostly it was how you thought. Do you remember, can you possibly remember, how when Nuada's hand was cut off and Mother explained that he couldn't become king then, how you said, 'Melkorka can become queen.' Do you remember? A woman alone, unmarried, queen! That's how you were. Wild. Thank heavens, or you wouldn't have survived."

"We're almost there!" shouts Óláf, who runs ahead with my goat Cadla at his heels.

They call him Óláf pái. Lots of people here have little extras added to their names. One man has *rauði*—red. Another has *djúpauðga*—deep-minded. Another has *magri*—lean. And, oh, another has *tordýfill*—dung beetle—the poor thing. The extra on Óláf's name is because when Mel was at the gigantic trading market in Miklagard with the Russian slave dealer Gilli, she saw a strange bird called a *pái*. He had long tail feathers that dragged on the ground behind him, until he got excited and held them up in a huge arc behind him, all blue-green with eyes painted on in beautiful patterns, the most exquisite animal Mel had ever seen. She'd forgotten that one instance of beauty in the long horror of those days, until Óláf was born, and he seemed more exquisite than any other human being could be.

"I'm jumping in!" Óláf pulls his tunic over his head. He disappears around a hillock.

"No!" I scream, and run for him.

Mel grabs my arm. "Whatever is the matter with you?"

"He could drown, Mel!"

Mel gawks at me. Then she laughs. "We're not swimming in the river. That would be fatal at this time of year. No, no. No one could get hurt where we're going." She lets loose my arm, and we run together to Óláf.

The boy sits in a small pool of water in the middle of ferns and grasses. Steam rises around him. His face is flushed and content. Mel undresses and joins him.

I dip in a hand. "It's hot! I've heard of warm springs—in Eire there are warm springs—but this is positively hot." And now I wish Alf had come along. Foolish me, I asked him to give us some time alone.

"The whole of Ísland is speckled with hot springs. Or all of this huge country that I've seen is. Some are large enough to swim in, milky-blue with white mud. Others are just overgrown puddles—like this, which is better, because then no one else comes to use them." She pats one of the black rocks that edge the spring. "Our private soaking puddle."

"It's not a puddle," says Óláf. He leans back, yields himself to the water, and floats.

"What better proof?" I say. And I grin. This boy is quietly clever. He reminds me of Hakon, my dear adopted brother back in Heiðabý. I have suppressed thoughts of Hakon, but now I miss him strongly. And I miss my queen mother, and Beorn and Ástríd and Búri and Alof. And Alf, though he's only back at Mel's home. But what a fool I am. I am here, soaking with my sister and my nephew—I must think about them, and this place and this time.

We have been speaking Norse, but I switch to Gaelic now. "Please change your mind. Please. Come back with me, Mel."

"And do what?" she answers in Norse.

"*Immalle*," I say. "Remember how Mother told us to stay together? Remember?"

"We were children then," she says steadfastly in Norse. "We spoke Gaelic, like I do with Óláf. My life is here now. And I speak Norse with adults."

"You're a slave," I say, surrendering to Norse. She's right. This is the language of our adulthood.

"I am also the mother of a boy who will grow into a powerful man. He will be important, I promise you that."

I check to see the effect of these words on Óláf. But the boy still floats, his ears underwater. He shows no sign of listening. He looks as though he's comfortable enough to fall asleep and keep floating. "He could be important in Jutland, too."

"Jutland? Don't be silly, Brigid. He will be a king in

Eire as soon as he's old enough to sail there and claim his birthright."

"A king in Eire! Will he want to live in Downpatrick? Really?"

"Of course he will. And until then, I'll keep him safe here, so he can grow strong and wise and tough—tough enough for whatever lies ahead."

"But, Mel, if he lives here until he's adult, he'll be totally Norse. He won't be Irish at all. Even I don't feel Irish anymore, and I lived there till I was eight."

"He will rule in Eire. He will not be the son of a slave there. He will satisfy his ambitions."

"Or do you mean yours?"

"Dear Brigid, you are still so very honest and direct." She hesitates. "I have lived with humiliation a long time. I want vindication. This is true. But I am sure, absolutely sure, Óláf pái will have his own ambitions too. He's bright. He's perfect. He will stay here and grow. You can tell Mother and Father why." She rests her head on an edge stone and closes her eyes. The goat Cadla comes and nibbles at her hair, but she swats her away.

I sidle over next to her and whisper in her ear, "Let Alf buy your freedom, at least."

She smiles without opening her eyes. "He can save his money. Hoskuld doesn't deserve any of it. Someday I will marry, and my husband will buy my freedom. I am waiting only until Óláf pái is old enough to leave me."

"Leave you? You mean you won't return to Eire with him?"

"I'll never set foot on a boat again."

"Oh, Mel. You'll be alone here."

"Stay with me." She opens her eyes and sits tall. "This is a land of fire and ice—volcanoes and glaciers. In some places you can see volcanic tabletop mountains in the middle of ice all year round." Her voice grows bright with enthusiasm. "There are vast meadowlands for grazing. There's bog iron in bogs and heaths and marshes. We have high mountains and low river valleys, and on the south coast there are sandy beaches. You can have a farm on any coast, or in a river valley. It's there for the taking. Just burn off the forest and plow the land. If you want forest, birch and willow and rowan all grow here—shorter than normal, it's true, but strong. And driftwood litters the shores, so there's never a lack of firewood even if you live far from forests. Streams and lakes burst with salmon and trout. The sea gives whales, walruses, seals. Imagine what it's like to stand on a high spot in winter, the world white with snow, and look down on a deep canyon. It's majestic. There's no other word."

I laugh. "Catch your breath, Mel. I believe you."

"And, Brigid, there's a waterfall so high, it kicks up a wall of spray. On a sunny day a rainbow arches over it. You can count on that."

I turn my head so I'm facing into the wind. "The wind has been blowing from the east ever since I got here."

"It's always that way."

Always? And I think of the fjord up near the first Jutland home I lived in—the pit house. The wind there always blew from the west. Winds can be funny like that. They can characterize a place. I think of Jutland. I've lived in the north and the south, in the west and the east. I know that peninsula. Places can come to mean so much.

"I don't—"

"Stop, Brigid. Don't say it. Think about it. Talk with Alf. Spend the winter here together and see how you like it."

"I want to go back to Eire with him—and, we had hoped, with you—for the wedding. I want to be married in a church, even after all this time."

"Alf has agreed to that? Then he's a better Norseman than any I know. We have no churches here. Lots of Irish people, but no churches; all the Irish are slaves. You can marry Alf here the Norse way. Then, if you still want, you can get remarried in Eire later."

Óláf splashes us. "Let's go home and eat. And afterward I want to take you to see something. Just you." He points at me. "Mother can't come."

I look at Mel.

She smiles and raises an eyebrow. "I think my son likes having an aunt."

"Can Alf come?" I ask Óláf.

"Can he keep a secret?"

"A secret?" says Mel. "Hmmm. Now I'm getting curious."

"You can't know," says Óláf. "But Aunt Brigid can. And maybe Alf."

"Definitely Alf," I say. "I trust him."

"All right," says Óláf solemnly. "Then I trust him too."

So after dinner we set out, Óláf and Alf and I. I have warned Alf that he must earn Óláf's trust. He has vowed to do precisely that.

It's past dusk—the reds and yellows of the autumn leaves are neutralized to grays. The boy leads us through trees to a lagoon where icebergs float in gentle moonlight and colors can be seen again—stark white against the deep blue of the water. I graze Alf's hand with my fingertips, and he moves closer to me till our arms touch through our sleeves.

"It's beautiful here, Óláf. Thank you."

"It's better when the icebergs crash into each other."

He picks up a rock and throws it. A funny black-and-white bird with an orange bill and feet takes to the air. I hadn't noticed it before. "Watch," he says with urgency, pointing up. "Something good is about to happen."

And then the clear, dark northern skies dance with color. It's a spectacle, a festival of the heavens.

"It goes on all through winter, way till spring comes again." Ólaf laughs. "Mother told me you both watched the lights as girls, but then you disappeared. So, ha! Now you have the lights again."

"Enchanting," I say. I don't have the heart to tell him that the northern lights grace Jutland, too.

Ólaf takes my hand. "But there's more. Come on." He pulls me a bit, then walks ahead in his impatience.

We follow. A brown-gray fox with a white tail and tummy and white on the insides of his ears appears from nowhere and walks along the rocks beside us. I hurry and catch Ólaf's arm. I point and whisper, "He seems to have no fear of us."

"Why should he?" Ólaf says in a normal voice. "I'd never hurt him. Would you?"

"No. But how can he know that?"

"No one hurts him," says Ólaf.

"What about predators?" asks Alf.

"What are predators?"

"He is, for one," says Alf. "A predator is an animal that eats other animals."

"Then he's the only predator here, except for us," says Óláf. "And, like I said, I'd never hurt him. He knows that. He was stalking the puffin, so I threw the rock to warn the bird. But he never would have got it, anyway. He's foolish; that fox can't catch birds." Óláf turns away from the lagoon and walks through a rocky area and around trees. He stops.

In front of us is a low hut made completely of stone. My breath is gone.

"What is it?" asks Alf.

"An Irish hermit's hut," I say.

"Who built it?"

"My friend," says Óláf. "They'd kill him if they knew he was here. Not even Mother knows. I'm the only one. You must never tell. Want to meet him?"

I can't believe he says all that so casually. I nod.

Alf nods.

Óláf crawls into the hut. His high-pitched voice carries to us, speaking Gaelic. Mel was good to teach it to him. He comes out followed by a small man with long white hair. It's so dark now, I cannot really see his eyes. Or maybe that's because my own are blurred with tears. This man walks stooped like Papi did, back in Ribe. I wonder how he feeds himself, though I can see he survives on practically nothing. He's skin and bones.

"Good evening," I say in Gaelic.

"Good evening, aunt of Óláf." He looks at Alf.

"Say something to him," I say to Alf in Norse.

"Greetings, old man," says Alf in Norse.

"Do you live here all alone?" I ask.

"The Lord is with us. We are never alone."

"Are there other monks here?"

"Three of us came together. But we separated. I don't know if they are still of this world."

"How? How did you come here?"

"In a skin boat with a twig frame."

"I have just spent ten days in a ship on that raging ocean, and sometimes I feared for my life. How could a skin boat make the journey?"

"How can a bird fly over the seas? We all have his help."

I feel at a loss. "Do you want to go home?"

"I am home."

"Can I do anything to help you? Get anything for you?" But I know his answer before he says it.

"The Lord gives me what I need."

"Thank you for talking," I say.

"Speaking Gaelic is always worth the effort." The monk crawls back into the hut.

"See?" says Óláf. "Mother was wrong. Not all the Irish here are slaves."

"What was that all about?" asks Alf.

"Our future," I say, keeping the tremble from my voice.

"Explain, cryptic woman."

"Let's leave for Eire tomorrow, if we can."

"Good. This is sounding good." He puts his arm around me and pulls me to his chest. "I cannot wait to wed you." His voice is gruff with desire.

My eyes are on those lips, so close and delicious. "The boy," I whisper.

Alf releases me gently. "Would you like a ride on my shoulders, Óláf?" He goes to stoop, but Óláf climbs his back like a squirrel up a tree.

"Immediately after the wedding," I say, "we'll go live in Jutland. Jelling if you want. Or Ribe. Or Heiðabý."

"I'm allowed the choice? Are you sure, imperious one?"

I grin. "I don't care, as long as I can visit the people I love in Ribe and Heiðabý."

"Then I choose Heiðabý. That's where we met. And Hakon will be so glad to have you back for good, not just visiting."

"Have you talked to Hakon?"

"It was his idea to light fires up and down the land as signals for having spotted the women pirates. He didn't know you were their captain, of course. He just wanted to help strategize. He's a natural at it."

And now I'm sure. I'm so completely sure. "You and Hakon together, you will help the kings of all the cities of the Dan people understand that Christians are no threat."

"Was that old man a Christian?"

"An Irish monk."

"He's no threat."

"Exactly. You'll explain to everyone. Let's go home, Alf. Let's go home."

Old Norse Glossary

alf: elf
bjór: fermented cider
borg: height
byrnja: shirt of mail
Dan: Danish
djúpauðga: deep-minded
draug: ghost
dreng: king's aide, usually young
dróttinn: military leader
feræring: fishing boat
fuðflogi: homosexual man
Heiðabý: Hedeby
hempægar: king's personal fighting men
hild: battle
hjálm: iron helmet
høggorm: serpent
hval: whale
Kristinn: Christian
Írland: Ireland
Ísland: Iceland
járnbrák: iron slick

krage: tree-trunk ladder
magri: lean
melrakki: white fox
mjøð: mead
Nóreg: Norway
øg: terror
pái: peacock
papi: hermit; monk
rauði: red
sefask: be calmed
sjøvættir: sea spirits
skald: bard
þegn: king's aide, usually old
þing: assembly
tordýfill: dung beetle
valsham: hawk-plumage cloak

POSTSCRIPT

This book is a companion to *Hush: An Irish Princess Tale*. The heroine in the first novel is Melkorka, a character who appears and reappears briefly in the Icelandic sagas *Land-námabók* and *Laxdœla*. Her younger sister, the heroine of the present novel, was made up in the first novel, and so I was free to create whatever story I wanted for her. I blended her story with the well-known story of Alfhild, the first Norse woman pirate so far as anyone knows, and the character I find most striking in the Norse Amazon tradition.

Melkorka and Brigid were princesses in Ireland in 900, but that doesn't mean they lived in a castle. Castles didn't come to Ireland for another couple of hundred years. In fact, there were no castles in Denmark at this time either. Instead everyone lived in homes made of wood and mud, often just branches and straw stuck together with soil, clay, sand, or animal dung, usually with only a couple of rooms. Royal families had plenty to eat and nice clothes and jewels. But their lives were not totally leisure; they helped out with chores, even though they had servants to cook and clean for them. And whole families (and often others as well), rich or poor, slept together in a single room in both Ireland and Denmark.

The people of Ireland had organized themselves into alliances of families, called tribes or clans, of perhaps a few thousand people spread across hills and valleys. They lived in private homes and owned private land, but they also shared public land. The clans each had a king. A king's home was usually fortified by a wall and often larger than the ordinary home, perhaps with some extra rooms. Clans further allied themselves to form larger confederations with nearby clans. There were four main confederations in Ireland at this time, with four main kings. Melkorka and Brigid's father was a lower king.

Vikings had raided the island for a little more than a hundred years, stealing wealth from monasteries, massacring many, raping and plundering. In sum, they terrorized the Irish—they were criminal. But not all Norse were this way. Some of them established towns and settled down to mix civilly with the Irish. Dublin was such a town; it was huge compared to other towns, perhaps around three thousand inhabitants just within the town walls, and many more outside in the hills and valleys. It was in Dublin that Melkorka and Brigid's family met the problems you learn about in this book. When a Viking leader wanted to marry Melkorka, their father planned a trick to slaughter him and his men. Since the plan was dangerous, the girls' mother tried to protect them by dressing them in peasant clothing and sending them off on a horse, not to return until the event was over. But while the girls were hiding out, a Russian slave ship captured them.

The custom of capturing people, particularly women and children, and keeping them as slaves or selling them into slavery was common in this time period (and, interestingly, was probably responsible for the spreading of certain genetic tendencies, such as the appearance of multiple sclerosis in places the Vikings traveled). The slave trade thrived, with captives moving between Europe, Asia, and Africa. In the Icelandic sagas, the slavers who stole Melkorka are Russian, so I kept them Russian in my story. However, the Russians were only one group of many who scanned the shores for slaves. Often captured women and children were brought to Miklagard, which is now called Istanbul and which was said to be the biggest city in the world at that time. People from east and west, north and south, met there for trade. That's what happened to Melkorka. But instead of being sold in Miklagard, the Russian slaver kept her as he headed back north, and he ended by selling her to a Viking, who took her off to Iceland. Iceland was, essentially, a Norse colony at that time. Starting in the late 800s, the Norse had been settling there, although there is archeological evidence that Irish monks had settled there earlier.

Brigid, however, never traveled to Miklagard. She jumped out of the Russian slave ship as it passed through the Limfjord, way near the north of Jutland, in Denmark, straight into the icy water. Hence begins her tale, told in this book. Denmark at that time consisted of the same landmass as today plus the western coast of what is now Sweden. Across the southern border were the Franks, a people who had adopted Christianity and were viewed as a major threat by the Danes. Denmark, while a small and unimposing country today, was important at that time if for nothing else but its geographical position. It jutted up between the two seas and thus was in a position to control commerce between lands to the east and lands to the west.

Brigid could have followed many paths, for she was only eight when her life was so completely disrupted. But there was something in her character in the first book, *Hush*, that made me believe she would revolutionize her world. So I went searching for evidence of revolutionary women at that time. And I found Alfhild.

There are many variants on the story of Alfhild—with her living anywhere from the fifth century to the eleventh, with inconsistencies over who her parents were and what role snakes played in her time in the tower, and with debates over whether she was, in fact, a single historical figure, or a blend of several, or a complete fiction. Given these uncertainties, I felt I had some license to use those aspects of the various tales about her that made the present story cohere the way I wanted it to.

The prince Hakon in this story is also made up. However, there was a King Hakon of Norway (the third king of all Norway) around the time that this young Hakon might have become a king. That King Hakon erected beacons on hills to send messages up and down the country quickly. Also around the time of our boy Hakon's prime, the attitudes in the Norse countries toward Christianity changed. The real King Hakon himself was in favor of Christianity, although he did not manage to make Norway accept it. Meanwhile, King Gorm, who was the first historically recognized king of all Denmark (ruling at least ten years and perhaps more than twenty, until his death in 958), was not opposed to Christianity, and his son, Harald Bluetooth, who ruled from 958 to around 987, was reputed to be baptized by a cleric who went simply by the name Poppa or Poppo or Papi.

The views of Norse mythology put forth in this book are based on materials from a few centuries later. My assumption (which is shared by many scholars of Norse culture) is that those materials were in large part based on oral traditions that predated them by hundreds of years. The first recorded versions we have of the Norse myths are in Icelandic sagas that date from around 1180 AD. But somewhere around 1225 the Icelander Snorri gave us a major work called the *Snorra Edda*, also known as *Prose Edda*. Most modern ideas about Norse mythology are based on that work. Alongside Snorri's work is another collection called the *Poetic Edda*. It contains a collection of anonymous poems performed by all sorts of people on all sorts of occasions. As I was writing this book, I consulted translations of both works.

BIBLIOGRAPHY

Abram, Christopher. *Myths of the Pagan North: The Gods of the Norsemen*. London: Continuum, 2011.

Barrett, James H., ed. *Contact, Continuity, and Collapse: The Norse Colonization of the North Atlantic*. Turnhout, Belgium: Brepols Publishers, 2003.

Becker, C. J. "Viking Age Villages and 'Manors' in Denmark: Recent Discoveries." In *Proceedings of the Eighth Viking Congress*, edited by Hans Bekker-Nielsen, Peter Foote, and Olaf Olsen, 25–36. Odense, Denmark: Odense University Press, 1981.

Blindheim, Martin. "The Ranuaik Reliquary in Copenhagen: A Short Study. In *Proceedings of the Tenth Viking Congress*, edited by James E. Knirk, 203–218. Oslo: Universitetets Oldsaksamling, 1987.

Brodeur, Arthur Gilchrist, trans. *The Prose Edda, by Snorri Sturlason*. London: Oxford University Press, 1916.

Byock, Jesse L., trans. *The Saga of the Volsungs: The Norse Epic of Sigurd the Dragon Slayer*. Berkeley: University of California Press, 2012.

Chisholm, James Allen. "The Eddas: The Keys to the Mysteries of the North." Accessed November 3,

2013. http://www.heathengods.com/library/poetic_edda/ChisholmEdda.pdf.

Clarke, Howard B., Máire Ní Mhaonaigh, and Raghnall Ó Floinn, eds. *Ireland and Scandinavia in the Early Viking Age*. Dublin: Four Courts Press, 1998.

de Paor, Liam. "The Age of the Viking Wars (9th and 10th Centuries)." In *The Course of Irish History*, edited by T. W. Moody and F. X. Martin, 91–106. Cork: Mercier Press, 1967.

Douglas, T. *Lives of the Most Celebrated Pirates and Sea Robbers*. London: J. S. Pratt, 1845.

Duffy, Seán. *Medieval Ireland: An Encyclopedia*. New York: Routledge, 2005.

Einarsson, Bjarni F. *The Settlement of Iceland: A Critical Approach. Granastadir and the Ecological Heritage*. Doctoral dissertation: Göteborg, Sweden: Göteborgs Universitet, 1994.

Englehart, Deirdre Sheridan. "A Story to Tell: The Culture of Storytelling and Folklore in Ireland." *Childhood Education* 87, no. 6 (2001): 409–414.

Etchingham, Colmán. *Viking Raids on Irish Church Settlements in the Ninth Century: A Reconsideration of the Annals*. Maynooth, Ireland: Department of Old and Middle Irish, St. Patrick's College, 1996.

Foot, Sarah. "Remembering, Forgetting and Inventing:

Attitudes to the Past in England at the End of the First Viking Age." *Transactions of the Royal Historical Society, Sixth Series*, vol. 9, 185–200, 1999.

Frank, Roberta. "Skaldic poetry." In *Old Norse-Icelandic Literature: A Critical Guide*, edited by Carol J. Clover and John Lindow, 157–196. Toronto: University of Toronto Press, 2005.

Graham-Campbell, James, and Dafydd Kidd. *The Vikings: The British Museum, London, the Metropolitan Museum of Art, New York*. New York: William Morrow, 1980.

Grammaticus, Saxo. *The Danish History, Books I–IX*, late twelfth century. Translated by Oliver Elton. (New York: Norroena Society, 1905.) Douglas B. Killings, editor, electronic edition. Kindle Edition.

Hallencreutz, Carl F. "Missionary Spirituality: The Case of Ansgar." *Studia Theologica* 36, no. 1 (1982): 105–118.

Helle, Knut, ed. *The Cambridge History of Scandinavia*, vol. 1. Cambridge: Cambridge University Press, 2003.

Hodges, Richard. "Goodbye to the Vikings?" *History Today* 54, no. 9 (2004), 29–30.

Jesch, Judith. *Women in the Viking Age*. Woodbridge, Suffolk, UK: Boydell Press, 1991.

Jesch, Judith, ed. *The Scandinavians from the Vendel Period to the Tenth Century: An Ethnographic Perspective*.

Woodbridge, Suffolk, UK: The Boydell Press, 2002.

Jochens, Jenny. *Old Norse Images of Women*. Philadelphia: University of Pennsylvania Press, 1996.

Jones, Gwyn. *A History of the Vikings*. Oxford: Oxford University Press, 1984.

Kenny, Michael. "The Geographical Distribution of Irish Viking-age Coin Hoards." *Proceedings of the Royal Irish Academy. Section C: Archaeology, Celtic Studies, History, Linguistics, Literature* 87C (1987), 507–525.

Klinge, Matti. *Ancient Powers of the Baltic Sea*. Ontario, Canada: Aspasia Books, 2007.

Laing, Lloyd Robert. *The Archaeology of Celtic Britain and Ireland, c. AD 400–1200*. Cambridge: Cambridge University Press, 2006.

The Laxdaela Saga. First published 1899. Written around 1245 AD. Translated from the Icelandic by Muriel Press. Charleston, SC: Forgotten Books, 2008.

Lindow, John. *Norse Mythology: A Guide to Gods, Heroes, Rituals, and Beliefs*. Oxford, UK: Oxford University Press, 2002.

Lynch, Patricia. *Enchanted Irish Tales*. Dublin: Mercier Press, 1989.

Madsen, H. J. "Introduction to Viking Århus." In *Proceedings of the Eighth Viking Congress*, edited by Hans Bekker-

Nielsen, Peter Foote, and Olaf Olsen, 69–72. Odense, Denmark: Odense University Press, 1981.

Nyberg, Tore. *Monasticism in North-Western Europe, 800–1200*. Aldershot, UK: Ashgate, 2000.

Oakley, Stewart. *A Short History of Denmark*. New York: Praeger Publishers, 1972.

Old Sailor. *The Log Book; or, Nautical Miscellany*. London: J. Robins and Sons, 1827.

Olrik, Axel. *The Heroic Legends of Denmark*. London: Oxford University Press, 1919.

Pearson, Andrew. "Piracy in Late Roman Britain: A Perspective from the Viking Age." *Britannia* 37 (2006), 337–353.

Poser, Charles M. "The Dissemination of Multiple Sclerosis: A Viking Saga? A Historical Essay." *Annals of Neurology* 36 (1994), S2, S231–S243.

Randsborg, Klavs. *The Viking Age in Denmark: The Formation of a State*. London: Duckworth, 1980.

Roesdahl, Else. *Viking Age Denmark*. London: British Museum Publications, 1982.

Rose, Jamaica, and Captain Michael MacLeod. *The Book of Pirates: A Guide to Plundering, Pillaging and Other Pursuits*. Layton, UT: Gibbs Smith, 2010.

Rowley-Conwy, Peter. "Rye in Viking Age Denmark: New Information from Øster Aalum, North

Jutland." *Journal of Danish Archaeology* 7, no. 1 (1988): 182–190.

Sheehan, John. "Early Viking Age Silver Hoards from Ireland and Their Scandinavian Elements." In *Scandinavia and Ireland in the Early Viking Age*, edited by H. Clarke, M. Ní Mhaonaigh, and R. Ó Floinn, 166–202. Dublin: Four Courts Press, 1998.

Short, William R. *Icelanders in the Viking Age: The People of the Sagas*. Jefferson, NC: McFarland & Co., 2010.

Stanley, Jo. *Bold in her Breeches: Women Pirates Across the Ages*. London: Pandora, 1995.

Walpole, Charles George. *A Short History of the Kingdom of Ireland from the Earliest Times to the Union with Great Britain: with Five Maps and Appendices*. New York: Harper & Brothers, 1882.

Wolf, Kirsten. *Daily Life of the Vikings*. Westport, CT: Greenwood Press, 2004.